WHERE'S OURS?

For Shelley —
Enjoy it!

Natalie

McKelvy

8-11-90

WHERE'S OURS?

Natalie McKelvy

Published in 1987 by

Academy Chicago Publishers
425 North Michigan Avenue
Chicago, Illinois 60611

Copyright © 1987 by Natalie McKelvy

Printed and bound in the USA

Library of Congress Cataloging-in-Publication Data

Mckelvy, Natalie A.
  Where's ours?

  I. Title
PS3563.C375W44   1987   813'.54   87-19447
ISBN 0-89733-278-4
ISBN 0-89733-277-6 (pbk.)

To Charley

Marcia stretched in the shower and watched the soap fall away toward the drain. "Oh drat," she said. "It's going to be one of those days."

Carmen, her green-eyed cat, rubbed against the door.

"Gin, would you bring my bathrobe? It's behind the bedroom door."

The warm water coursed down the back of her neck and cut through her short hair. She closed her eyes and enjoyed its warmth. After all, it would be the only pleasure of the day.

A hairy male arm thrust a blue-green bathrobe through the door. "Your robe, madam."

"Thanks, Gin. Just throw it on the toilet." Marcia cut the water and grabbed the big white towel off the rack, stepping into the open. She appraised herself in the mirror.

"Diet time," she mumbled, as she looked at the smooth white flesh and the soft spots around the waist. "God damn it, why can't I ever keep the weight off?" Last night's binge of popcorn, rye bread and a whole package of Maurice Lenell cookies came back to her. "Christ, it's like racial memory. I always eat the same damn stuff."

She was of medium build and fair-skinned, "frog-belly white," as she called herself to her friends, all of whom seemed darker, and thinner, and better married, and making more money, and having entirely better lives than she could ever hope to have. She always felt this way when she was ten pounds over where she wanted to be and she was always ten pounds overweight.

All she had to do was lose ten pounds and she would feel so much better, a woman able to deal with everything.

She had told herself this every morning for the last six months—and most of the previous fifteen years. She had been on diets ever since she had hit puberty and her hips boomed out and her rear broadened. She could make it through the eight hours at the bank, but by the time she had hiked the stairs to their Chicago apartment, all she could think of was rye bread, slathered with butter and jam. She would kiss Gin, drop her coat on the floor, and head for the bread, perched on the refrigerator like her nemesis.

Within fifteen minutes, half of it would be gone.

Marcia cringed and stared at the mirror, at the ten pounds that she had lost only twice in her life and that always came back. "Today, today, I'll try to do it. This is my new leaf. I swear it. I'm going to lose this damn weight.

"All I need is will power, and I can do it."

Will power had gotten her through everything, she thought to herself.

All you have to do is want it bad enough and you can have it. Just grit your teeth. If only she looked like a skinny, fifteen-year-old boy. Life would be so much easier if she didn't look so fat, so much like a woman.

Will power would get her through the day. It would walk her through the big doors of the Chicago headquarters of the First Midwestern National Bank and up to her desk on the fifteenth floor where the real estate department was. It would sit her down at her small neat desk in the corner and it would give her the grace and the poise and that savoir faire that other women and even some men seemed to have and she never did.

She would perform brilliantly; she would handle them all—all the real estate developers coming for money for their next big project, annoyed that they had to deal with a loan analyst, but trying to act patient. They would even deal with some stupid woman smiling blandly in a grey suit with a tie at her neck, like she was gift-wrapped, if they could get the money out of the bank.

They would deal with her, one of the lowest on the department's pecking order, to get that money. Somehow, no one at the University of Chicago MBA program had ever told her how to respond to customers who treated her like a mildly retarded twelve-year-old. She was a banker; she controlled the purse strings; they were coming to her for money. So why did they make her feel like she couldn't walk and chew gum at the same time?

Another mystery of the ages, she sighed, part of the magic of making it in the business community. "Low self-esteem, that's my problem," she muttered to the mirror, examining her face. It wasn't making it either this morning. Every pore stood out. "I look like a sponge with eyes and a mouth."

And so it went. Seven o'clock on a wintry Monday morning in February at the Bernthals'.

"Come and get your coffee, Marsh," Gin called. Hodgkins Bernthal III, "Gin" to his friends, stood in the kitchen, surrounded by his coffee grinder and special drip coffee pot that required expensive paper filters. He loved grinding the beans and brewing his coffee. It gave him a reason to get up and get going in the morning.

"Preparing my life-giving fluid for the day," he thought, yawning and filling up the school thermos. The stuff they had in the teachers' lounge would kill anyone. And, on Monday mornings, he really needed chemical help to get moving.

Damn that Marcia; she was still in the bathroom.

"Marcia, honey," he called. "Get your sweet little ass out of the bathroom. I've got to shave and get out of here."

He heard the door slam, and passed her in the hallway, her bathrobe flying open as she ran. Why couldn't that woman stay calm on Mondays?

Like me. He sipped his coffee and stared in the bathroom mirror. I'm so calm, I'm comatose. From boredom.

Eight years of teaching and three years at St Paul's Catholic High School for Boys and he was still just an English teacher. Sure, he headed the department, but so what?

The Jesuits who ran St Paul's would never make him a vice principal, even though the Nazi who ran the place, Father Dotson, had promised him the job when he had arrived. Otherwise, Gin never would have left Howard High School.

Now Dotson put him off whenever he asked about it. Well, what did he expect? He lathered up his face and began shaving his lower left jaw. He was only a nominal Catholic and never went to church. Maybe if he developed the Stigmata, he'd have a chance?

Hah, that was unlikely.

Not only am I bored, he thought, I'm starving. Thirty years old and he was making $16,000 a year. It was humiliating. Just how long did it take to "earn your wings," as Dotson put it, before you could move up in the ranks?

But if he left St Paul's, where was he going to go? The public schools were glutted with aspiring little vice principals. And they were cesspools of drugs, bad kids, and burned-out teachers. Who wanted to run that—for any amount of money?

He sighed and stared at himself in the mirror.

Six feet tall, with sandy hair, Gin was a handsome man, and he knew it. He flexed his muscles, sucked in his tight little belly, and admired his profile. All that swimming paid off. (Maybe he should become a professional stud).

He went back to his shaving. It might be time to change careers. Computers. Maybe he should get into computers. That new teacher, Morton something or other, had a brother-in-law who owned a Computerland in Niles. Morton said he was cleaning up.

Gin started shaving maneuvers around his lower right jaw. That cute blonde he met at Harvey's party last month used to teach history at Amundsen High School; now she was a customer representative for the computer division of Xerox. She said that lots of ex-teachers ended up at Xerox. He should look her up when he wanted to make a change.

He had asked her what a "customer representative" did. From her reply he gathered that she convinced businessmen to buy computers they didn't need and then soft-soaped them when the hardware broke down.

I'm the wrong sex.

"Gin, my boy," he said to his half-shaved face in the mirror. "The computer revolution is passing you by."

"Gin, you talking to me?" Marcia was hopping past the bathroom on one foot; she paused at the open door. Her other foot was half stuffed into one leg of her pantyhose.

"Just mumbling into the mirror, Marsh."

"I know that place is driving you nuts, dear, but when you start talking to yourself, you know your time is up."

"Yeah, I know." He looked depressed.

"What's the matter?"

"The usual. I'm thirty years old and I don't know what I want to be when I grow up. And I'm already grown up."

"Yeah, well," she said. She wished he didn't look so pathetic. It unnerved her to think that they were both unraveling at once.

Marcia hopped over and kissed him where he was clean-shaven.

"I've got to run. We can talk tonight, okay?"

"Yeah, sure." Marcia couldn't really help; they had been over all this endlessly. He just wanted to talk to someone, anyone, to relieve his anxiety.

"Don't worry. It will all work out," Marcia said, putting her arm around him and wondering if it really would. She didn't have time to discuss his problems now. She had fifteen minutes to breakfast, pack her diet lunch of carrots and celery and get dressed or she would be late for work.

She went to look through the bedroom closet for her navy suit. Gin picked up the cleaning twice a week on his way home from school; half the time he forgot to hang her clothes on her side of the closet.

Men. Why couldn't they be more considerate?

And in the case of Gin, more focused. The navy suit surfaced in the midst of Gin's collection of chinos and identical button-down shirts. As she dressed, she wondered what was happening to him. It had been love at first sight when they had met four years ago on a blind date. They married six months later.

Most teachers she had known had been sour old things, stupid people; but Gin was different. Teaching excited him; he was ambitious. He wanted to be a principal and run his own school—maybe some day a whole school system. When they got married he seemed well on his way: he had just taken the teaching job at St Paul's, the biggest Catholic boys' high school in the city. The principal had promised to make him vice principal within the year; he would be the youngest vice principal in the Chicago Catholic school system.

But that one year was dragging into three, and there was still no promotion. Gin's ambition seemed to be dying; he was like a deflated balloon. Christ, she thought, when's that man going to get off his rear end and do something?

Every now and then, she wondered if marrying him had been a serious mistake. Maybe all that talk about school systems, all that ambition, that drive, was really hot air? Maybe he was really just another teacher—sour and stodgy—and she was stuck with him. He was a loser and she would have to support him emotionally and financially their whole life. Whenever this thought crossed her mind, she felt as though someone had punched her in the stomach.

She grabbed her purse and briefcase and headed back to the kitchen, where she shoved a few vegetables and pieces of rye crisp into a plastic bag. Gin was eating Rice Krispies with skim milk. She pecked him on the cheek.

"'Bye hon. See you around six."

"'Bye."

And she left.

Gin was glad to see her go. He finished his cereal and peeled an orange. They had married for better or for worse, but in Marcia's book things were only supposed to get better. She wasn't being much of a sport about his school problems.

She listened to his complaints and suggested alternatives, but he didn't like her tone. It seemed as if she didn't believe he could solve this problem on his own; she had to save him. That made him angry.

But maybe she was right; he couldn't find his way out. She thinks I'm a failure—and I am. It was depressing.

Well, at least he knew what he was, unlike Marcia. She hated her job, too. She just wouldn't admit it, even though she dragged herself home from the bank and dominated the dinner conversation with complaints. He was tired of listening to her. Get another job he had said the other night, trying to finish his meal.

She was offended. She wasn't a quitter, she said; her voice took on a strident tone and her face went stony. She was going to try harder and "tough it out" at the bank.

Gin threw his orange peelings into the garbage and went into the bedroom to dress. Just my luck. I marry a woman for her intelligence and exuberance and she turns into a sado-masochist.

You pays your money, you takes your chances, he thought, pulling on his camel sweater. He threw on his overcoat and picked up his thermos. If he didn't get moving, he'd be late for Dotson's staff meeting.

TWO

Marcia ran up the stairs to the Elevated platform and made it just in time. She crammed herself on the train, getting a seat next to the world's fattest woman when the previous co-occupant got up to get off at the next stop. At least it was a seat, though one buttock hung off the edge.

At Fullerton, a small blonde with a cloth briefcase over one shoulder jammed herself into the aisle next to Marcia. The edge of the case missed Marcia's head by about three inches every time the train lurched around a curve on its serpentine way downtown.

Marcia had been riding the El for ten years. She hated it. How could one walk into the bank with dignity after sitting on the train dodging briefcases, bulky shoulder purses and occasional elbows?

In the winter, the heat never worked; her feet froze in their thin lady-like boots. In summer, she sweated through all six of her linen-look suits.

Here and there were women in fur coats and soft felt hats looking like aliens in the seas of frayed coats, dirty boots and tired faces.

Marcia wanted to live where the fur-coated ladies probably lived: in the suburbs. A nice suburb with big trees, wide streets; upwardly-mobile people with white faces and well-behaved children named Jennifer and Jason who lived in big Colonial houses set back from winding roads and at the end of long flagstone walks, and garages with small, expensive foreign cars. Not an unambitious dream for someone making only $28,500 a year. But they could do it if they only scrimped a little.

She wondered if she could talk Gin into it. He liked the city, but these days he didn't seem to care where he lived or where he was going.

She knew where she was going. She was going to be head of the real estate loan department at First Midwestern National Bank by the time she was forty-five.

The young men at the bank and the real estate developers were dynamic and sure of themselves; they knew where they were going. They had nice suits, nice cars, and nice, well-groomed wives working at moderately well-paying jobs as legal secretaries at good law firms. Maybe they even had a neat, well-behaved child in a good day care center. They were the kind of men a woman could respect.

Unlike poor old Gin these days. She felt guilty at her disloyalty, but he *was* depressed, disorganized, and underpaid.

He was gorgeous, though. And a good lover. She thought about their regular Saturday morning love-making. He was better at it than she was; he loosened up and enjoyed himself. She was still holding herself back; she could feel it. But she was relaxing a little more with his help.

Love-making and swimming were his great sports. He was as natural in the water as he was in bed: he enjoyed it so much that it embarrassed her.

In the summer, he would swim a half mile out into Lake Michigan, diving thirty feet to see what was on the bottom.

How did he do it? She could swim a mile at a time, but was terrified to let water close over her head. Someone at a party had once remarked that it was very Freudian, being afraid of deep water. "It's being afraid of intimacy." Marcia had cringed then, and cringed now. Gin could swim in deep water; she couldn't. Maybe he could teach her that, too?

If only she could wave a magic wand, solve all his problems and make him the happy, dynamic man she had married.

The cloth briefcase swung by her nose as the train screeched into the station. Marcia gathered up her briefcase, her purse, her plastic bag full of diet food, and headed for the door, ploughing through people in a litany of "excuse me's." She forced herself out the doors, past a teen-aged Puerto Rican with green hair and an earring.

The headquarters of the First Midwestern National Bank was a forty-story concrete high rise topped with a decorative turret.

It was set in a sunken plaza with a fountain, a stage and a bad mosaic sculpture from the down side of Miró's career.

During the summer, the bank hosted a noonday concert series and the plaza teemed with people. The other three seasons of the year, it was a desert. In February, the winds whistled through the half acre of dead, snowy space in the heart of the city.

"Welcome to the moon," Marcia thought, as she made her way to the granite elevator block.

Her mood lightened when she reached the fifteenth floor. The outside of the bank might look like a pile of cement, but inside it was warm red carpets, teak desks and floor-to-ceiling windows giving panoramic views of the city. But the desks were facing the wrong way. Instead of looking out over the city, they looked in toward the elevator bank. Marcia had once suggested that they turn their desks around. Her co-workers had looked at her blankly; no one had apparently ever thought of such a thing, much less said it.

Her small desk firmly faced a grass-cloth covered wall with a good, subdued etching hung on it, while behind her the entire south side of the city could be seen blazing in all its glory. When she had first come to the bank three years ago, Marcia tried to work on her lap, or even on the credenza behind her desk, to get a look out the window. But that hadn't lasted for long.

She needed desk space, lots of it, for what she did for a living. Analyzing real estate is a painful, slow process that generates mounds of paper for even the laziest analyst. And Marcia was very thorough: the bank wasn't going to lose money on any loans *she* worked on.

Several piles of real estate appraisals, computer printouts and financial spreadsheets covered with Marcia's careful pencilled numbers were heaped on her desk. Others were stuffed into drawers, strewn across the credenza and even spilled over onto the floor. Under her desk, next to her boots, lay a market study commissioned by a developer who wanted the bank to fund a construction loan for a $35 million office building in Tulsa.

Must have cost him $50,000 for that study, Marcia thought contentedly; slush dripped from her boots onto its matte red cover with raised gold lettering. She rummaged under a bank of drawers for her navy blue pumps, thinking, The revenge of the powerless. Probably a pack of lies anyway.

She sat back in her chair and wondered, as she did frequently these days, how she ever ended up working in a bank. She hated bankers, she really did. Why the hell was she here?

She was here because they had money, they had power, and she had none and she knew it. She loved buildings, building them and looking at them and arguing about their financing. It took a long time before you could accumulate enough money yourself either to go out on your own or have enough power at the bank to make them do it your way. She wouldn't mind running the real estate department; bankers make great minions. But it took years to get there. And she felt she was losing her sense of how you got from where she was—to where she wanted to be.

She had never planned to end up at a bank. For that matter, she had never planned to end up in real estate. No one had ever told her that she would have to support herself when she grew up; no one had told her to plan a career. So when she got out of school, she had scrambled for a job, become a trainee at a mortgage banking firm, analyzing property. And now she was here, at thirty, the oldest loan analyst in the real estate department, surrounded by a sea of bright young men, five years or more her junior.

She glanced up to see one of them smiling a greeting to her over his styrofoam cup of coffee. Fred Baxter had been at his desk since seven a.m. Even though the day didn't officially start until eight-thirty, all the bright young men came in at seven a.m. just to show how eager they were. All they ever did before eight-thirty was read the *Wall Street Journal.*

Marcia was sure they had mastered the art of sleeping with their eyes open and staring at the newspaper. It was a strange tribal custom. She had never adopted it. She had her own custom: she came in religiously every day at eight-forty-five, fifteen minutes late, feeling guiltily defiant.

She sighed. She really had to start getting in by at least seven-thirty if she expected to get anywhere at the bank. The competition was getting a good two hours on her.

"Hello there, Baxter, how are you?"

"Fine, Marcia." Baxter's white shirt glowed, his skin glowed, his shoes glowed and his neat brown hair glowed. He was a gratifying neatly-barbered sight in his well-pressed pin-striped suit. For a moment, Marcia hated him for being twenty-five years old, handsome and competent.

And he was smart, too. And a nice guy. He would go far. She was glad for him.

"Marcia, you got the appraisal on the Six Corners Center?"

"The regional mall in Sheboygan?"

"That's the one."

Of course she had the appraisal. What the hell did he want with it? She was working on that deal. She attacked a file on the northeast corner of her mountain range of papers and started rummaging through it.

Baxter smiled as she rummaged. God, he looked like the Marlboro man without the leather. She wondered if his young wife, Bridget, appreciated what she had here, a good-looking, dependable meal ticket who also happened to be a nice guy. Kind of bland, but a nice guy. She felt glad for Bridget, too.

"Uh, Baxter, I know it's here somewhere. Just wait a minute." She always felt so vulnerable sifting through papers in front of the pin-striped men. Their desks were always so neat, and hers was such a mess. Another New Year's resolution: clean up your desk. She would add it to the list.

"Sure, Marcia, no problem. I just need it as soon as you can find it. In fact, I really need the whole file. Ranier wants me to take a look at it before the ten a.m. staff meeting."

"He does?" Marcia looked up sharply, a shock of brown hair falling in her eyes.

"Yeah, he told me Friday night, after you left, that he wanted to put me on the project with you. He thought you might need a little help with it."

Baxter shifted nervously.

"Well, I, yeah, I suppose I could always use some help. Look, here's what I've got already." She thrust an overexpanded expandable file of paper at him. "I'll bring you the rest as soon as I can dig them out."

She gave him what she hoped was a friendly smile, flashing her marvelous set of cavity-free teeth.

"Yeah, sure Marcia, just drop it by." Baxter put the file under his arm and glided beyond a row of beige file cabinets on his way to his spotless teak desk in another neighborhood of teak desks.

Hot damn, that little twerp. See what happened when you left right at four-forty-five quitting time? The powers-that-be rearrange the universe at six and cut you out. Another New Year's resolution. Stay until six every night, just to protect yourself from sneak attacks.

Marcia needed help on Six Corners as much as fish needed help to swim. What was Ranier trying to do to her? The head of the real estate department had hired her three years ago, promising that he would make her a loan officer and let her do her own deals. He said he might even give her the authority to approve some small deals, $25,000 or less, on her own.

Now, here she was, three years later, still slaving away like a twenty-five-year-old financial analyst, reading office leases by the hour and running revenue projections on strip shopping centers in small towns in Illinois. Clerk work.

Lots of real estate developers her age were building office towers with their names on them in Manhattan and Dallas. Here she sat trying to figure out how much some two-bit contractor-turned-developer had lied on his projections for constructing a million-dollar mini-warehouse near the airport.

"Now, Marcia, we all have to pay our dues," Ranier had said, when she had complained to him six months ago. He was such a nice man. He reminded her of her father, quiet and good at what he did, with terribly high standards for his staff. "You just keep up the good work and I'll make sure you get to work on a big deal coming up."

He had kept his word. When the Six Corners deal had come up two months ago, he had put Marcia on it. It was a big loan for a big customer. Harry Morris, the developer, had financed construction of all four of his other regional shopping malls through First Midwestern. At about $35 million a shot and an interest rate of over fourteen percent, the loans made a lot of money for the bank. The real estate department was a big profit center; they were proud of themselves.

Ranier himself handled the negotiations. Marcia did the analyses, happily burrowing through eighty-five leases and running miles of computer printouts on the project's feasibility. The project disturbed her. She knew Sheboygan from her days at the mortgage banking firm, and she wasn't sure they needed another regional shopping center there. And even if they did, the numbers on this center didn't look right. They seemed far too optimistic.

Owners of shopping centers derive much of their profit from percentage rents. Once the tenants achieve a certain volume of sales, they begin to pay percentages of their profits to the landlord. To reach the profit levels Morris was predicting, Six Corners' tenants would have to sell twice as much as any other center she had seen in years.

"Christ," she had said to Gin, "Morris expects inflation and future sales to make the numbers work on this deal." Gin had given her one of those pleasant, distracted smiles that meant he didn't understand what she was talking about. And he didn't want to.

Damn that man. Why didn't he take an interest in her work? She felt so alone.

She had mentioned her problems with the project to Ranier three weeks ago. "I know I haven't been close to regional malls for a while, but when you work the numbers back, his sales figures are way too high," she had said and gone on to express doubts about the leases and even the size of the parking lot. She ended by telling him that Sheboygan didn't need another two million square feet of retail space.

Ranier had listened closely. "Well, Marcia," he had said, "those are all good points."

And now she had a little helper.

She needed a cup of coffee.

She gathered up the four remaining files on Six Corners and on the way to the cafeteria, dumped them on Baxter's desk, startling him. He was bent over the appraisal file, making neat rows of figures on a clean yellow pad. He looked like a Boy Scout building an Indian village out of toothpicks.

"Here you go, Baxter," she said. "See you at ten."

THREE

St Paul's was a squat complex of red brick buildings that took up a complete city block. Its interior was a rabbit warren of rooms—some old, some new—connected by miles of corridors with linoleum floors. As the school had grown over the years, the Jesuits had added a wing here and a room there. In 1968, when enrollment exceeded two thousand, they had built a concrete and steel auditorium, two physics labs, and thirteen extra classrooms.

Now enrollment was down to fifteen hundred and additions were out of the question. To save heat, half a dozen classrooms and a physics lab were locked up and not used. Still, you had to hand it to Father Matthew Dotson, S.J., the principal. School enrollments everywhere were dropping and the archidiocese was closing schools, but St Paul's appeared to be prospering.

Gin drove Vivian the Volvo into the teacher's parking lot. She stood out there—a shiny, new car the color of gun-metal—among the ten-year-old Dodge Darts and rusted-out Datsuns. Gin and Marcia had talked each other into getting Vivian last summer when their old Toyota died.

It really was ludicrous, he thought, locking up Vivian. What had possessed them? They had giggled as they signed the papers for Vivian, and afterward they had toasted their new car with champagne. He was driving a car that cost as much as his annual salary. The euphoria was growing fainter each time he wrote out the monthly car payment checks for $350.

Gin trudged through the snow toward the side door off the gym, his coffee thermos under one arm and his old briefcase under the other. Classes started at eight-thirty, but every other Monday, Father Dotson held a staff meeting for his teachers at seven-forty-five. Today was an early Monday.

What a waste of time, Gin thought morosely. The old guy calls us out just to troop the colors, not to tell us what's really going on. Gin was dying to find out if the school was running at a profit. At the last meeting, Dotson had talked about the new plastic coffee-cup holders he had ordered for the teachers' lounge; about where they should park when snowfall was over two inches, and about the never-ending battle to keep the kids from smoking in the bathrooms. Gin had never been so impolitic as to ask directly about the school's financial condition: teachers were not supposed to be interested in that.

He dropped his briefcase in front of his locker. Up and down the corridor, faintly lit by two rows of fluorescent tubes in these pre-class hours, most of the school's fifty teachers were hanging up their coats and shaking snow off their boots, filling the hallway with the pleasant murmuring of male conversation. All students and teachers at St Paul were male. After three years, Gin still couldn't get used to it. He often felt as though he were in a monastery, or under a glass bell, cut off entirely from the opposite sex. It made him uneasy.

Everyone, except the gym instructors, carried bulging leather briefcases. A true sign of a teacher, Gin thought, especially an English teacher. In his own ancient bag, along with a well-worn copy of the *Odyssey*, were essays from his seven daily classes. They ranged from the remedial sophomores' efforts to write letters to local newspaper editors on national issues to essays by his accelerated seniors on symbolism in Homer.

He would spend all day Sunday working on them.

Gin shivered despite his heavy sweater. It must be fifty-five degrees in here, he thought. Archie the janitor had forgotten to turn the heat up for an early Monday—again. Par for the course. From janitors to gym teachers, Dotson hired only the cheapest help he could find. So he attracted only the incompetent, the inexperienced or the desperate. He also got a few mavericks, like Gin and Harvey Teitelbaum, who didn't want to teach under the public school bureaucracy.

"A little brisk in here this morning, hey Bernthal?" Gin turned around and found himself eye-to-eye with the grey, bloodless face of Ron Franklin. Fortyish and thin, with slicked-back brown hair, Franklin taught algebra to mystified freshmen. He lifted their cloud cover by tutoring them for fifteen dollars an hour after school and on weekends. That was one way to supplement your salary. The students pay in cash and you don't declare it on your income tax.

"Hi, how are you, Ron? Ready for our big meeting?" Gin had trouble keeping sarcasm out of his tone.

"Words from the Holy Father are always welcome to my ears," Franklin said mildly. Gin could never tell whether Franklin was serious or not. The man reminded him of a talking clam.

"Yeah, I suppose. How's the tutoring business these days?"

"Oh, very good indeed," Franklin said in his low monotone. "It's amazing the difficulty many children have with algebra."

Especially if you can't teach, Gin thought, smiling politely. If he ever became vice principal, Franklin would be among the first to go.

"Well, see you at the meeting, Ron. I gotta run." He pointed to his thermos. "Got to go try out one of Dotson's new coffee cups."

Gin, waving to some of his colleagues, saying hello to others, walked down the corridor toward the stairs leading to the second-floor teachers' lounge. People liked Gin—and sympathized with him. Everyone knew that Dotson had stuck it to him on the vice principal's job and Gin knew they knew. He tried to ignore it and sometimes, for an entire day, he could. But often he felt embarrassed walking past a group of his colleagues. He hated to be pitied.

The "teachers' lounge" was actually just an old classroom. The spring-green paint had faded and a big patch was peeling off one wall. The acoustical tile on the ceiling was spotted from leaks. The furniture—folding chairs and three long trestle-tables—dated from the Depression. In a far corner an ancient coffee urn sputtered and groaned. Gin found it hard to believe that he had spent so much of his spare time in this ugly room.

About a dozen teachers, standing around in small groups or sitting in the old chairs, were sipping coffee from styrofoam cups nestled in new, brown-plastic cup holders.

Ted O'Connor, the oldest member of the English department, sat alone at a table, scowling over some student papers and marking away furiously with his red pen. O'Connor had been at St Paul's since the Dark Ages. He prided himself on never taking work home with him over the weekend. Instead, he graded papers during every spare moment of the school day, including Dotson's Monday staff meeting. While the others sat politely listening, O'Connor scratched away at his papers, breathing heavily and arching his bushy eyebrows every now and then.

By right of seniority, O'Connor and not Gin should have been head of the English Department. But O'Connor didn't seem to care. He rarely spoke to other teachers and if he was trapped into conversation he would mumble and leave as soon as he could. He was sixty-three years old; he had heart problems and a sick wife. The teachers' pension plan at St Paul's was a joke, and Gin doubted that O'Connor had any savings. He wondered what it would be like to have to eat dogfood. How about Purina Chunky bits au gratin? Your financial future at St Paul's. Just trust the good fathers of the Society of Jesus to take care of you. Put your faith in God and he will provide. Unfortunately, not in this life. In this life, you'll starve.

"Cheer up, Bernthal, you mope. You look like a truck hit you. The prospect of Father Flotsky's big meeting got you down?" Harve Teitelbaum smiled broadly and slapped Gin across the back. Gin's face lit up. The plump little history teacher with the Colorado ski tan was his best friend at St Paul's.

"Hey there, Harve, how you doin'?"

"Christ, better than you, Bernthal. What were you thinking about? The second coming of Christ and your future in hell?"

"Just contemplating O'Connor over there."

"From a distance, I hope."

O'Connor didn't seem to bathe much. Everyone gave him a wide berth at meetings.

"Harvey, what's that man going to live on when he retires?" Gin stared his friend intently in the eye, startling him.

"Don't worry, Gin. He's such a mess he'll drop dead soon."

Gin kept staring at Harvey. "Harve, you think I should ask Dotson about that vice-principal job again? You know, take one more shot at it?"

"God, you're a real laugh-a-minute this morning, Bernthal. Monday at seven-thirty and you already want to talk about life-threatening situations. What's with you?"

"Well, I was shaving this morning and I was thinking that maybe I should give up this whole teaching schtick and go into something different like computers or something. I don't know."

"Christ, Gin, you're beginning to sound like the rest of the walking wounded around here."

The St Paul staff complained constantly about their long hours and lousy pay. At any gathering at least two people would say that they were going to get out of teaching and into something more profitable, like manufacturing silicon chips or developing management-training programs.

But with the exception of John Saylor, the music teacher who went back to school to become an accountant, no one had left teaching in the three years that Gin had been at St Paul's. A half dozen had taken jobs at other schools. Three had retired; and Carl Gluckman, one of the lay religion teachers, had decided to become a Jesuit—at the age of fifty-eight. That was one way to retire comfortably. The Society of Jesus took care of its own.

Gin poured some coffee from his thermos into two styrofoam cups, mounted in their new cup holders. He handed one to Harvey and lifted his cup in a toast.

"Well, Harve, here's to our latest perk. Never let it be said that the Society of Jesus didn't spend the bucks on its staff."

"Here, here."

They solemnly sipped their coffee.

"Do you think it would help if I talked to him again, Harve?"

"Boy, you don't give up easy."

"I just have to get it off my chest. It's driving me crazy."

"Don't do it, Gin. Don't. Dotson doesn't want to hear about you and his broken promises. He just wants you to shut up and rot in a corner, teaching *Silas Marner* to the illiterate for the rest of your life. You start rocking the boat, and he'll make life real hard. And I mean *real* hard."

"Give me a break, Harve. The man's a professional educator. He wouldn't treat me like that just for asking where I stand here."

"He knows where you stand. You're slime on the bottom of the sea. You just don't know it yet."

"But we never really ironed that all out."

"He doesn't have to iron it all out. He's been sending you death rays on those Jesuit brain waves of his for three years."

"But then why is the job still open, tell me that, wise guy?"

"I don't know. Maybe he doesn't want to fill it at all. It's been vacant two years, ever since Father Hodson retired. He's hardly in a rush to fill it."

"Yeah, but maybe it's something political. Maybe he's been waiting for some orders from his superiors. I still might have a chance at it."

"A chance like a snowball in hell. They're going to give the job to another Jesuit."

"How do you know?"

"Just a feeling. The Jesuits take care of their own."

"But then why did Dotson bother to lure me here in the first place?"

"You got me. Why did the Jesuits start the Inquisition and torture Spain into becoming a cultural backwater? There's no logic there."

"Harvey, this isn't the Inquisition. If I'm not going to get that job, I've got to start thinking about getting out of here. I've been more than patient; I should have had that job a year ago. The man can't hang me for asking where I stand. I've got to know what's going on."

"Yeah, I suppose so. But you better be prepared to sell shoes for a living." Harvey lifted his cup again. "Here's to your career suicide, Bernthal."

"Harvey, for God's sake. I really think you're overdoing it." As usual, Gin thought. For Harvey, life was a huge tapestry, filled with wars, great issues and the struggle between the forces of good and evil. It was "human drama". Harvey loved teaching History because it gave him a chance to play all the parts. One of his favorites was Napoleon; Harvey's re-enactment of the Emperor leading the retreat of his ragged army from Moscow had everybody on the floor at parties.

And Harvey was a good teacher, maybe even a great one. But with an income of fifty thousand a year from a family trust fund, Harvey could afford to concentrate on his teaching. He could spend two years in the Peace Corps and summers in Europe and go skiing in Colorado over semester break with his wife Dominique and the two kids. He didn't have to worry about money or the course of his career. Unlike the plebian teachers who had to work for a living.

Harvey loved Roman history. His classes were always making model Roman war fleets out of paper cutout kits and re-enacting the Battle of Actium. Harvey liked to declaim Mark Antony's oration from his desk; the kids ate it up. Last year *Cleopatra,* with Richard Burton and Elizabeth Taylor, had come to a revival movie theatre and Harvey had taken all three sections of his ancient history class, along with Dominique and Gin and Marcia, to see it. The Battle of Actium was great; Taylor's cleavage and the love scenes were just as good. The kids loved it.

Dotson had given Harvey a severe dressing down because of that. The Church had condemned *Cleopatra* when it first came out twenty years ago, and it was still considered immoral even though what the kids saw on TV every night was just as sexy and a lot more violent. Harvey had sat before Dotson's desk, stone-faced and wordless. In all his eight years of teaching, no principal had ever spoken to him like that.

Since that time he had hated Dotson. Gin had tried to explain that Dotson had to stand up for what the Church said. It was his job. Harvey had replied that Dotson was a twisted old man with homosexual tendencies who enjoyed humilating his staff. "A system where doing your job makes you act like a hostile lunatic isn't worth supporting," Harvey had said.

More and more, Gin was growing afraid that Harvey was right.

Gin looked up at his friend, who was watching him quizzically.

"Welcome back to the world of the living. Where'd you go so suddenly?"

"Just thinking, Harve, just thinking." Gin picked up his thermos and coffee cup. "Time for the big meeting, amigo. Let's hit the road."

They walked down the hall together.

FOUR

Marcia couldn't believe she was hearing it.

"And so, Baxter here will pick up the remaining analytical work on the Six Corners project, while Marcia can start work on the Cully warehouse deal tomorrow." Ranier removed his horn-rims with a statesman-like flourish. He shuffled his papers back into a manila folder, indicating the meeting was over, and smiled benignly at the seven young faces smiling back at him.

Marcia felt as though she had just been blown out of the water, like one of those battleships in the World War II movies that Gin loved to watch.

"Uh, Mr Ranier, could I have a few moments with you?" she asked, as he turned toward the door.

"Of course, Marcia. I have another meeting at eleven, but I can spare you a few moments." Ranier lived in meetings. He was always on his way to or from one, or going out to lunch with customers, or going somewhere where it would be difficult for his bewildered staff to find him when they needed him. Marcia always felt she was interrupting him on his way to something important. All the conversations she had ever had with him about her career at the bank had been sandwiched into five-minute segments between his meetings and phone calls.

She knew he treated everybody that way, from the blue-eyed boy wonder, Tom Paxton, to Henrietta Ratner, the department lost cause. The men seemed to take the boss's distraction in stride, but it threw Marcia off. She felt especially thrown off, and guilty, when she came into his office to complain about something.

She felt terribly guilty right now.

Ranier strode into his corner office, stopping off en route to pick up a bundle of pink message slips from Marge, his secretary, who shouted instructions after him from her desk as he moved away.

"You're supposed to call Franklin Howard by noon. He says he can't make the meeting in Fort Lauderdale on Friday—how about next Tuesday? But he's catching a plane at one today; he needs to know before he leaves. Melville Evans called; you can reach him at his car phone this afternoon. He's going on to the Chambers Center this afternoon to talk to his appraiser about the refinancing. Herbie Cohen called; the Freilich deal will close in two weeks if he can straighten out the title mess by then."

Marge rattled through another four complicated messages involving airplanes, car phones and something about a loan commitment from Aetna Life Insurance that might not be going through. Marcia's blood rushed. This was where she wanted to be. She wished that all those messages were for her.

"Marge, just hold on a minute and I'll be right with you." Ranier closed the door to his office, motioning Marcia to one of the deep upholstered chairs in front of his massive teak desk. Marcia noted that his desk faced the right way: he had a great view of the lake. She looked at his tanned face and exquisitely graying hair against a background of grass cloth and an abstract painting.

Bosses got oil paintings; the troops got etchings. Everybody got grass cloth.

"Well, my dear, what can I do for you?" Ranier said.

"Look, Mr Ranier," she began. Her hands were cold, but her neck was hot. "I really don't understand why you're pulling me off the Six Corners project. I thought I was doing a good job, and I was getting along with the customer, and I really enjoyed working on it. So why did you pull me off?"

"Well, of course you were doing a good job. We just thought it would be better for Baxter to pick up the ball from here. He needs the experience of working on a regional center, and we needed you to work on the Calderelli deal."

"Cully deal." Marcia corrected him. The Cully deal, as revealed during the magic moments of the staff meeting, was another construction loan on another warehouse out near the airport. Only instead of being just a one-million-dollar loan, it was a two-million-dollar loan. Real progress she was making here.

"Yes, the Cully deal." Ranier began to shuffle through his fluffy pink pile of phone messages. "You're our expert on industrial parks." He looked up suddenly into her eyes, startling her. "After all, we have to let the others work on the big deals too. We have to let others work on deals that are exciting. Besides, I need someone who can get along with the customer."

"But I got along well with Mr Morris, Mr Ranier."

"Well, you didn't seem as enthusiastic about the deal as I thought you should be." His voice was developing an impatient edge.

"Enthusiastic? Mr Ranier, of course I'm enthusiastic." Before the words came out of her mouth, it hit her. Oh, my God. Now she knew what had happened. She had criticized the deal, the biggest deal in the shop, the one that Ranier himself had talked Harry Morris into bringing to them instead of giving it to those maniacs at Continental where they'd lend to anybody as long as his knuckles didn't drag on the ground when he walked. Morris was a good First Midwestern customer, but he had been ready to jump ship. Ranier had promised him he would stretch on the deal.

And she had come in with complaints about leases, the retail demand in Sheboygan, and even the size of the parking lot. How could she have been so stupid? She was lucky Ranier hadn't shot her instead of giving the deal to Baxter. First Midwestern would do that deal even if Morris had to rent the whole center to Zoo World to fill it up.

It's one thing to criticize a crummy warehouse deal from a nobody customer. It's quite another to go after the boss's pride and joy. It would be a cold day in hell before Ranier gave her another big deal to work on.

She sagged in her chair. Ranier glared at her.

It was time to take evasive action, patch up the troops, and retreat.

"Well. . . I . . . uh. . . can see that you would want to give Baxter a shot at working on something big like this. I enjoyed working on it; I hope you give me a shot at another one soon, Mr Ranier." She smiled the smile she always gave her father when he reminded her, as he did regularly when she was a child, that she just wasn't measuring up to his high expectations. Her smile said she would try harder.

She hoped it would help. It did.

"Well, Marcia." Ranier's voice softened. "Of course you'll get more of the big deals to work on. You just sit tight and do a good job on this Calderelli deal and we'll see what comes down the pike. Now if you'll excuse me, I have to make some phone calls."

He showed her to the door and she floated out in a haze, past Marge who barrelled in as she left. "Mr Feinstein and his lawyer are here, Mr Ranier. They're in the blue conference room."

"I'll be right there, Marge." He grabbed a legal pad and charged down the hall to the conference room in a cloud of subtle male cologne and energetic male efficiency.

Marcia drooped as she watched him sprint off. Why can't I be like that? she thought. So efficient, so in control, so successful. She had never seen Ranier say "uh" and look at his hands. Even the twenty-five-year-old men were poised and joked easily with one another. She always felt like the fifth wheel, the only one who didn't get the joke in an elevator full of laughing men.

Well, business was a man's world. She was just going to have to try harder. She threw back her shoulders and tried to feel confident. Her current late-night reading, *Management in a Cut-Throat World*, advised her never to give up in the face of business problems. Always press on. It was persistence that separated the winners from the losers in the business game. That was good advice. She would do better next time. Maybe Ranier would allow her to redeem herself.

Redeem herself from what? From doing a good job? From being a competent analyst and pointing out that the deal was a bomb? The problems with the deal were all too obvious; Ranier would never have taken it on if he hadn't been anxious to do it regardless of quality.

How could she have been so dense? Now that she thought about it, he had never appreciated her detailed analyses of the property.

"Oh, thanks, Marcia," he would say, and put her Six Corners reports to one side on his desk. And she would never hear anything about them again. Her feelings had been hurt. She had done her best crayon drawing for dear old Dad and he hadn't even told her she was the best little artist in the second grade. She had dropped a few hints to Ranier about going over the reports. He always said he was busy, or would get to it tomorrow, or that he was studying them. But he said that about everything she gave him. How the hell was she supposed to know that he didn't want to be told about Six Corners? She wasn't clairvoyant.

But she was sure that the baby loan analysts around her would have picked up the hint. Why hadn't she? She was never going to learn how to play these business games. She was a failure again.

She drooped her way back to her desk. Compared to Ranier's office it looked tiny and cluttered. She wished she could talk to Gin, but she wouldn't see him until tonight.

She fished her diet food out of a drawer: carrots and cauliflower at room temperature. She couldn't face that. She needed a nice big hamburger with fries, washed down with a chocolate shake. She shuffled papers around, glued some new labels on some files, and at eleven-thirty ambled over to Frances Klein's desk.

FIVE

Frances Klein was lucky. Sometimes new bank customers didn't know she was a woman. They would call up, gruff male voices asking for "Frank Klein," and would be surprised to hear a poised female voice slipping along the phone wire. It was helpful: the customers were usually thrown off enough so that Frances got a slight negotiating edge.

That's why Frances is a real estate loan officer and I'm not, Marcia thought in her uncharitable moments. Maybe she should change her name to Leslie? That was another of those hermaphrodite names.

Who was she kidding? Frances was a loan officer because she was good.

Customers liked her. She negotiated hard enough to get a good deal for the bank but not hard enough to drive customers into the arms of the competition. Frances was twenty-nine, pretty and red-haired. She had been made a loan officer five months ago. She was making only small deals now, but Marcia was sure she'd go far at the bank, although maybe not in Real Estate.

Real Estate was a good department, but all the real action was in Commercial Lending. That was where the big fees came from. Everyone who was anyone at First Midwestern came up through Commercial Lending. Frances would definitely end up there, arranging hundred-million-dollar loans to big-name companies in Chicago and jetting to Rio, New York and Paris to handle negotiations with the companies' foreign subsidiaries.

Marcia could envision Frances lunching with the company vice president of finance in Paris. She would nibble at her foie gras, her delicate white fingers entwined around the stem of a crystal wine glass, and charm him into accepting an extra half-percentage point in loan fees or into putting up more collateral. That's real talent, Marcia thought.

Frances would go far. She was just stretching her young wings in Real Estate, picking up some pointers on net-leased industrial buildings before moving on to the ultimate glories of Commercial Lending.

Frances was in the bank's five-year management-training program with only one hundred and fifty young bankers. They had been tested, interviewed, and the men probably had to give sperm samples before they were accepted. They were management's hope for the future. The fledgling managers of tomorrow rotated through all the major departments of the bank, spending a year in the Trust department, and nine months in Real Estate, and six months in Cash Management, and four months here, and eight months there, and so forth. It reminded Marcia of a European tour: wake up, travelers, this is Wednesday; you must be in Foreign Currency Trading.

How could anyone learn anything about anything in six months? It had taken Marcia two years just to figure out how to detect holes in heating and air-conditioning expenses in warehouses. And she was a fast learner. But Frances had been in Real Estate Lending for six months, and they had made her a loan officer after she had been there for only a month.

She had come to Real Estate from the Personal Trust department. There she had explained their dividend checks to little old ladies with blue hair; now she was negotiating with the borderline criminal types known as real estate developers. And she seemed to be doing just fine. Marcia hated her for it.

Frances was friendly, but reserved and discreet. She never said "uh" and stared at her hands; she exuded quiet self-confidence. Marcia knew that she lived alone in the trendy part of the city with a cat and a tank of exotic tropical fish. She was engaged to some guy about Marcia's age who was a rising star in the International Lending department. They had just bought a house in Barrington, the horsy, woodsy suburb for bank executives like the Rising Star who were making over eighty-five thousand a year.

Frances and the Star were always going to the opera or the theatre, or signing up for personal improvement classes. Frances was now attending a class on using your home computer to develop your own tailored financial plan. This was in addition to finishing her MBA at night at the University of Chicago, where she was in Marcia's Cost Accounting class.

Both Marcia and Frances were in their last quarter of the program. Marcia was exhausted and bored with it; Frances looked as though she could hardly wait to start on her PhD so she could be going to school three nights a week for the rest of her life. When did she and the Rising Star get enough time to get it on, Marcia wondered, watching Frances' red curls bob on her shoulder as she talked on the phone. She hung up.

"Hello, Frances, how are you?" Marcia said. "You free for lunch?"

Frances was the only Frances Marcia had ever met who wanted to be called Frances and not Fran, Franny, Fanny or Muffy.

"Oh, Marcia, I'd love to, but I have a lunch with a customer in the dining room." Her blue eyes sparkled and her milky skin glowed with that porcelain look that only redheads have. Loan officers used the executive dining room to entertain customers; loan analysts could entertain themselves in the employee cafeteria or at Wendy's.

"Well, maybe next week sometime, Frances," Marcia said. "Oh, Frances, you're coming tonight to the Cost Accounting meeting, aren't you?"

A group of students from the class were meeting at Marcia's apartment after dinner to work on an assigned problem, due after the holidays. The rest of the world took a Christmas vacation, but University of Chicago MBAs never rested.

"Of course, Marcia. At seven, right? Got to run now. Mr Ferlingetti is waiting for me. See you tonight."

Such a pretty woman, and talented too. Why can't I be more like her? Marcia went into the ladies' room and stared in the mirror at her dark cap of hair, falling the wrong way over her forehead, as usual. Her skin, like the skin of most brunettes, had a yellowish cast. Under fluorescent light, it looked like yellowed parchment. The Dead Sea scrolls, Marcia thought, pulling a comb through her hair. She wore a knit cap to keep warm on the El, and it always mashed her hair down. Maybe a little water would revive it?

She bent over the faucet but straightened suddenly as the bathroom door swung swiftly open, narrowly missing her backside.

"Oh, Marcia, I'm sorry, I didn't know you were there."

It was Henrietta Ratner, hurrying in with a pile of packages. Her coat was open, her hair straggled out from under her beret, and her blue scarf—the one with the Pac Man on it, the one her son Timmy had given her for Christmas—dragged on the floor.

"No problem, Henrietta, I'm not hurt, " Marcia murmured, trying to get out the door before Henrietta geared up. But it was already too late.

"Oh, Marcia, I'm so glad to see you. You know I never see you much any more, now that you're on the other side of the elevators. Listen, I've got some new pictures of Timmy and Suzanne here somewhere—I've been meaning to show them to you but I haven't had the chance."

She began rummaging in her overstuffed handbag. "You know I'm just running all the time. Running, running, running. Never stops. You know how it is with us working moms. I was just now going out to take back Christmas presents. You know the kids' father never gets them the right size for Christmas and I always end up being the one who has to exchange the stuff."

Her voice took on a plaintive tone. "He gets the kids twice a month on weekends and he still can't take the time to find out what sizes they wear. Isn't that just like a man? Oh wait, I can't seem to—I hope I didn't leave them home. . . "

She dropped her boxes on the floor and began digging violently into her bag, contorting her face into an agonized frown as she excavated. She looked tired. It was hard to believe that Henrietta was only twenty-nine, the same age as Frances.

Henrietta was the other female loan analyst in the department; she made even less money than Marcia and was destined for oblivion at the bank. Until she retired she would remain a loan analyst, laboring away in her corner on the deals no one else wanted. Everyone else thought of himself or herself as having a "career" in banking. Henrietta was just struggling to survive.

She drove Marcia crazy with her vulnerability and her quiet despair over everything that happened to her. It was a relief when the department was redesigned and Henrietta's desk was moved to the other side of the elevators. The woman depressed the hell out of Marcia.

"Wait, wait! Success! I found them, I found them. Here they are."

She flourished a stack of dog-eared color snapshots secured with a rubber band. The stack was at least a half-inch thick. An ugly baby with a pink bow in its limp blond hair stared open-mouthed at the camera. A four-year-old boy with sad eyes made rabbit-ears with his hands behind his baby sister's head.

"Now here's Timmy and Suzanne at my sister's house at Christmas. And here they are opening their presents. And here's Suzanne with her favorite stuffed doggy with the ratty ears. You know, I got her a Cabbage Patch Doll for Christmas and she just ignored it. We couldn't get that ratty old dog away from her."

Every report on Baby's First Christmas that Marcia had ever heard contained expressions of the mother's amazement at her child's preference for an old stuffed bunny over a new toy, as if her kid was the first in the universe to behave that way.

"And here they are with my mother." The sad-eyed boy sat next to a nasty-looking old lady at a heavy wooden table, a big spoon in his tiny hand poised over the soup bowl.

Marcia wondered if he looked sad because he had figured out that his mother was a dingbat. Four years old and he knew the score already. Poor kid.

Henrietta flipped through the remaining photos, showing her children from various angles, as if she were shuffling a deck of playing cards. Her voice was rapturously self-involved; she seemed to forget she was standing in a public restroom showing pictures of her children to a virtual stranger. She thought she was back home with Mom, watching the kids open their presents.

Marcia did what was expected. She made cooing noises as Henrietta flipped the snapshots, in that whiney soprano women use when they admire other women's children. It was only polite for childless women to praise the progeny of their progenitive sisters, and after years of doing it, Marcia played her part well. The trouble was, the progenitive sisters never returned the favor and admired her beautiful loan reports. But then, of course, she'd never asked them to do it.

Henrietta was relentlessly cheerful as she chatted on about her children. That was part of being a good mom when you were divorced, Marcia thought. Your life is falling apart, your ex hates you, you've sunk into poverty, and you have to put on this big act for the kids. After all, they've been traumatized.

What about you? Can't you just say, Look kids, we're screwed. We're living on fifteen hundred dollars a month before taxes and only because I work full-time. You're going to have a real rough childhood: baby-sitters, crummy day care, lousy schools, the works. I'm sorry, but there's nothing I can do. Now why don't you just go out and get jobs to help out poor old mom?

Henrietta's four-year-old could roam the streets at four a.m. delivering newspapers. Marcia was chuckling to herself at the notion of the poor little guy trying to pull a red flyer wagon down the street when she noticed that Henrietta was staring at her.

"Well, Marcia, how about it?"

"I'm sorry, Henrietta, what did you say?"

"I said how about getting some lunch?"

Every time she ran into Henrietta, Henrietta asked her to lunch. And each time Marcia did not know how to say no. She felt so sorry for the woman. If she said no, she was sure Henrietta would fall apart right in front of her.

"Sure, Henrietta." The bank cafeteria offered a mean cheeseburger for ninety-five cents.

"Look Marcia, do you mind if we run a few errands before we eat?" Henrietta was gathering her packages off the floor.

"Uh. . . Sure, Henrietta. No problem. Let me get my coat."

How do I get roped into this stuff? she thought, while she traipsed behind Henrietta through two major department stores and watched her wrangle with sales clerks like a fishwife. All of the clothes had to be exchanged for a larger size and apparently one or two items had been worn for a while.

"We carried that snowsuit with the itty-bitty green trim last year," the black clerk at Carson's said. "What you trying to do here, lady? This here is old clothes."

Henrietta puffed up. Of course, she had no receipts. "Look here, miss, that's the snowsuit my child got and that's the snowsuit I'm returning. And if you won't take my word for it, I want to talk to the manager."

The manager appeared, Henrietta raged, and Suzanne got her new snowsuit. Marcia was mortified. All the way back to the bank Henrietta complained about the intransigence of black sales clerks.

By the time they got to the cafeteria, Marcia had twenty-five minutes left to eat lunch. Henrietta moved on to new topics, including the vast logistical problems involved in shipping a four-year-old to nursery school and a baby to day-care and getting ready for work all before eight-fifteen on every working day.

"You've got to be organized, Marcia," she said, over her grilled cheese sandwich and fries. "You women without kids and with a man in the house don't know how lucky you are. You don't have a care in the world; you can go anywhere you want, do anything you want. . ." She stared hard at Marcia, rebuking her for being so carefree.

"Well, Henrietta, that's not quite true," Marcia said. "You know I had a run-in with Ranier this morning." It was a relief to turn the conversation to her own problems.

"Oh, really? That old warhorse; he just hates women. I wouldn't let that bother me, Marcia." She stood up and hoisted her tray. The conversation was over. Marcia felt cheated.

"It's been great having girl-talk; I've got to run now. I have to call Mom to make sure that Timmy got home all right from nursery school. I worry about him all the time; did I tell you I'm trying to find a new baby-sitter? Mom's great, but she feeds him Chee-tos and fried foods. I've said to her a million times, 'Look Mom, a four-year-old kid should eat good stuff, like fruit, not potato chips and Ho-Hos.' But that's Mom—I can't do anything with her. I got to get him out of there before she poisons him. Okay, see you later." She walked off to the conveyor belt filled with soiled lunch trays, her ill-fitting skirt clinging to her legs.

If that woman invested as much time in her job as she does in her kids and her problems, she'd run the bank in five years, Marcia thought. She put down her half-eaten cheeseburger. She shouldn't have ordered it. She had hardly tasted it during Henrietta's rapid-fire discourse on her many trials, and now she had eaten all those calories. It would go right to her hips.

Everybody gets what he wants, she thought. Henrietta gets her kids, Baxter gets Six Corners, and Frances gets her brilliant career, the Rising Star and lots of money. And what do I get? A ticket to nowhere in this bank, a husband in a funk, and fat thighs. Thirty years old and I don't even own my own house yet.

She felt tired and she had a headache. She popped two aspirin, bussed her dishes, and headed back to the fifteenth floor.

SIX

The teachers' meeting that Monday had been the usual boring affair. The St Paul staff sat and shivered in the main science lecture hall, its seats arranged in tiers like bleachers, as Dotson worked his way down the list of announcements. He was a tall man in his sixties with silver hair, a formal manner, and a smooth, well-modulated voice. Just like a radio announcer on one of those easy-listening music stations, Gin thought.

Dotson announced new schedules for teacher supervisions of the lunchroom and study halls. The late busses that took the boys home after their extracurricular activities would now leave from a different corner. The teachers should encourage kids to take up musical instruments; St Paul's needed more bodies in the school band.

The archdiocese was asking children in Catholic schools to contribute to a special fund for the African Missions. The collection would be taken up next week; it was part of the Holy Father's program to encourage more missionary work on the Dark Continent.

The teachers smiled politely. In the back row, O'Connor graded sophomore grammar homework.

Dotson continued with his list for a good half hour, ending up with his usual plea that the teachers work harder to keep the kids from smoking in the bathrooms. Every offender should be brought to him for a personal rebuke.

"After which he will be crucified," Gin whispered to Harvey, who chuckled.

"And now, my fellow teachers, go with God and our holy patron, St Paul, in shaping the minds of these young Catholic men of tomorrow," Dotson said. "God bless you." He gave them a fishy smile, blessed them, and walked out. He finished every Monday meeting with some similar encouragement to labor in God's vineyard and then blessed them. After all, he was a priest.

Forget God and the vineyard line, Gin thought. Dotson held these meetings just to rub it in that he ran the show at St Paul's. With a little help from above. But not much.

First period, Gin had a sophomore class. Teacher and students nodded through fifty-five minutes of faltering discussion of *Great Expectations*. Tom O'Malley was actually asleep in the back row, his chin resting on his chest and his arms crossed.

As long as he didn't snore, Gin would let him sleep. Dickens had the same effect on Gin; everything was overwritten and the armies of characters gave him a headache.

After first period Gin hurried up to Dotson's office and made an appointment to see him at three-thirty, right after school. It was time to lay it all out on the line, to find out where he stood.

Second period was another round of sophomores and *Great Expectations*. Third period was his favorite class, the accelerated seniors. They were bright and Gin could choose most of the reading list himself. He liked contemporary fiction. The class was devouring Joseph Heller's *Catch 22*. They would never be able to listen to their fathers' war stories with straight faces again. No parents had complained—yet.

Fourth period, he supervised a study hall. The room was too hot and he dozed at his desk while the kids mumbled to each other and shot a few rubber bands. Fifth period he ate lunch with Harvey and Will Henderson, who taught American History. They discussed in detail the problems of the Cubs' pitching staff. Gin told Harvey privately that he was meeting with Dotson; Harvey wished him luck, looking alarmed.

A class each of seniors and juniors, followed by another study hall, filled Gin's afternoon. By three-twenty-five he was sitting in a worn chair outside Dotson's office, his stomach churning, rehearsing what he wanted to say. Their previous encounters had been brief and rather strained, even when Dotson had approached him to come and teach at St Paul's.

Gin had done well at Howard, a tough public high school in a melting pot neighborhood on the northwest side. He had won a teaching award and had been part of a group that worked to develop a program to teach English as a second language. Koreans, Vietnamese, Cubans, Mexicans and a few Thai were in the Howard student body. Most spoke only pidgin English and couldn't read it at all.

Gin and five other Howard teachers had convinced the principal and their colleagues to petition the School Board to set up a special language program for kids. For months, Gin filled in forms, wrote proposals and met with bureaucrats at the Board of Education. Finally the Board allocated the funds and the staff. The *Chicago Tribune* did a long story on the program in their *Sunday* magazine, running big pictures of Gin and the other organizers. That was four years ago.

After that piece ran, he got the letter from Father Dotson, on fine white vellum headed with the school's crest. Dotson had read about Gin's work at Howard; it was really impressive and St Paul's could use a man like him. He would like to meet with Gin and talk it over. By the way, was Gin Catholic?

Gin was intrigued. He phoned Dotson and set up an appointment. Yes, he was Catholic; he did not add that he was not a practicing Catholic.

When they met, he found Dotson rather cold, but not impossibly so, and his promises were great. Come to St Paul's, head the English department, and we'll make you vice principal in a year. The aged Jesuit who had held the position for twenty-five years was retiring. As vice principal, Gin would be responsible for the school's day-to-day management, including discipline.

Gin couldn't believe it. It sounded like a gift from heaven. Classroom teaching bored him; this was a chance to try his hand at running a school, a chance he would never get in the Chicago school system with its glutted bureaucracy and ponderous seniority system. It would take him twenty years there just to get the authority to supervise the bathrooms.

He asked why they didn't want a Jesuit to take the position.

"Our numbers are small," Dotson had said. "We believe it's time to move talented lay people into lower administrative positions." Of the school's fifty teachers, fifteen were Jesuits, and eight of them were over fifty years old.

The money was about a third less than what he was making at Howard—and he wasn't making much at Howard. But Gin would have paid the Jesuit for a chance to be a vice principal. He accepted on the spot. They shook hands and it was agreed that Gin would join the staff in the next school year.

In his excitement, he hadn't thought to get anything in writing. Dotson seemed so trustworthy. And he had approached Gin with these promises; Gin had not initiated them. So why shouldn't Dotson keep them?

In that meeting Dotson had not asked him about how he thought the school should be managed, nor had he answered Gin's questions about the school's financial condition. If Gin was going to run the place, they needed to talk about things. He thought maybe they would discuss them when Gin finally got the job.

Gin liked St Paul's, although the all-male environment and the religious atmosphere made him uneasy. The first thing he would do as vice principal would be to convince Dotson to open the school to girls and drop the compulsory religion classes. Half the kids and at least ten of the teachers weren't even Catholic. The Catholic teachers treated their religion like an in-house labor union. It was something you joined to get promoted on the job.

The kids were better behaved than public school students; their parents were paying fifteen hundred a year in tuition and three hundred for books. Those who had gone to Catholic grammar schools read and wrote better than those who had come from public schools. But most of the kids were no better or worse than his students at Howard. The same applied to his fellow teachers. Gin felt right at home.

Dotson was a good—if strict—administrator who got along pretty well with the faculty. As long as you followed the rules, you could teach the way you wanted to. Nothing seemed to change much from year to year; sometimes Gin felt as though the school were firmly wedded to teaching methods that were at least thirty years out of date.

Despite that, he happily awaited the anniversary of his first year and his ascent into the vice principalship. The anniversary was marked with a small raise and no promotion. Gin had asked Dotson about his promise. Dotson said he didn't remember having promised him that the new job would begin at any specific time. "Patience, Mr Bernthal. You have to earn your wings before you can fly."

Gin began to be depressed. Six months later he had gone back to Dotson and asked again, receiving nearly the identical answer. On his second anniversary at St Paul's, just last autumn, Gin received an even smaller raise than he had the first year—and no promotion. He was so upset that his studied calm cracked; he complained to Dotson about the money.

"Pay peanuts, get monkeys," Gin said.

"Well," Dotson replied coldly, "I know the raises were small this year, Mr Bernthal, but we need to save money everywhere we can while we do the Lord's work. All of us are making sacrifices. Besides," he continued, lighting a cigarette with a silver lighter and fixing his watery blue eyes on Gin, "if we're all monkeys here, what does that make you? Good afternoon, Mr Bernthal."

Dotson ushered him politely out of his office, closing the heavy door behind him. Father Santucci, Dotson's young, dark secretary, sniggered as Gin walked out in a daze. Gin hadn't even had a chance to mention the vice principal's job.

Now, here he was again, for round four, or whatever it was. Maybe Harvey was right and it was fruitless. But he had to know what the hell was going on. This was getting ridiculous.

Father Santucci smiled impishly at Gin and kept typing, his fine black-haired head bent over the machine. Was that a come-on, Gin wondered as he fidgeted in his chair. "Father" Santucci was twenty-six years old. Gin had a hard time calling anyone his younger brother's age "father," and just settled for "Santucci."

The door opened. "Come in, come in, Mr Bernthal," said Dotson, standing in the doorway. "I hope I haven't kept you waiting too long."

Of course he had: it was 4:00 and his appointment had been for 3:30.

"No problem, Father," said Gin.

Dotson's office looked like a gloomy, Gothic chapel. The walls were panelled in old dark wood all the way up to the high ceiling. A stained glass window jammed with saints and symbols overlooked the school courtyard, and a heavy, ivory crucifix about two feet high hung on the wall behind Dotson's desk. It was an old Italian cross, so lifelike that Gin shivered.

Above a dark leather sofa was a large portrait of the order's founder, Saint Ignatius of Loyola, looking to be in his mid-twenties, with soft brown eyes and the effeminate manner of a Spanish grandee. He reminded Gin of Santucci. Why didn't they paint saints to look like linebackers instead of gay boys?

"Do sit down, Mr Bernthal," Dotson said, pointing to one of the small upholstered chairs in front of his ornate oak desk, on which all twelve apostles were carved.

Dotson settled behind the desk in a high-backed leather chair. Up close, he was an elegant, fastidious man with fine features.

"Now, what can I do for you?" he said, lighting a cigarette from a marble lighter on his desk. His graceful hands flicked an ash into the marble ashtray sitting next to it. He looked amused.

Gin had the sudden feeling he was playing out of his league. He plunged ahead.

"Well, Father, I've been doing a great deal of thinking about my position here at St Paul's and I would like to clarify where I stand."

Dotson nodded, the smoke drifting out of his nostrils.

"I came here three years ago, under the impression that I would be made vice principal in a year. I feel I've been doing a good job in the English department and I want to know when you intend to make me vice principal, as you promised."

There. It was out. Gin tried to look friendly and looked Dotson right in the eye, or where his eye would be if cigarette smoke wasn't blurring his face.

"Mr Bernthal," came the cold, formal voice from behind the desk. "I never made you such a promise."

Gin's jaw dropped.

"Excuse me, Father, but what are you talking about? Three years ago, you sat in that chair and promised me the vice principal's job."

Dotson shifted in his chair, an impatient tone in his voice. "Mr Bernthal, haven't we had this discussion before? As I recall, and correct me if I'm wrong, I believe we talked about this just over a year ago. At that time, I said that I may have indicated to you, when you were hired, that you would be seriously considered for the vice principal's position then available. But in no way did I ever 'promise' you the position, as you put it."

Dotson leaned forward slightly in his chair, his face a mask of affected concern. "I am terribly sorry, but I do believe there's been some misunderstanding here." He settled back in his chair, an action clearly saying to Gin that the issue was settled.

"Father Dotson, that is not how I remember the situation at all," Gin said, his voice growing colder. God, this guy would deny that the sun rose in the East.

"You promised me the job. That's why I left Howard. And you led me to believe I would get the job once I 'earned my wings,' as you put it."

Dotson looked perplexed and annoyed. "Young man, I never led you on in any such way and I'm sorry that you see it like that. I was simply encouraging you to be a better teacher. You were just starting at St Paul's. You have a great deal of potential, but I knew you were nervous in your new position as head of the English department."

Dotson drew on his cigarette, exhaling delicate lines of smoke through his nostrils.

"We were—and still are—delighted to have you working with us in the Lord's work of educating young men. But you *are* very young and inexperienced. You were having some trouble fitting in at first."

Dotson smiled. He was the famous theologian who had just made clear some complex point in the Gospels to a simple parish priest. Now all the priest had to do was smile back and pretend he understood.

But Gin didn't understand. What the hell was Dotson talking about? He hadn't had any problems at St Paul's. He stared at Dotson.

"What do you mean?"

"You mean you don't remember?" Dotson said, his voice registering true surprise. "Surely you must remember our conversation about the nature of Catholic education and the role of the teacher?"

"What?"

"When you first came here, we had an interesting conversation about your views of where the school should be going. Frankly, I found your ideas somewhat disturbing, but attributed them to your newness to the Catholic system of education."

Gin looked at the Jesuit, calmly smoking his cigarette. The only time they had ever discussed Gin's views on anything had been during a casual conversation at the annual staff banquet when he first came to St Paul's. Over cocktails, Dotson had asked him what he would do to improve the school.

Gin had spoken freely. He would like to open the school to girls, drop the compulsory religious classes, and add special classes to help the foreign-born and slower students learn how to read and write. They should add classes in drivers' education and consider getting the alumni more involved in raising money for the school. Perhaps they should consider an alumni drive to raise money to buy computers?

He was going to offer his ideas on improving the athletic programs, when Dotson politely excused himself to go to mingle with the other teachers. It was only then that Gin heard the ice in his voice and noticed the hardness around his eyes.

He had offended the man. But he had not known how much—until now. They had never discussed the topic again. He couldn't believe Dotson was that petty.

"Sir, you mean you won't consider me for the vice principal's job because of comments I made during a cocktail party?"

"Mr Bernthal, it makes no difference where you aired them. I am a quick judge of character and frankly, I did feel that your ideas would not fit in with the Catholic, and specifically, the Jesuit view of education."

"What is the Jesuit view of education?" Gin asked. He was in deep water. He might as well dive down and see what slime was on the bottom.

Dotson stubbed out his cigarette in the marble ashtray and folded his hands on the desk. His face became hard as he lectured Gin about how the school was really Christ's body and everyone was a different body part. He, Dotson, was Christ's head.

"Mr Bernthal," he said, "the Body couldn't run at all if each of its parts did as they wished. The Head must direct it all, just as our Holy Father directs the Church from Rome.

"In other words, the Body is not a participatory democracy, Mr Bernthal, and neither is this school." He flicked open a silver case, picked out another cigarette, and lit it with the matching silver lighter from his pocket.

Gin's head ached. he felt his face redden and his hands go cold. This was it; something was breaking.

"With all due respect, Sir, what the hell does Christ's anatomy have to do with the Jesuit theory of education?"

"What?" Dotson looked shocked.

Gin leaned forward over the desk and glared at him.

"And for that matter, what the hell does the Jesuit theory of education have to do with you promising me a job that you never had any intention of delivering to me?

"You just dangled it in front of me to entice me here; another dumb public school teacher lured in by promises of promotion. It's the only way to get us to accept your lousy pay and half-baked religious theories. By the time we discover we've been duped, you've wrung a good five or six years out of us and you hope we're dispirited enough to stay another five more. By then, we're really rooted in and can't leave at all. That's a great way to run a school, Dotson, that's really terrific. A real pillar of God, you are."

Gin was surprised to discover he was nearly shouting. He stopped abruptly.

Dotson stared right through him, unblinking.

"Young man, just who do you think you're talking to?" He looked like the Grand Inquisitor about to pronounce judgment on a wretched Spanish Jew. Gin thought of Harvey.

Dotson's voice fell to a near-whisper.

"Mr Bernthal, in my thirty years at St Paul's, none of my staff has ever spoken to me in such a hostile and inappropriate manner.

"I am sorry to discover that my impression of you as a dedicated teacher was sadly mistaken. You are one of those selfish, misguided young men blinded by ambition and self-importance. The teaching profession is a noble calling, Mr Bernthal, a noble calling that demands a selflessness and devotion to others that you apparently lack."

Dotson stood up and walked over to the window. The room was quiet except for the sound of the late busses leaving at the corner.

"In view of your comments about me and the school, I am relieving you of all your responsibilities at St Paul's effective immediately. Please remove your belongings."

Gin stood up, giddy and trembling. "With pleasure, you old fraud."

He turned and left.

SEVEN

"My God, Bernthal, he can't do that to you. You have a contract."

"You ever read those things, Harvey? They're documents of indentured servitude. They can fire you for just about anything, including insubordination, but you can't quit unless you're dead. They've got you by the balls."

Gin fingered his glass of beer. Hard to think this was the last time he and Harvey would be drinking after school at the long, stained bar at the Dog Run Inn.

"Harve, I wouldn't go back even if I could. The place was making me sick." He took a long swig of beer. "I'd rather be broke than sick."

Harvey turned on his stool and grimly watched two young men in pink trimmed mohawks play a video game.

"What are you going to do now?"

"I don't know."

"What's Marcia going to say?"

"I don't know, but I have a hunch she isn't going to be too thrilled."

Gin chuckled to himself.

"Harve, if I didn't have to tutor my remedial kids tonight, I'd love to get stinking and really celebrate my fall from grace. How about tomorrow night? Or tomorrow at noon, for that matter."

He squinted at an imaginary datebook in his hand, and said, in a voice like Dotson's, "My schedule seems to have opened up considerably, thanks to Our Lord's mercies and the intervention of His Blessed Mother who has taken a special interest in my future calling as a selfless teacher laboring in Her Son's vineyards."

In the midst of their laughter, Gin croaked, "Free at last, Lord, God Almighty, I'm free at last."

"I'll drink to that," said Harvey, wiping his mouth and raising his half-empty glass.

They clinked their glasses. Gin called to the bartender for another round.

"Harve, what the hell am I going to do?"

"How are you at selling shoes?"

"Seriously, Harve. I'm in trouble." The relief of having spoken his mind was leaking away. Pure, numb terror was replacing it.

"Do you want to stay in teaching?"

"I don't know."

"Well, why don't you let your subconscious work on it while we have one for the road?"

"Good idea."

They raised their fresh glasses of beer and downed them quickly.

"Well, Harve, I'll see you tomorrow here, then, ready for some heavy drinking?"

"Absolutely, you turkey. I've got Latin Club but I can get here by 4:30, ready for battle." He put his arm on Gin's shoulder. "Lighten up, Gin. It's all going to work out."

"I sure hope so, Harve." He slipped into his coat while Harvey paid for the beers. "See you tomorrow."

On the street, Vivian the Volvo sat jammed to the gunwales with Gin's possessions. The sight of her nearly made him weep. He felt like a refugee, nameless and homeless in a world that didn't care.

He unlocked the driver's side and shoved over *The Complete Works of the Lake Poets*, which had slid down from the great pile of books now tottering on the passenger seat. Three cardboard boxes from the cafeteria, hastily requisitioned from Archie, sat on the back seat. They were filled with the contents of his desk. An old blue sweater lay crumpled on top of one.

He had left his files, grade book, and stacks of graded essays neatly piled on his desk, along with all his lesson plans. The substitute teacher would need them all. He had left the box of *Playboys* he had confiscated from the boys over the last three years outside the door of the chapel; the reverend fathers could throw them out themselves.

His only remaining responsibility to St Paul's was to tutor his remedial English students tonight. He had started tutoring in the fall to help the kids out and make a little extra money. That was one part of his teaching career he wouldn't miss. The remedial students depressed the hell out of him. But he would need the money, so he might as well keep tutoring.

He marveled at how quickly and easily the break with St Paul's had been made. This morning he was there for years ahead; now, he was out.

As usual, Vivian started up right away. Her new car smell soothed him.

I hope we don't have to sell her, he thought.

God Almighty, what have I done?

*　　*　　*

The rush hour trains were all messed up, as usual. Marcia stood in the cold and watched two "A" trains in a row go by. Even the trains pass me by, she thought. An "A" train finally stopped and Marcia forced her way on, jamming herself between a thin Chinese man in a cheap coat and an old lady with two tattered shopping bags.

She had spent the afternoon shuffling through the files on the Cully warehouse deal. It looked like every other warehouse deal she had ever done. And the way things were going, it looked like the only type of deal she was ever going to do. If only she hadn't shot her big mouth off on the Six Corners deal.

She sighed. She was just going to have to try harder to be a team player and to give Ranier what he wanted. Team players got promoted; women with big mouths didn't. They undermined team spirit and ruined the bank's earnings. She had to learn to fit in if she was going to be a success at this banker business.

"Keep your mouth shut, Marcia," she hissed under her breath, startling the lady with the two shopping bags, who had been whispering to the Angel Gabriel during the entire ride.

Marcia elbowed her way out at the Addison stop and marched homeward. Compared with the glass and steel buildings around the bank, her neighborhood looked tired and grey. She cringed at the thought that her cost accounting group would be on her doorstep in an hour. After the splendor of their suburban homes, her apartment would look like a slum. Until tonight, she had managed to avoid hosting a study group, but this one was made up of real egalitarians who insisted that each host a session in turn.

When she had told them how to get to her apartment, four of the five had looked confused. One even pulled out a city map and asked her to put an "X" where she lived. They came from the suburbs; for all they knew they might be travelling to Calcutta.

She climbed the grey wood stairs of the porch, conscious of the peeling paint on the landings and the rusted light fixture near the door, bent and bulbless for years. In a window on the first floor, a plaster Blessed Virgin prayed intensely while a stringy green plant sprouted out of her back. "Let Us Pray" was printed under her breasts. Marcia prayed that the Virgin would shatter and disappear before her guests arrived.

The smell of rancid cooking oil and fish filled the lobby. Mrs O'Connell, her landlady, was a great fan of Smacky Jack's Fishsticks, which she fried up in lakes of Wesson Oil. The stench drifted up to the Bernthals' apartment and lingered there for hours. It was Smacky Jack night tonight. Marcia groaned.

Heavy rock music grated on her ears as she walked into the apartment. Gin was sitting on the couch drinking a beer and staring out the living room window. Three cardboard boxes and stacks of books were spread over the floor. They looked like his schoolbooks.

Marcia's eyes widened in alarm.

Gin turned to her calmly. "Hi, Marsh. Dotson canned me."

"What?"

"He canned me. Defunct. Kaput. No more St Paul's and the Holy Angels for me. Dotson threw me out effective today." He motioned toward the books on the floor. "Voilà, my worldly possessions spread about me." He chuckled and sipped his beer.

Marcia unzipped her boots and dropped her coat on the floor. Her heart was racing.

"Good grief. Why'd he can you?"

"Insubordination."

"You're kidding."

"No. I accused him of luring me to his school with the vice principal's job when he never had any intention at all of giving it to me."

Marcia pattered over to the old stuffed chair opposite the sofa and sat down. "For telling the truth, he fires you? That old jerk is a lot dumber than I thought. What happened?"

Gin replayed his conversation with Dotson, including his own offensive remarks. Marcia couldn't believe her ears, especially when Gin got to the part about Dotson bearing a grudge against him just for suggesting changes in the school's operations.

"That man's crazier than Ranier. He thinks he's God."

"At that concentration camp, he is God."

"But you have a contract; he can't just fire you like that."

"Oh yes he can. He can dismiss me for insubordination. Who's going to argue with him?"

Marcia's heart sank. "You mean a court of Jesuits would arbitrate the case?"

"You got it. They're certainly not going to decide in favor of a heathen like me. Besides, I don't want to go back. I've had enough."

He felt relieved. Marcia felt confused. They sat silently for a few moments and then she sighed and said, "I need a beer. You want another?"

Gin nodded and she headed for the kitchen. Numbly, she popped open two Old-Styles and returned to sit next to Gin on the couch.

"Oh, yuck," she said, looking into his eyes and kissing him lightly.

"Oh yuck is right, Marsh."

"Now what do you do?"

He kissed her on the forehead. "I don't know. Here's my chance to try all those other jobs I've been talking about for the last year. Maybe get out of teaching altogether."

"That might not be a bad idea."

"Maybe computers, or some sort of business management position, or something. Maybe I should go into electronics, get my MBA, I don't know."

"You sure you wouldn't want to go back to a public school? Maybe you could get reinstated at Howard?"

"I don't know if I'd want that or if I'd even have a chance at it. Old lady Rodriguez was pretty upset when I left." When Gin had announced that he was going to St Paul's, Maria Rodriguez, Howard's principal, had treated it like a personal betrayal.

"Maybe if you cut your balls off and handed them to her on a platter she'd be happy."

Gin laughed. "Maybe."

"Well, we were busy little beavers today, weren't we?" Marcia said. "Ranier pulled me off the Six Corners deal today."

"You're kidding. That was your baby."

"Well, I'm a mom without a baby now. He gave it to one of the little twerps to work on."

"He can't do that."

They turned and looked at each other. "Oh yes he can," they chimed together, affecting bass voices. They laughed.

"Gin, my darling, do you think we have trouble with authority figures?"

"You bet your sweet bippy, we do." He kissed her again.

She sighed. "What are we going to do about money?"

"We'll have to live off your salary for awhile."

"I don't know if it's enough—there's Vivian, and the rent, and the heat, and everything. We just barely make it as it is."

"Well, what about that money you've been saving up?"

Marcia felt betrayed. Her throat tightened. "Oh Gin, not that. I was saving that for buying a house. It took me forever." Marcia had managed to save $10,000; it was now sitting in a money market fund. "I mean we'll never be able to buy a house if we touch that."

"I know it's important to you, Marsh. I feel terrible asking, but we may have to use it for living expenses." Gin felt humiliated.

Marcia started to cry. "No, Gin, no."

"Marcia." He put his arms around her while she dabbed at her eyes with the sleeves from her suitcoat. He hated it when she cried: she looked so pathetic. "Maybe we won't have to touch it at all. I'm going to go out and find something as soon as possible. Don't worry."

"I'm sorry, Gin. I didn't mean to lose my grip." She sat up and forced a brave smile. "But I'm terrified."

He looked into her red-rimmed eyes and smiled. "So am I."

She gave him an amused look and lifted her beer. "A toast. To your future career, whatever the hell it's going to be."

Gin laughed, took a sip from his beer, and set it on the coffee table. "Come here and give me a hug, you goofy broad." He wrestled her down to the couch and playfully kissed her, his moustache tinged with beer foam.

EIGHT

Elaine Schuster was sure she got the address right, but how could this dump be the place? The other business students in her group who lived in the city all had cozy apartments close to the lake, filled with Victorian charm and twentieth century plumbing. On the ground floor of their neat, tuck-pointed buildings were florists and cute little pasta shops. No cappucino cafes here; only a Jewel supermarket on the corner, and endless blocks of brick two-flats and houses with asphalt siding. . . .

Elaine dragged her huge briefcase out of her grey Toyota and started up the steps. She did a double-take at the Virgin Mary and gagged on fish fumes in the hallway. The doorbell sounded as if two feeble monks were hitting pieces of wood with felt-wrapped hammers. Someone buzzed her in and she dragged herself up two flights of stairs, weighed down with her cost accounting books.

Suddenly, she froze. She must be in the wrong house, the wrong neighborhood and the wrong place at the wrong time. The largest Puerto Rican kid she had ever seen was standing in the doorway to what was supposed to be Marcia Bernthal's apartment. He was scowling at her.

This was it. Her mother had warned her about wandering around the city at night. Elaine's golden curls trembled. She was sure these crazy Latins liked perky little Anglo blondes. She'd seen *Evita*. She knew.

"Excuse me, señor," she said with a limp smile. "I have the wrong apartment." She turned quickly and ran down the stairs.

"No problema, señora," Enrique Mendoza called politely, wondering who the washed-out-looking gringa with the suitcase could be. Maybe somebody's sister-in-law coming to visit? An ugly little chicken. Enrique liked tall, dark women with wild black hair and a penchant for leather.

He closed the door and returned to the help-wanted ads in the *Sun-Times*. Mr Bernthal's remedial English class was learning how to read the want ads and apply for a job. Before Mr Bernthal had sent him to answer the door, Enrique had been puzzling over an ad for someone to teach grades "K to 8" in "W. Chgo." Reading English was bad enough, but this squeezed-together version was worse.

"Who was it, Enrique?" Gin asked. He was helping a short young man with acne and a head of dry, dirty-brown hair who was sitting at the kitchen table, halfway through an ad for a welder at a canning factory in "Arl. Hts."

"Some lady. Said she had the wrong place," Enrique said.

"Oh, thanks, Enrique," Gin said. "That's an abbreviation for Arlington Heights, Mike."

"Where's that, Mr Bernthal?" Mike asked; he hoped it was somewhere he could get to on a bus. He had done some welding in shop class. Maybe they'd take a chance on him?

"Sorry, Mike, it's out beyond the airport," Gin replied. "The land beyond O'Hare. You'd need a car."

Mike's shoulders sagged. He picked up his magic marker and inked a black "X" through the ad.

"Well, the problem is we're looking in the wrong place, Mike." Gin refolded the paper. "See here on the tops of the columns it says 'city' and here it says 'northwest suburbs.' You want to look under the 'city' column."

Suddenly Gin stood straight up. "Oh my God," he said.

He ran into the living room where Marcia was rearranging her bowls of pretzels and potato chips for the third time. "Marcia, I think Enrique scared off one of your business group when he answered the door."

Marcia hurried to the door and made it down the stairs just in time to see the grey Toyota turning the corner and scurrying in the direction of the expressway.

Back to the suburbs, Marcia thought. When she had scheduled her study group, she'd forgotten that Monday was the night the apartment turned into the "Planet of the Apes," with six of Gin's remedial students hunched over her kitchen table.

Why don't they just give up and join a street gang where they belong, Marcia had asked Gin when he set the group up in the fall. He had laughed and said they probably would anyway, but they could use the money.

What was her business group going to think of this?

Before she reached the apartment, she heard the feeble monks knocking on wood again. She raced for the buzzer, but no one tried to beat her to it. Gin had locked himself in the kitchen with his students and left the door patrol to her.

About thirty seconds later, two well-groomed male heads followed by two well-dressed male bodies appeared on the stairs. It was Mike Levinson and John somebody. . .Wolin or Wallen or Valenski or something like that. She could never keep her classmates' names straight; they all came and went so fast. Courses lasted only ten weeks and people were always dropping in and out of the program.

"Maria?" said Levinson.

"Marcia," Marcia said. "Marcia Bernthal."

"Hi, I'm Mike Levinson and this is John Walsauer."Levinson was short and Jewish. Walsauer was tall and Jewish. They both had on dark blue suits and red silk ties. It was uncanny, Marcia thought. Two guys who don't even know each other show up wearing practically the same thing just by accident.

Maybe they really were twins? Twin body snatchers? Twin diamond merchants? Twin baby investment bankers?

"Levinson, you're with Goldman Sachs, right?" Marcia asked, remembering that one actually was an investment banker.

"Right. And John here is with Cresap, McCormick," Levinson said.

"Management consulting to silicon chip manufacturers," Walsauer said, extending a bony hand in a fine leather glove. Marcia shook it. "You're with one of the big banks?" he asked.

"Yeah, First Midwestern, in real estate lending." No MBA student ever introduced himself to another MBA student with just his name. He had to tell you where he worked, whose colors he draped across his armour. Then you could fit him into the salary and power pecking order. Management consultants and investment bankers outranked bankers in real estate lending. They probably make twice what I do, Marcia thought sullenly.

"Come on in. Let me take your coats," she said. She ushered Levinson and Walsauer into the living room where they perched uncomfortably on the edge of her worn, Haitian cotton couch. Carmen, her grey cat, immediately jumped up on Levinson's lap. Cat hair floated onto his pants.

"Carmen, you bad cat, get down." Carmen shot Marcia an aggrieved look and went back to sharpening her claws on the back of the couch.

"Sorry about that," she said.

"Oh, don't worry about it," said Levinson. He tried to pick off some of the dozens of cat hairs now permanently attached to his trousers. He used to torture cats when he was a kid.

"Can I get you something to drink? I've got coffee or Diet Coke or Perrier."

"I'll take a Diet Coke," said Levinson.

"A Perrier for me," said Walsauer.

Marcia went into the kitchen and Levinson and Walsauer opened their leather briefcases with expandable locks. Each pulled out a calculator, a legal pad, an expensive mechanical pencil, and the weekly case study for introductory cost accounting. Each made his pile neatly on Marcia's rickety coffee table, and sat back on the couch. They looked like two international bankers ready to transact business with some Berber chieftan under the mud walls of Timbuktu. They looked bloodless.

Marcia pattered over to the refrigerator. She popped open a Perrier and a Diet Coke. Though the room was quiet, she could almost hear the brain waves of the six frustrated young men grappling with a foreign language. They were writing letters, applying for jobs they had found in the paper. Gin sat in the corner on the kitchen stool, chewing the end of his pencil and daydreaming.

She stuck her tongue out at him. He stuck a thumb in each ear and wiggled his fingers at her. She giggled, Gin smiled, and she disappeared into the living room with her drinks.

The twin body snatchers hadn't moved.

The phone rang.

"Marcia, this is Elaine Schuster of the cost accounting group," a high-pitched female voice said. "I'm afraid I got lost and well, I strayed into a borderline neighborhood and nearly got raped by some Puerto Rican."

"Uh, Elaine," Marcia said, "do you drive a grey Toyota?"

"Well, yes."

"Well, uh, you had the right place."

"I did?" Clearly, Elaine thought this impossible.

"That was Enrique who answered the door, one of my husband's students, and a very nice boy. I tried to catch you, but you had already pulled away."

"Oh, dear. Well, that was silly." Elaine laughed nervously. Maybe this Bernthal woman ran a gang of white slavers? Cost-accounting was just a front for her to lure in her prey. Elaine's mother had warned her that white slavers liked blondes.

"Well, Marcia, I don't feel so well anyway. I think I'll just take a pass tonight. See you in class on Thursday. 'Bye." And Elaine hung up.

What a strange woman, Marcia thought. She pulled a folding chair up to the coffee table. "That was Elaine Schuster," she announced to the gruesome twosome. "She can't make it tonight." No one cared.

The doorbell intoned again and then again. Frances Klein swept into the room with apologies for being late, followed by a thin, pale young woman with long straight hair down to her waist. Marcia recognized her from her Women's MBA Group. Kathy Morton, she said her name was; she was an assistant internal auditor at Borg Warner, somewhere in the plastics division. In the MBA pecking order, internal auditors were somewhere near the carpet lint.

Marcia fetched more drinks, stealing a kiss from Gin on her way, and passed around her bowls of pretzels and chips. They munched distractedly as Levinson read aloud the case history they were supposed to analyze. The three-page narrative was followed by a set of questions they had to answer as a group.

The case involved some company that manufactured bolts in England and shipped them to a subsidiary in Madagascar, with stopovers in Dar Es Salaam and Zanzibar where they refueled the ship and picked up coconuts or something.

Zanzibar! Marcia thought, envisioning palm trees, white sand beaches, and half-naked African men in wildly patterned loin cloths. Their black skin gleamed in the tropical sun.

Everyone else envisioned crates of bolts and piles of dried-up coconut.

Levinson droned on about shipping costs, docking fees, and the costs of storing or selling forty-four tons of bolts in Zanzibar. Apparently, while the good ship Krakatoa steamed toward Dar Es Salaam, back in London management had decided the bolts were obsolete. Madagascar didn't need them. What should they do with the bolts now? Store them, sell them, return to England with them, or what?

Just like management, Marcia thought. The right hand doesn't know what the left hand is doing. Then, while you're floating in the South Atlantic they decide that whatever you've done is wrong. She fumed and stared at Carmen. Damn cat. Damn Ranier. Damn Dotson.

"Throw the damn bolts into the sea and dead-head for the Cape Town beaches," she muttered. "The surfing's great and you could live off the coconuts for months."

Everyone stared at her.

"Just joking, guys." She flashed her team-player smile. Who cared what was the cheapest and best thing for this stupid company to do? What the hell were they doing in Madagascar anyway?

Frances, Kathy and the twins embarked on a long analysis of the comparative costs of shipping bolts back to England and selling coconuts in Madagascar. Calculators clicked and mechanical pencils scratched. Yellow legal pads filled up with the numbers.

The twins came up with fifteen alternative scenarios one of which involved splitting up the shipment into five packages and shipping thirteen tons of bolts by Land Rover to the Sudan. They would ship the coconuts back to England and sell them to a company in Dorset that made canned coconut frosting.

Marcia was amazed. The twins could keep all fifteen scenarios in their heads at once as they argued the pros and cons of each. Frances made diplomatic, supportive noises for three of the scenarios; the twins listened to and included her suggestions. Kathy smiled blandly and didn't seem to have any idea what was going on. The twins ignored her.

Marcia hated women like Kathy. Her women's MBA group was filled with quiet, mousy women. They smiled a lot, wore cheap wool suits, and were so desperately seeking male approval it made Marcia sick. "Am I doing all right, guys?" they seemed to be asking. "Can I play too?"

The twins were lecturing the women on the benefits of Scenario Twelve, setting up a coconut processing subsidiary halfway between Zanzibar and the London home office, when raucous laughter and loud punk rock music emanated from the kitchen.

Eight-thirty and Gin and the kids were calling it quits.

The kitchen door swung open and a giant, 18-year-old black kid, Laetril Johnson, stepped into the living room with a long, looping stride. He slung his leather jacket with the ten zippered pockets over one shoulder. A black stocking cap covered his woolly head.

Laetril was a nice kid, Marcia thought. One of the few black kids at St Paul's who was actually a Catholic. His family must be from the West Indies, she thought, turning back to the group.

They were staring at Laetril.

Kathy Morton looked terrified and tried to blend into the back of the couch. Levinson's eyes widened; Walsauer kept rubbing his. He had just gotten contact lenses and couldn't see too well. He thought he saw a giant black man walk out of Marcia's kitchen, but that was impossible.

"Hi there, Mrs Bernthal," Laetril boomed in a deep, bass voice.

It wasn't impossible. Walsauer's jaw dropped.

Only Frances kept her cool. Her stare turned into a polite smile, as if it was the most natural thing in the world for a six-foot black kid with a tattoo on his right arm to walk through her cost accounting problem set.

The nobility always behaved well when they were trapped in a backwater for two hours while the peasants fixed the Mercedes. Marcia wondered if Frances would give Laetril a dollar as a tip.

"Hello there, Laetril," Marcia said.

The boy hesitated in the living room. Marcia could see Kathy's body tense.

"Second door on your right down the hallway, Laetril," she said. "The light's overhead on a pull string."

Laetril strode off to the bathroom.

"One of my husband's students," Marcia said. "He's running a tutorial tonight; I guess they're finished." A "tutorial" sounded impressive as if Gin was leading a discussion on Chaucer instead of trying to help six illiterates find jobs.

"Well, yes, he just surprised me a bit," said Walsauer.

"Yes, quite a surprise," laughed Levinson. He was angry that he had let Laetril frighten him. "Well, let's get back to business, here. I think we should pick Scenario Eleven-B, the one with the shipping subsidiary. . ."

They were interrupted again, this time by Mike Callahan, roughhousing with Enrique in the kitchen doorway. Two Puerto Rican kids stood behind them, talking in Spanish.

Someone switched the music off and Gin's voice filled the living room. "Well, see you guys next week. Bring your letters and we'll clean them up. If we get done early next week, we'll work on *Pet Sematary.*" The group loved Stephen King novels.

"Hey, all right, Mr Bernthal. Great!" they said.

Marcia winced. No chance of teaching Chaucer now.

"Now you guys go right home. No messin' around. Your mommas would kill me." And what looked like an entire Puerto Rican street gang with one scrawny Irish recruit rumbled through the living room, mumbling shy "Hello Mrs Bernthals" all the way. Gin followed them to the front door.

"Uh, hi, everybody," he said. He crossed the living room, smiling weakly and waving a hand at the cost accounting group. It looked like a meeting of the Future Undertakers of America. "Hope we didn't disturb you."

"No, hon, no problem," Marcia said, wishing that she could have rented an office for her meeting. "This is my husband, Gin, I mean Hodgkins Bernthal."

Everyone nodded politely at Gin, and mouthed some "pleased to meet you's" while Gin nodded politely back. Marcia's jaw was getting tired from smiling so much. Gin ushered the kids out the door. They laughed and joked down the stairs and Marcia heard the lobby door creak as they disappeared into the dark.

Thank God they were gone, she thought. Gin disappeared into his office in the back and the sound of buzzing Messerschmidts came through the door. Time for *World At War* on channel 9.

She turned back to her own private war. She couldn't figure out which scenario to choose because she hadn't the foggiest notion what was going on. She would support the same scenario Frances supported. Frances could follow this stuff.

Levinson proposed a vote, knowing everyone would support his pet scenario, which involved shipping the bolts back to England and selling them for scrap. They voted, they agreed, and Levinson said his secretary would type up their answer. Marcia retrieved the coats and the group departed quickly, leaving her coffee table with a litter of sticky glasses and greasy bowls.

* * *

On Tuesday, Marcia worked on her analysis of the Cully deal. Gin worked on his resume, made an appointment to see Mrs Rodriguez at Howard High School on Friday, and then got stinking drunk with Harvey at the Dog Run Inn. Harvey's wife, Dominique, picked them up at nine o'clock. She had to help Gin up the stairs to his apartment and physically hand him over to Marcia. He gave her a boozy kiss that nearly corroded her eyebrows.

On Wednesday, Marcia worked on the Cully deal. Gin nursed his hangover, retrieved Vivian from her parking place in front of the Dog Run, and worked on his resume some more. Two teachers from St Paul's called, ostensibly to offer their sympathy, but in reality to fish for details. His sudden exit had been the talk of the school. Gin gave them blow-by-blow accounts. They listened silently, made a few sympathetic comments and then hung up quickly, as if they had been caught consorting with the devil.

Thursday, Ranier came back from Fort Lauderdale, spent five minutes looking at Marcia's work and told her to add more marketing analyses. Marcia ground her teeth and did it. Gin called up the blonde ex-teacher he had met at the cocktail party, the one who was supposed to be selling computers for Xerox. She had left the company.

At Marcia's cost-accounting class that night, the overworked young lecturer announced the answer to the problem the group had worked on on Monday night. The company should have just dumped the bolts in the sea or given them away for free to the first taker. They had no conceivable use for the things, why ship them around the globe?

He didn't say anything about surfing in Cape Town.

NINE

The Chicago Public School System had been good to Maria Rodriguez. At thirty-five years of age, she was principal of Howard High School, one of the largest and most polyglot high schools in the city. She was well-liked by the leaders of the Latino community, the Superintendent of Schools, and two members of the School Board; in a year, the Superintendent would pull her in from the field and give her a high-ranking position with the Board of Education.

Maria was Mexican-American; her family had been poor. She had spent her childhood babysitting her seven brothers and sisters, an experience that prepared her for handling children and bureaucrats and discouraged her from ever having children herself. She had won a scholarship to Boston University where she met and married Hernando Rodriguez, also from a poor Chicago Mexican family who had won a full scholarship to Harvard Law School. Now he was one of the youngest partners of a big-name law firm with a big-name corporate practice. They lived in a wealthy, woodsy suburb on the North Shore.

Maria was fine-boned, dark and pretty. She favored subdued, expensive silk dresses. In good weather, she drove an expensive Italian sports car. During the winter, she drove a royal blue Mercedes sedan.

Friday morning at 9:45, Gin drove Vivian into the visitor's parking area at Howard High School, pulling up only four cars down from Maria's gleaming Mercedes. He winced when he saw it. Maria had been friendly enough over the phone, agreeing to talk to him, but he wondered how much help she could, or would give. He wondered if she was angry because he had left Howard.

Oh well. He had nothing to lose by asking. You could do a lot worse than be under Maria's wide wing, especially if you were Latino. Gin, another man, and four Latino women had been the six teachers responsible for setting up Howard's special classes for foreign-born students. Maria encouraged them all, but took special interest in the Latino women, drawing them aside after meetings and speaking softly to them in Spanish.

The women had done well. With Maria's help, two now worked for the Board of Education, drafting plans for similar classes at other Chicago schools. The other two ran Howard's program; they were also "special consultants" to their two friends at the Board of Education.

The other man was still teaching sophomore English.

And Gin was unemployed.

"Well, Gin Bernthal, I'm so happy to see you," Maria said in her warm pleasant voice, as she extended a delicate hand and welcomed him into her office. She wore a blue silk dress and soft grey pumps with lizard trim. Her office was bright, with a few abstract prints on the wall and fresh tulips in a vase on her desk. Hernando had flowers delivered weekly.

"Maria, it's good to see you," Gin said, flashing a smile and trying not to look desperate. He wore his best grey wool suit and carried his nicest briefcase, a thin leather envelope containing five copies of his resume in a new manila folder.

They exchanged polite inquiries about their health and their spouses. Maria sat down in one of the small grey chairs in front of her metal desk, gesturing to Gin to take the other.

"So, what can I do for you, Gin?" she said, smoothing the blue silk of her dress over her lap. "You are planning to leave St Paul's?"

Gin cleared his throat. "Well, Maria, I left already. And unfortunately, my departure was not under the best of circumstances."

Maria arched her diminutive eyebrows; she looked like an alarmed mouse.

Gin continued. "The principal there never came through on his promise to make me the vice principal. When I challenged him about it, he fired me for insubordination. It all happened last week."

"I see." She paused. "It's most unusual for an administrator to dismiss a teacher in mid-term."

"Well, I did say that he had lured me there with a promise of a job that he never had any intention of giving me. I think that upset him."

"I would think it probably did. That's quite a serious charge. Did it occur to you that he might have intended to give you the job, but couldn't because of the present political situation at the school?"

Boy, she's madder at me than I realized, Gin thought.

He smiled. "Well, when I asked him about his promise, he denied that he'd ever promised me anything. Besides, I had been pretty patient. I waited three years for a job he promised I'd have after two."

"I see." Her voice took on a condescending tone. "Gin, the Superintendent promised me a job as his assistant two years ago; I still don't have it. But I'm not running back and throwing it in his face."

Gin did not like the direction of this conversation.

"Maria, whether or not it was politically appropriate for me to challenge Father Dotson about the vice-principal's job, the point is that I am now out of work. As they say in the newspapers, I am 'free to pursue other options.' " He chuckled; she didn't.

"I would like to stay in education, but I want to be an administrator, not a teacher." He cleared his throat. "Could you help me get a position at the Board of Education?"

Maria clasped her fine hands together on her lap and pursed her lips. "Gin, I would like to help, but I think you give me credit for more power than I really have. I could put in a few good words for you with a few people I know, but I couldn't guarantee anything."

In other words, go take a flying leap, Bernthal. She wasn't going to help. "I would appreciate anything you can do on the administrative front," he said.

She nodded politely.

"I would also consider taking another classroom job, if one comes up."

"I will see what I can do," she said primly. "But knowing that you don't really want to teach anymore, I would be reluctant to recommend you. There are many qualified teachers looking for classroom jobs."

Me Tarzan, you monkey puke, Gin thought. This woman is really playing hardball. So much for baring your soul to your former boss.

"You have, of course, notified the School Board and the Teachers' Union of your desire to be reinstated in the system?" she continued.

Gin nodded. He hadn't notified anyone of anything, yet. He had hoped to resurrect Maria as his patroness before he'd jumped into the bureaucratic jungle. Now he would have to dive in on his own.

Maria stood up, sporting her best professional smile. She extended her hand. "I'll see what I can do for you, Gin. If I were you, I would also contact some of the suburban school districts. Their budgets are not as tight as ours."

In other words, Gin thought, maybe some of the peasant villages surrounding our magnificent city will throw you a bread crust. We won't.

He stood up, slightly off balance as he simultaneously shook her hand and fished out a resume from his briefcase.

"Just in case something does come up, here's my resume. Thanks for your help."

"Any time, Gin. I'm glad to help. Give my best to your wife. Oh—and best of luck."

In the parking lot, Gin spat on the windshield of Maria's Mercedes.

You couldn't blame her. What good would it do to push some guy ahead who'd left the system three years ago? Dozens of Latinos and other allies were eager to get the same jobs. They would loyally back their patroness in her future power struggles; he was a deserter.

He had never dreamed she would hold a grudge against him. When he left Howard, she had wished him luck, saying she was sorry she couldn't offer him the kind of opportunity he would have with Dotson. He should have guessed she was angry. He had won a teaching award, started an innovative program and then in unholy haste left the school that nurtured his young talent for five years. It didn't look good to Maria; it was biting the breast that nursed you.

Gin gunned Vivian and roared out of the visitors' parking lot.

* * *

The answering machine light was blinking when Gin stormed into the apartment in the late afternoon. He threw his briefcase on the floor and dropped two bags of groceries on the kitchen table. He had been too angry to come home and job hunt. So he had run some errands and gone grocery shopping, muttering as he pushed his cart up and down the aisles.

Oh well. Maybe Maria would come up with something after all. It was a long shot, but you never knew.

He fed Carmen and then rewound the tape on the answering machine; maybe someone had called to offer him a high-paying job running a major school system? But only his mother's chirpy voice came over the tape. Were he and Marcia coming to dinner on Sunday?

Of course they were. They had agreed to it just last week, but Alice Bernthal always called two days before any family get-together, "just to check up," as if everyone would have changed their minds and decided to abandon her at the last minute.

He shrugged his coat off onto the floor and dialled the familiar number.

"Hello, mom?"

"Hello dear. How are you?" she said sweetly.

"I'm fine, mom, fine. Listen, we'll be there on Sunday," he said, anxious to get off the phone.

"Yes dear, well, I just wanted to double-check. Claudia and Jack are coming with little Fay around three for drinks and we'll have dinner at five."

"Of course, mom, we'll see you at three then," said Gin, wondering if he really wanted to go. He sighed. Maybe this time it would be different.

"You know Jack just got another promotion at the SEC last week," Alice said. "He's so excited, dear. He's such a good attorney; Claudia is doing wonders with their new house out in Riverside. Fay got three new teeth and Tommy Hampton from over on Oak Park Avenue, you remember him from third grade, dear? Well, I ran into his mother the other day at the Jewel and she said Tommy's wife was pregnant again and he's doing real well at the insurance company."

Alice chattered on for another two minutes, providing updates about people whose names Gin couldn't even remember, much less the details of their lives. She had an encyclopaedic memory for completely useless information.

Gin heard himself make polite and appropriate noises about his brother Jack's new job, Tommy Hampton's pregnant wife, Harry Bourse, the Cullerton twins, and at least five others who could have just landed from Mars for all he knew.

"And how's Marcia, dear?" Alice was winding down.

"What? Oh, real well, mom. Just working away like a real beaver as usual."

"That's good, dear. Well, tally ho and all that. We'll see you on Sunday."

"Bye mom."

As he hung up the phone, he realized he'd forgotten to tell her he was out of a job. Not forgotten, was afraid to. What would the family think?

Alice wouldn't care, just so long as he showed up for family functions well-dressed and without leprosy. But his father, Hodgkins Bernthal, Jr, would be furious. He had made no secret of his disappointment in Gin's choice of careers: teachers were wimps. Why didn't Gin become an accountant, or go into business, or become a lawyer for the federal government like his younger brother, Jack? Jack was now one of the many young, inexperienced attorneys writing regulations on laws they didn't understand at the Securities and Exchange Commission.

Hodge had perked up when it looked as though Gin was going to become a vice principal at St Paul's. As the job seemed to be slipping out of Gin's grasp, Hodge's disappointment grew. Now, he sent Gin newspaper clippings about the oversupply of teachers and the potential of careers in computers. A package of these love notes from Dad arrived at least once a month.

Gin wondered what he was going to say to him.

Marcia came home around six. They dined on canned peaches, a meatloaf Gin had made that afternoon, and half a head of iceberg lettuce tossed with diet California dressing. Marcia was depressed; Ranier was still picking apart her Cully analysis. More punishment for criticizing Six Corners.

She complained to Gin.

"Marsh, maybe you should look for another job," he said, chasing a slithering peach around his plate. "You're not going anywhere there."

"I don't know. I still think I have a chance. Banks are just real slow at promoting women."

Gin raised his eyebrows.

"Well, they do promote them eventually."

"Like the Jesuits. You get your promotion in the next life."

"Gin." Marcia gave an exasperated sigh. She played with a lettuce leaf. "It's not that bad."

"So why do you complain so much, if it's such a bed of roses?"

"It's the same everywhere, Gin. I'd have to fight the same battles everywhere else. I might as well fight them here. Besides, I don't know where else to go at this point."

They chewed in silence for awhile.

"And I don't think I should rock the boat too much at the bank until you find another job."

"Probably not." The hushed tone in her voice irritated him; she sounded as though she were humoring a small child.

"How was your meeting with Maria?"

Gin groaned.

"That good?"

"She won't help me. She's still mad at me for leaving."

"A real forgiving nature that woman has."

"She said she would see what she could do, but she couldn't guarantee anything. I spent a grand total of about ten minutes in her office." He felt like a failure.

Marcia stared at her plate. "Now what do you do?"

"I don't know. Stop asking me that. I don't know," he said, his voice rising with frustration.

"I just asked." It's not my fault you're out of work, you jerk, she thought. Was this the replacement? Instead of crabbing at her about Dotson, would he crab at her now about his job search?

"Sorry, I didn't mean to take it out on you."

"Okay, forget it."

Gin cleared the table and washed the dishes; Marcia dried. They listened to the music on the radio and tried to joke around, but they could generate only a little forced laughter.

"My mother called," Gin said, handing Marcia the meatloaf pan to dry. "Drinks at three, dinner at five."

"Did you tell her about your run-in with the Grand Inquisitor?"

"No. I'm saving that for Sunday."

"Uh, oh. Just so I'm out of the line of fire." Marcia couldn't stand it when Gin and his father argued. No one in her family battled like that.

"What makes you think we'll fight?" Gin said angrily.

"Just a nasty hunch, dear." She took a quart of butter-pecan ice cream out of the freezer and divided it into two bowls.

"Marcia, I can't eat all that ice cream."

"Then I will." She scooped out a third of his bowl and plopped it in her own. Gin couldn't understand his wife's obsession with food. Every now and then he would find her in the pantry, stuffing herself with cheap cookies, and looking embarrassed at being discovered.

That night, they watched a string of public affairs and wildlife programs on the educational TV station. Marcia felt sick from all that ice cream; they went to bed early.

Marcia dreamed she was married to a handsome, high-powered real estate developer. They lived in a big house in a ritzy suburb along the lake and had lots of money. She spent the whole dream trying to charm him into making love to her. She woke up feeling pleased; she had gotten him to smile at her.

Gin dreamed that Marcia was being eaten by giant ducks with suits on. Now they were coming after him, and they had turned into members of his family. He woke up sweating.

Saturday morning they made love, tentatively. Marcia was feeling guilty about her dream; Gin was angry about the day that lay ahead.

They spent every Saturday cleaning the house, doing the laundry and running routine errands. Gin hated Saturdays; Marcia just attacked everything with the same determination that got her through her job five days a week. Despite Gin's complaints, Marcia refused to get a cleaning woman or send the laundry out. It was too expensive, she said.

Gin's cleaning never met her high standards. Today, he knew she was on good behavior; after all, he had just lost his job. He could tell she didn't like the way he had cleaned the bathtub, but she smiled her bank smile and said it was fine.

She wondered why Gin was such a poor housekeeper. She found cleaning relaxing. For the first six months of their marriage, she had done all the housework. She would have been happy to continue, but she felt on principle that Gin should do half of it. So, one Saturday, she had insisted that he do his share. They had argued about it all day, until finally he gave in. Every month or two, Gin suggested they hire a cleaning woman and Marcia shot down the idea.

Watching her mop the kitchen floor, Gin felt despair. Now that he had lost his job, they really couldn't afford to hire help. He would be swabbing out the toilet for years to come.

By Saturday night, Gin was so tired and depressed that he almost looked forward to seeing his parents for Sunday dinner.

TEN

Sunday broke clear and cold, a beautiful winter day with white snow and brilliant sunshine. Gin and Maria slept late, ate a huge breakfast, and read the Sunday paper. Around one, Marcia suggested they go for a short drive before going to the Bernthals. Gin readily agreed. Riding in Vivian, they felt affluent; Gin's unemployment was filed away in the backs of their minds.

Hodge and Alice Bernthal lived in Oak Park, an old, affluent suburb just west of the city. Gin and Marcia took the long way to Oak Park, winding through miles of suburban streets and stopping at a forest preserve on the way. Marcia loved to look at all the houses. And, though he disliked the suburbs, so did Gin. You had to admit, some of them were beautiful. They looked so quiet and peaceful, straight out of a Norman Rockwell painting, not like their crowded street in the city, where your bathroom window was less than three feet from your neighbor's. On summer nights, Gin and Marcia could hear every word as the Palestinian next door screamed at his six-year-old daughter.

"Oh Gin, look at that one," Marcia said; they were passing an old, three story clapboard house. It was set back on a wide lot filled with giant oak trees. With its cornices, overhangs and porches, it looked like the House of the Seven Gables, Gin thought. Comforting, a good place to lay down your bones at night and rest. He could see himself swinging on a hammock on the front porch. Marcia would have to get a cleaning woman if they lived in a place that big.

Gin's parents lived on a wide, oak-lined street only two blocks from the gabled house. Their old, blue-shingled house with white shutters sat on a hillock back from the street. It was a big house; a wide veranda ran its length and curved around one end. An old oak leaned precariously over the veranda. Hodge refused to cut it down. "Let it fall down," he would remark when some well-meaning relative suggested that it would blow over in a windstorm some night and crash through the front-bedroom window. "The old lady and I don't mind leaving this world with a tree branch embedded in our brains, do we old girl?" he would say, and take another swig from his Scotch and soda and throw an arm around Alice's thin shoulders.

Alice would smile weakly. She had no intention of being killed by a tree, but she always smiled and agreed with her husband in public. She was adept at blending into the wallpaper if she had to.

"My blessed first-born. It's good to see you again," Hodge said, as Alice scurried to collect their coats. He pumped Gin's hand vigorously and kissed Marcia lightly on the cheek. "Marcia, you look marvellous as usual."

Marcia and Gin smiled hard. "You look pretty good yourself, Old Man," Gin said. Hodge was a fatter, shorter version of his eldest son. With his red face, Gin thought, he looked like a prime candidate for a heart attack. If he kept gaining weight, in ten years Hodge wouldn't be alive to retire from his job as the best life insurance salesman the Tillman Insurance Agency had ever seen.

"Gin, honey. Marcia, how good you both look," Alice said, in a high, sing-song voice. She had returned from depositing their coats in one of the upstairs bedroom. She was a thin, nervous woman with wispy blonde hair and blue eyes. Gin had her eyes.

"Well, what can I get you two to drink?" Hodge boomed, heading for the liquor cabinet in the dining room. "We've got Scotch, Bourbon, vodka. . ."

"Scotch and water for me, Dad."

"A Bloody Mary, Hodge."

A young man with thinning blonde hair strode into the room. Gin grinned. "Jack, you turkey, where you been hiding out?"

"Same place you have, you jerk. Where have you been since Christmas?" Gin grabbed his brother's hand and shook it hard.

"The press of business, my good man, has kept me quite busy."

"Give me a break." He cuffed Gin behind the head and the two of them started roughhousing around the living room. Alice made clucking noises and glanced nervously at her collection of china figurines in a mahogany case on the wall.

Horace "Jack' Bernthal was five years younger than Gin, but looked and acted older. He had Hodge's blustery good humor. It didn't suit him; it was an act from another generation. Jack was doing well. He had a beautiful house in Riverside, a devoted wife who was helping with dinner in Alice's kitchen, two cute daughters, and a decent job as an attorney for the SEC. Gin liked Jack, especially on the few occasions when he caught him staring out a window with a drink in his hand, looking bewildered. Probably worrying about his bills, Gin would think. Jack was mortgaged up to his eyeballs.

The brothers threw their arms around each other's shoulders and went into the TV room, Hodge taking up the rear with a plate of cheddar cheese and crackers in one hand and a Scotch and water for Gin in the other. They settled down for an afternoon of football, basketball and golf, with Hodge changing the channel during every commercial to catch the scores. Gin nestled into an old overstuffed chair, sipped his Scotch, and let masculine camraderie wash over him. He hoped to make it through the visit without letting his father know he had lost his job.

"Well, dear, should we go give Claudia a hand in the kitchen?" Alice asked, looping her arm through Marcia's. Marcia wasn't much of a cook and would rather have watched the football game with the men, but group cooking was her mother-in-law's idea of female fun.

"Sure, Alice."

Cooking noises and smells drifted out of the kitchen. "Caroline," a woman's voice said quietly, floating in an ocean of patience. "If you don't dry the silverware right away, Mommy will have to do it herself."

They heard the sound of silverware hitting the floor as the four-year-old decided that "Mommy" could do just that. A little girl in a red dress pushed past Marcia.

Claudia Bernthal, a quiet, plain young woman, crouched on the kitchen floor, picking up the silverware. She wore a perpetual bland smile and a beige dress to match. She was doggedly devoted to her husband, her children and housework. Between Claudia's catatonia and Alice's flighty chit-chat, Marcia felt like an inmate in an all-female lunatic asylum. Claudia was the one who had the lobotomy; Alice needed sedation.

Until Caroline was born, Claudia had taught the fourth grade in a west suburban school. Now, with little Fay just barely four months old, she would be a full-time mother for years, if she ever went back to work at all.

When she talked to Claudia, Marcia played a game. How long could she think of things to say before she ran out of topics and just ended up smiling blankly at the woman? Two hours was her best time so far.

"How are you, Claudia?" she said, kissing her lightly on the cheek. She hated all this damn kissing.

"Very well, Marcia, and you?" Claudia said tonelessly. She poked at the beef roast in the oven.

"Fine, just fine. Can I help?"

"Well, you can peel those potatoes over there."

"Here, dear, here's an apron for you," Alice said handing her a red gingham apron with a lace-trimmed pocket. It clashed violently with Marcia's red plaid wool jacket.

As Marcia peeled potatoes into a big aluminum pot, Alice and Claudia fussed over the roast and salads, vegetable casseroles and pies. Claudia unmolded raspberry jello with walnuts and tiny marshmallows in it. Marcia's stomach growled. She couldn't talk to these women, but she sure loved eating their cooking.

"You should see Claudia and Jack's new house," Alice said, hacking up a salad tomato. Claudia and Jack had moved to a new house in early February; Gin and Marcia hadn't been there yet.

"It's simply gorgeous, one of those colonials with four bedrooms and the most marvelous breakfast nook. Riverside is so beautiful—all those big trees and winding streets. Of course, Claudia is re-doing the whole place herself. She's a whiz at wallpapering. She even put up wainscoting in the dining room. She's just starting to reupholster the sofa in a tiny blue Williamsburg print and next week we're going to make all the curtains and draperies together.''

"You're really doing all that yourself, Claudia?" Marcia asked. "That's really impressive." Claudia sounded like a one-woman crafts fair. What the hell was wainscoting?

Claudia smiled and nodded her head. Except that she wore a beige dress, she could have been an Amish woman in severe black, pleased that someone had noticed she existed.

"I'm impressed," Marcia said, staring despondently into her pot of peeled potatoes. What she wouldn't give for a house like that.

Alice chattered on about a coffee cake recipe she had clipped from the paper; the new draperies she was helping Claudia make for her living room, and a new carpet store that had just opened on Oak Park Avenue. Maybe she and Claudia should go over there one day and see if they had the right shade of blue carpeting to match the sofa upholstery.

Alice had taught school for two years before Gin was born and had never worked since. Jack came along five years later, and then twin girls Lorraine and Berenice, who were now seniors at the University of Illinois in Champaign. Lorraine wanted to teach retarded children and get married; Berenice just wanted to get married. She was engaged to a nice young man who was promised a berth in his father's printing business at graduation; they'd be married in the fall. Marcia was amazed at the twins' lack of initiative.

She threw a big red potato in the pot and began to work on another. God, she thought, this cooking stuff took a lot of time.

Alice began to talk about African violets; they just weren't blooming this year.

That was it. Marcia had had enough of Alice. She attacked her last potato, fixed herself a double Bloody Mary, and excused herself. She went into the living room and plopped down in a big wing chair in front of the fireplace.

Alice's house was an inviting place, decorated in the colonial style. Heavy, braided rugs covered the dark oak floors and family bric-a-brac and tasteful water colors hung on the walls.

A fire burned in the big red-brick fireplace in the living room, casting a warm glow on the room's old woodwork and fine cherry furniture.

Marcia wished it was her house. The Bernthals' mortgage payments were probably something like $100 a month—if they didn't own it outright. After all, they had bought it thirty years ago, in the days of six percent mortgages. We'll never be able to afford a house like this, Marcia thought. Now, with Gin out of work, it was more out of reach than ever. She sipped her drink and stared sightlessly into the fire. They were supposed to be going forward in life, making more money every year. What had gone wrong?

Caroline crawled into her lap with a story book. Marcia read her a story about three anthropomorphic mice and their beautiful house in the country. Even the mice lived better than she did.

The clattering of serving platters in the kitchen indicated that dinner was on its way. She nudged Caroline off her lap and returned to the kitchen, where duty lay.

ELEVEN

Alice knew how to set out a meal; there was no doubt about that. The big trestle table in her dining room was covered with a heavy white tablecloth and china plates in a squared colonial design. Some of the silverware dated from the Revolutionary War; Alice's family had bloodlines reaching back to old Virginia. Carved water goblets and thin crystal wine glasses sparkled in the soft light from the chandelier.

Sunday dinners at his parents' house reminded Gin of the Last Supper: Alice made so much food, you'd swear you'd never want to eat again. After a week of Wheaties, Spaghetti-O's and hot dogs, he was glad to see it. Marcia couldn't cook to save her life.

The jello salad sat cheek-to-jowl with a potato salad, a tossed-greens salad, a marinated salad with artichoke hearts, and a basket of three kinds of bread. A heavy silver platter of roast beef circulated around the table, followed by a painted ceramic bowl of mashed potatoes and a matching tureen of gravy.

Creamed green beans with almonds and a bowl of buttered peas and carrots made the rounds; reinforcements sat on the carved sideboard under the dining room window. Bowls of sweet pickles, olives, and baby marinated corn perched in various open spaces.

The diners washed it all down with glasses of California burgundy.

Gin, Hodge and Jack held a spirited discussion of the draw-backs of the Chicago Bears' offensive line. Claudia and Alice gossiped about some relative Marcia had never heard of, and Caroline told Marcia all about the valentines she had made at nursery school that week. In Marcia's opinion, theirs was the most interesting conversation at the table.

Hodge told a story about how the disability insurance policy that he had sold a young man last year had just saved his family from financial ruin. Apparently, the poor guy, only thirty years old, had stepped off the tennis court and collapsed at the feet of his unfortunate wife. He had been in a coma for the last nine months.

"Without that policy, they'd have been in real trouble," Hodge announced to his attentive audience. The fellow had two infants and the wife had no job skills.

Gin rolled his eyes and looked at Marcia, who gave him a half-smile. Hodge's insurance tales, along with his lectures supporting the Republican Party, were standard at Bernthal Sunday dinners. According to Hodge, he had saved more than half the old ladies in the western suburbs from impoverished widowhood.

Near the end of the meal, Hodge rose from his chair at the head of the table and announced a toast. "To Jack's promotion," he said proudly. "May it be followed by many more."

"Here, here." Gin lifted his glass with enthusiasm, his cheeks flushed from the wine. "To the meteoric rise of my baby brother."

Everyone laughed and clinked glasses.

Marcia watched Gin with concern. Had he told his father about losing his job? He caught her eye and smiled at her as if he had just won the lottery.

She turned to her brother-in-law. "What exactly do you do now at SEC?"

Jack explained his new role in the real estate division of the enforcement department; it sounded like the same job he had before, only they were paying him three thousand a year more for doing it.

Such are the plodding successes of the Federal bureaucrat, she thought, eating marinated salad. Jack described in boring, baroque detail the regulation he was presently working on—something about publicly traded limited partnerships and whether or not promoters could use pictures in their mailings of the properties they were offering for investment.

Everyone listened as if he had just discovered a cure for cancer, except Caroline, who was stirring her jello salad into her mashed potatoes, and Marcia, who couldn't believe that someone could happily devote his entire life to such trivia. She glanced at Gin again. He drooped over his plate and picked at a slice of roast beef; he looked like a deflated balloon.

Jack ended his monologue with a story about how SEC regulations had saved some old lady from losing her life savings to a crook. Like father, like son. Hodge saved the old ladies from poverty; Jack saved them from their own stupid greed.

Suddenly, Gin perked up. "How about some more wine?" he suggested. Marcia thought he was starting to sound manic.

"Great, a great idea," boomed Hodge. With three Scotch-and-sodas under his belt and two goblets of burgundy at dinner, Hodge was in an outgoing and accepting mood.

"Another toast," he said generously. "To my eldest son and heir, the Socrates of the classroom, the hero of young men, and the right arm of the good Jesuits."

"Here, here," boomed Jack, magnanimous after his fifteen minute performance in the family spotlight. Time to let the also-ran get his time in.

Gin turned white and weakly lifted his glass.

"So," said Hodge, his eyes alive with alcoholic sparkle. "How's it going at St Paul's?"

"Well." Gin bit his lower lip and looked pained; his voice was flat. "Well, Dad, I don't work there anymore. I was meaning to tell you earlier, but we were talking and watching the game and everything and it just slipped my mind."

Hodge eyed him quizzically for clues. "Son of a gun, Gin," he laughed. "You really keep your old man hopping. You must get your modesty from your mother. Big-mouth guy like me, if I got a new job, I'd be crowing about it to the entire world."

He swished some more wine around in his mouth and sat back in his chair, his arms folded across his chest. He smiled. "Now you just tell us all about this, son. What have you been cooking up? You finally seen the light and gotten out of teaching? Got something in computers I bet. Christ, it's about time. I always said you were wasted in teaching. What is it?"

All eyes were fixed on Gin.

Gin cleared his throat. His lips were dry. "Well, it's not exactly like that, Dad." He paused. "Dotson canned me last week," he croaked.

"Speak up, son. I can't hear you."

"I said Dotson fired me, canned me, cut me off from the trough. I don't work there anymore," Gin said loudly, in an irritated voice.

"Well, where do you work then?" Hodge asked, puzzled.

"Nowhere, I'm out of work."

"What?"

"I said, I'm out of work, old man," Gin yelled. "Christ Almighty, don't you ever listen?"

The table was completely silent. Everyone looked at Hodge. Marcia felt her stomach turn over.

"I heard you, son. I heard you loud and clear," Hodge said evenly in a normal speaking tone. "You're the one sitting there screaming like some banshee and disrupting our family dinner."

Hodge grabbed the edge of the table on both sides of his plate and turned to his wife. "If that doesn't take the cake, Alice. If that doesn't take the cake, I don't know what will. What's going to become of this son of ours?" Alice looked straight ahead, expressionless.

Hodge turned to Gin. "I knew you were a fool, son, I knew it from the time you told me you wanted to be a teacher. Of all the fool stupid things you could do, becoming a teacher was one of the worst." His voice was starting to pick up volume.

"I told you it was a job for losers; you'd go nowhere, make no money, do the same thing year in and year out, but you wouldn't listen to me. No, you had to go out and ruin yourself on your own.

"Now, not only are you stuck in a loser profession, you can't even keep a job in it. How can a schoolteacher get himself fired in mid-term? What did you do, threaten to sodomize the Pope?" he screamed.

"Oh for Chrissakes, Dad, Dotson was a jerk," Gin screamed back. "I just asked when he would give me the job as vice principal, and he just canned me for it."

"Right, you just walked in and said politely, 'Let's discuss this like rational men, Father Dotson,' and he canned you for it. You expect me to believe that?"

Gin gave an exasperated sigh.

"Well?"

"I told you. I tried to explain my position to him and he wouldn't listen. He became unreasonable and just canned me." Gin was trying to keep his temper. "For God's sake, Dad, give me a break."

Hodge sat back in his chair and looked in disgust at his eldest son. "I had such plans for you, Gin, and now look at you. Thirty years old and your wife is going to have to support you. How can you stand the shame of it? I'd never have let Alice support us."

"Keep me out of this, Hodge." Marcia was surprised to hear her voice; it sounded cold. Hodge ignored her.

"When I was your age, I was well on my way in the insurance business. I already had two kids and a house and responsibility," Hodge said, his voice filled with disgust. "But you're acting like a kid. What have you got to show for your years in teaching? Nothing. Just nothing. You're turning into a real loser. And I'm sorry to see it."

His voice became sad. "This is really the last straw. I've done everything I can to help you, but you won't listen. I wash my hands of the whole affair."

Gin fingered his water glass and stared at his plate. Marcia tried to catch his eye but he refused to look up. Hodge's oration had been one of his most vehement in years. A stellar performance, she thought.

The table was quiet.

Hodge turned to his wife. "How about some coffee and dessert, Alice?" he said, pleasantly, as if the entire argument with Gin had never occurred. He turned to Claudia. "So, Claudia, how's your house decorating going?"

Before she could answer, Gin stood up, and turned to Hodge. "Okay, Dad, this is it," he said evenly. "I've had enough insults for one night. Thanks for dinner, Mom."

He pecked Alice on the cheek, then Claudia. He shook Jack's hand. Everybody looked relieved. When Gin and Hodge fought, they either screamed themselves hoarse or one of them left. This was a leaving night, which everyone preferred.

"C'mon, Marcia, let's get the hell out of here." He stepped back from the table so firmly that his chair tipped over. By the time he had retrieved their coats from upstairs, she had said good-bye to everyone and was standing by the front door. She was sorry to miss dessert: Alice's peach cobbler with vanilla ice cream.

Marcia could hear nervous laughter and the clinking of dessert forks. As they walked out, Claudia was calmly describing her wainscoting project.

*   *   *

"Another quiet dinner at the Bernthals," Marcia said, scooting into the car. The screaming dinners used to shock her; now they disgusted her. Why did he let his father talk to him like that?

"Oh shut up, Marcia."

"Oh shut up yourself, you should hear how ridiculous you two sound."

"My family is my business."

"You drag me along and they're my business, too."

"What do you want me to do? Shoot him? That's the way he is. Your family is no piece of cake either." Marcia's father was a quiet, depressed man. His wife, Marcia's mother, was one of the coldest women Gin had ever met.

"At least we don't have screaming matches every other time we have dinner."

"That's because you're all clinically dead. Your old man couldn't scream if his life depended on it."

They rode home in silence. Every time he fought with Hodge, Gin was mad for a day and a half. He'd snap at Marcia, kick the cat, and fume. Then, he'd call the old man up and they'd have lunch together or go golfing. They'd be formally polite, never mentioning what they had fought over tooth and nail only the week before. It was insane behavior; he knew it.

If only Hodge would listen to him, he thought. He knew he would, one of these days; he just had to keep trying. And maybe the old man had a point. Maybe he should get out of teaching and try something new, like computers or even insurance sales. Maybe he really was throwing away his life.

His throat choked with fear. The old man had been telling him he was an incompetent for years. Maybe he really *was* incompetent. He would never amount to anything. Only Marcia had any faith in him.

"I'm sorry Marsh," he said softly. "I didn't mean to scream at you."

"Sure. Don't worry about it." She stared coolly out the window.

He took her limp hand in his and then dropped it. Now she was mad at him, too. Damn them all.

TWELVE

February moved into March and Gin made his move into computers. Marcia thought it was worth a try. And when he had lunch with his father two Saturdays after the big fight, the old man blessed his decision. "Computers. That's a business worth being in," he said; he bought Gin an imported beer as a sign of approval. After all, *Time* and *Newsweek* were running regular stories on the fortunes being made in computers and he personally knew four men whose sons were doing well in the field.

Each week-end, Gin answered all the help-wanted ads for computer programmers and analysts in the Sunday papers. He answered over seventy-five ads, but no one ever called back. He tried three employment agencies that specialized in computer personnel; two told him he needed to take courses or get some experience before they could place him. The third came up with a minimum-wage job as a computer operator for a mail order house on the midnight to 8 a.m. shift.

The job sounded awful; the operator spent the whole night moving from one giant machine to another, changing computer tapes and disc drives. Gin interviewed for it anyway, losing to a twenty-year-old kid with two years of computer courses from a junior college. Every student with a technical mind and a desire for a steady paycheck was majoring in computers. They read *Time* and *Newsweek,* too.

He called up Xerox, IBM and Digital Equipment, asking about possible sales jobs. Yes, they were still hiring ex-teachers to sell their equipment, but they had waiting lists for the jobs. He'd added his name to the rosters—number 4,324 at Xerox. They would probably offer him a job in Cleveland at the beginning of the next Ice Age, he thought. He hung up the phone, and called his father for moral support. "God damn it, Gin," Hodge had yelled. "Just get off your ass and go out there and sell yourself. You just got to get out there and hustle."

He called up the teacher at St Paul's whose brother-in-law ran a computer store in Niles; the brother-in-law wasn't hiring. He went through the yellow pages and began calling computer stores. Several were hiring salesmen, but they all worked on straight commission. No sales; no salary. They seemed to go through sales personnel like wealthy women go through interior designers.

In April, he tried a commission job, selling for a Video Circus store in the northern suburbs. The store was part of a franchise chain catering to the low end of the market. Gin spent his days selling video games to teen-aged boys and cheap home computers to parents trying to turn their children into over-achievers. The store did sell a few high-priced systems to a few businessmen who were stupid enough to buy from such a poorly stocked store, but none bought from Gin.

After a month and a half of mind-numbing work, he had made $634.46. The owner promised that his earnings would improve, but Gin couldn't see how. He had learned nothing about computers, made no money, and worked from 11 a.m. to 8 p.m. six days a week. Marcia complained that she never saw him and when she did he was dead from fatigue.

With her encouragement he decided to quit and take some computer courses; maybe he could get a better job then? That summer, he took two night school computer classes at one of the city's junior colleges. At the same time, an ex-salesman from Video Circus called him up and got him a job selling computers at Computer World, a better-quality computer store in the suburbs. He thought his luck had finally turned.

He worked until five each day, raced to his classes, and didn't get home until ten at night. When he wasn't asleep, he was doing homework or poring over some computer at school. Marcia was distraught; he was distraught and exhausted. Both chalked it up to laying the groundwork for his new career.

Then, sometime around the Fourth of July, his new world unraveled. He discovered that computers bored him silly.

He had thought of computers as being like robots—incredibly sophisticated machinery that made the modern office and business hum with efficiency. Now that he had studied and sold them, he found that they were big, dumb adding machines with programs, printers, systems and discs that didn't match, wouldn't work, or were just so stupidly designed that they were impossible to use.

His colleagues were enthralled with the challenges of making the whole mechanical mess work; Gin was disgusted. He hated tinkering; he couldn't see spending his life hooking together mismatched machinery with fancy names or supervising the people who did. Nor was there much money in selling the stuff. Competition was fierce and his store handled mostly losing brands. He was lucky if he sold one or two systems a month. He was making less than half his salary at St Paul's.

By August, he was disgusted and depressed. He was also broke: he and Marcia had used up all their meager savings except the $10,000 she had saved toward buying a house. Gin didn't dare suggest they use that. He had the terrible feeling his marriage wouldn't survive it.

He was sure that Marcia had started to lose interest in him. She had decided that he was never going to amount to much; now it was time for her to pull out and make other plans. She didn't say anything to him about it. She still smiled and nodded when he told her about his day; she was pleasant when they shared Sunday, their one free day together.

But more and more, her inquiries seemed polite formality. As he talked, he saw her eyes wander and her face go blank. He could still bring her back to him when he made love to her on Sunday mornings, but she responded with growing reluctance and a kind of sadness. He felt that she was saying goodbye.

Late one night, when it was too hot to sleep, he had suggested that they take a walk. They had ended up at an all-night grill, and over a glass of instant lemonade he had blurted out his fears about their marriage. Her face softened. She took his hand and assured him that she loved him. It was just that his long hours and low pay were taking their toll on her. Once he was well on his way in his new computer career, it would all be only a bad dream.

But he had said that he didn't want a career in computers. Computers were beginning to bore him. She had turned white, and that distant look had come back to her eyes. Well, she had said coldly, just what was it that he did want to do with his life? He said that he didn't know, but it wasn't computers.

That was last week and it had been the cold war ever since; he was living with a female iceberg. They were so wary and carefully considerate of each other that Gin felt as though he were living with someone he had just met at a bus stop. It was driving him crazy; he missed his wife. Short of immediately finding some job that paid him fifty thousand a year and made him deliriously happy, he couldn't see how he could get back into Marcia's good graces.

That was why it seemed like a miracle when he came home from school at nine-thirty one night and found a phone call from Maria Rodriguez on his answering machine. He had called her from work that morning.

She had not one, but two job leads for him. He wondered how he could ever have doubted her good intentions. At least he wondered that until she gave him the details of the jobs.

The first one was at a high school in the heart of the black ghetto on the West Side—a job teaching freshman English. That was one of the roughest schools in the city. He could see why the principal would need him—to help get all the knives, guns and drugs away from the wild illiterates posing as freshman students.

Maria was offering him what was possibly the single worst teaching job in the entire Chicago public school system. No wonder it was still open two weeks after the start of the school year.

How could her second lead top that?

It didn't. It was a job in a high school in a suburb about fifty miles northwest of the city. . . called Glass Lake or Crystal Bay or Toot's Corner or something, probably in an area full of small marshy lakes, truck farms and cheap track housing. Anyway, the principal was an acquaintance of Maria's; she hadn't seen him in years and then she bumped into him at a principals' conference in Milwaukee a month ago.

He needed a utility man, someone to teach freshman English and a little Drivers' Ed on the side. And maybe sweep the floors at night too, Gin thought.

But what did he have to lose?

He called the principal, a Mr Bellicosi, immediately. Apparently the man who had held the job had died suddenly from a heart attack a week ago, and of course Mr Bellicosi was having a hard time finding a competent replacement on such short notice.

Gin found that hard to believe; the metropolitan area was crawling with unemployed teachers.

He asked what the job paid.

Ten thousand a year, Bellicosi replied in a low voice. He sounded embarrassed.

No wonder there were no takers. The clerks at the public schools got more than that just to show up and breathe all day.

Oh well. Gin agreed to drive out the next day for an interview.

He disliked teaching, but he hated computers. Anyway he was making so little money selling them that the job at Bela Lugosi's or whatever his name was, actually paid better. It was also steady pay—that might just convince Marcia that he wasn't a total lunatic and was worth keeping as a husband.

He hung up and cursed himself for not having tried to line up a teaching job sooner, just in case his computer career didn't get off the ground. But he had been so convinced that computers were the answer. Marcia and his friends thought so and his father was sure of it. His father. He cursed him too.

* * *

Marcia came home late that night; Gin had been waiting for her since ten, but she cruised in about midnight, giddy and smelling of beer. She was surprised that Gin was waiting up for her; he was surprised that she came home so late. She had been out late the night before too. Two nights in a row was a real party roll for Marcia.

"Where have you been?" he said. "I thought something might have happened to you. I was worried." He sounded disapproving. He had been trying to reach her at the bank all afternoon; she had been out of the office and hadn't returned his phone calls. "Didn't you get my messages?"

"Sure, but by the time I got back to the bank, you would already have been on your way to school. After work, a few of us went out for drinks." The whining undertone in his angry voice unnerved her.

"You never used to go out drinking with these guys," he said. "You said you couldn't stand them. Now you've been out two nights in a row."

"Well, I never see you anymore, so I have to do something to occupy my time."

"Oh for Chrissakes, Marcia, you sound like a character from a soap opera."

"Well, I'm lonely," she said. "I don't see you much. And I get tired of sitting alone at home. We got a new guy in the department and we all went out for a few drinks after work; a few of us stayed out, that's all." She fingered her wedding ring.

"Say, what is this? The third degree?" she asked angrily.

"I just wondered where you were. You were out late the night before, too. I haven't been able to talk to you for two days."

"I get this feeling you're watching me. I don't like it."

"I'm not watching you," he said, knowing that he was. He had been so anxious about their marriage that he had found himself unwittingly tracking her movements. She'll be at the bank by now, he would think as he straightened up the store before opening each morning. Or: She's at lunch now, he would think around noon. He felt tired. His big announcement seemed anticlimactic.

"Anyway, I've got good news," he said, sitting down on the couch in the dimly lit living room. Marcia sat down next to him. "Maria Rodriguez called me last night and I talked to her this morning. It looks like I might have a teaching job for the coming year."

"Oh really? That sounds promising," Marcia said; her tone said it didn't sound promising at all. Gin's long search for the ideal job was boring her. All that energy spinning itself in circles. If he had used it to become a real estate developer, they would be rich by now.

"You don't sound too thrilled."

"Neither do you."

"Well, at least it gets me out of computers and back into teaching again," Gin said. "I should never have left teaching to begin with." He sounded dejected.

There was a time when Marcia would have disputed this, would have replied that he needed to follow his instincts and find his own way in the world. Now, she thought he might be right: maybe he should have stuck with teaching in the first place.

Maybe her parents were right about not rocking the boat and sticking with a steady job at a good company—or a steady teaching slot at a good school—even if you hated it. She was sticking it out at the bank. He should have stuck it out at St Paul's.

"Well, what's done is done," she said, patting Gin's knee. "Live and learn. We'll just have to see what happens."

That was all she could come up with? Gin thought. His dejection deepened. He had hoped for a burst of enthusiasm from her to buoy him up. "That's marvelous; oh what good news," anything but "Live and learn." This job was supposed to push her back into his arms, or at least push her in his direction.

"Where is this school, anyway?" she asked, getting up from the couch.

"Somewhere out in the northwest suburbs. I forget the name of the place. I wrote it down," Gin said. He followed her to the bedroom. "I interview for it tomorrow."

"Well, good luck."

"Thanks," he said sarcastically.

"I'm sorry, Gin, but I'm so tired I can hardly think straight." She feigned a yawn. Well, she thought, it was partially true. She *was* tired—tired of propping him up. "We'll talk about it tomorrow," she said, before she closed the bathroom door.

She hadn't even asked how much the job paid, he thought. That was a bad sign; normally it was her first question.

They each slept badly that night, far apart in their big bed.

THIRTEEN

The next morning, Marcia was ashamed of herself; as a reparation, she kissed her sleeping husband on the cheek and left a note on the kitchen table: "I'm sorry. Good luck. See you around six. Much love, Marcia. xxx"

She shouldn't pick on Gin; he had had a rough summer. It was hard not knowing what you were going to be when you grew up—and then discover you were grown up. She ought to know, she was starting to feel that way herself.

Gin at least had had the courage to go out and look for something else. He tried on the computer business for size and found it didn't fit. She was still treading water at the bank.

Yes, she thought, but he couldn't be so fancy-free if my money wasn't holding him up. A wave of hot resentment rolled through her. She couldn't just go out and quit the way he did: they would starve without her income. She had to play Rock of Gibraltar to his sea nymph.

He's supposed to be supporting *me,* not the other way around, she thought. It's the American way. Other men changed jobs and careers with grace and ease; hers was floundering around in the tidal flats like a wounded walrus.

Why oh why hadn't she married a nice, rich, real estate lawyer?

Because she hadn't been asked.

She looked in the mirror. A pair of bloodshot eyes stared back. "These late nights have got to stop," she mumbled. Drinks with the guys were a bore, but it was better than staying home alone with Carmen or working late at the bank. How many late nights could you work when you had already finished all the work they had given you by three in the afternoon?

Her summer had been hell. Ranier had banished her to the dog house. Every small-change real estate deal that came into the shop was channeled to her desk, while Baxter and the other baby loan analysts labored away on the really important deals. The Six Corners loan was pulling in a fortune in loan fees. Baxter was now a Golden Boy; she was the Tin Woodman.

She had thought things would improve in June when she finally got her MBA degree. Hah! The Personnel department sent her a congratulatory form letter signed by the president of the bank. When she told Ranier she had the degree, he patted her on the back, muttered "Good going, Marsh" and rushed out to catch a plane for Houston. Only Henrietta was enthusiastic. She bought Marcia a cheeseburger in the bank cafeteria and complained all during lunch that her ex-husband was falling behind in his child support payments.

Marcia spared Gin the details of her sagging career in real estate banking. She knew they bored him. He would dutifully ask her about the bank and she would make a few comments about how lousy things were. Then she would steer the conversation to Gin's problems, which he was happy to unload on her. She pumped him for details of his job search, listened patiently to his complaints and lived and died by his every trauma and upset. She had to; Gin was having a rougher time with life than she was.

Wasn't he?

She splashed cold water on her face; now it looked blotchy.

He would fall apart without her. Wouldn't he?

She paused, bending over the sink, to think about that one. A tiny little voice in the back of her head whispered that she had been toadying to her husband, meddling in his affairs and trying to run his life because it beat looking after her own. Who was taking care of her while she was taking care of him?

But she didn't listen to the tiny voice. She listened instead to the big booming voice in the front of her head that said she had married an idiot whom she would have to take care of for the rest of her life.

No wonder she didn't want a child. She had married one.

She sighed. Her father had warned her that she was "too much of a woman" and "too strong-willed" to get married. "You'd eat any man alive, my dear," he had told her when she started dating seriously. He had never approved of her marriage to Gin.

For that matter, he had never approved of any of her boy friends. "They're all such losers," he said to her, with a sad smile. It broke her heart, that he looked so sad. She had to take care of him, too.

On her way to work she wondered why all the men in her family were either depressed or incompetent—with the exception of her big-mouthed father-in-law. He was just a jerk.

She stared out the dirty window of the subway train and wondered how they were going to make their next car payment. Money was really tight. The landlord had raised their rent, she was still repaying school loans for her MBA, and she needed a winter coat.

By the time she reached her office, she was raging.

"Men," she muttered under her breath, slamming her briefcase down on her desk. The drawers rattled, and Tom Gavins, who sat at the next desk, almost jumped out of his chair.

"You guys are all useless," she yelled at him. Gavins stared at her through his horn-rimmed glasses.

"Excuse me?"

"I said you're all a bunch of stupid, useless wimps, Gavins. You can all go to hell." She fished in her purse. "Here's a quarter, punk, go get me a cup of coffee." She threw it on his desk and headed for the ladies' room before Gavins could say a word. There she ran into Henrietta, who kept her captive for fifteen minutes, complaining that Timmy had been roughed up at nursery school by some bullies. "Imagine, Marcia," she said, pulling a comb through her stringy hair. "The kid's only four and he's being hustled. If I only had the money I'd put him in a good nursery school instead of that dump."

When Marcia got back she found a steaming cup of coffee and a doughnut on her desk. They rested on a lace paper doily on which was scrawled in magic marker, "Have a nice day, you dumb bitch." Gavins sat at his desk, engrossed in a report.

"Thanks Gavins," she said. "You're a real sweetheart."

"My pleasure, you lunatic," he said, smiling.

"Where'd you get the doily?"

"I have my sources." He went back to his report.

Gavins was a slight man in his mid-thirties; he had curly blonde hair and was always well-dressed. He was one of Marcia's few friends at the bank. He had moved into the department early that summer from Letters of Credit; his boss there hated him and had palmed him off on Ranier. Gavins' job now was analyzing financial statements.

He knew he was going nowhere at the bank but, unlike Marcia, he wasn't upset about it. Marcia suspected that he was a homosexual with a vibrant after-hours life. He and Marcia had hit it off when it was apparent that he had a sense of humor and was on Ranier's dog list. Twice a week they had lunch together in the bank cafeteria.

"Gavins," Marcia said to him over lunch that day, "I think my marriage is falling apart."

"Oh?" He looked up from his salad with colorless eyes. "So what else is new?"

"I'm serious. I've had it up to here with Gin." She lifted her hand eyeball level. "Things don't seem to get any better. Now he wants to go back to teaching school again." She almost snorted in disgust.

"I thought he wanted to get into computers?" Gavins had never met Gin, but Marcia kept him posted on the ups and downs of her marriage. He found it amusing.

"Now he says computers bore him and he wants to get back into teaching."

"So why not?"

"But he keeps going around in circles and he isn't making any money."

"So maybe he likes to be dizzy and broke?" Gavins smiled sweetly.

Marcia sniffed and pulled her dinner roll apart. Gavins chewed on a cucumber slice.

"What the hell am I going to do with him?" she said.

"Shoot him?"

"Oh, for God's sake, Gavins, don't you have any better advice than that?"

He looked at her thoughtfully while he ate his lettuce. "Well Marcia, look at it this way. Does he play around with other women, beat you up, stay out all night, or steal your money? Is he a boozer or a drug addict," Gavins' eyes glimmered wickedly. " Or a homosexual?"

Marcia laughed. "No. Of course not. He's a great guy."

"So what are you complaining about?"

Marcia sat in her chair demurely, like a nun at Mass, and sipped her coffee. She had never thought of it that way.

Gavins pushed his plate aside, leaned forward, and whispered. "I think you want to cut his balls off and wear them around your neck."

"What?" Marcia was startled. She began to laugh. "Gavins, you twerp. You set me up for that one."

Gavins smiled and glanced at his watch. "Whoops. Time to go back to the salt mines. I have a customer meeting at two. Let's roll." They got up from the table. In the elevator, they discussed the weather and the latest episode of *Dallas* all the way back to the fifteenth floor.

*   *   *

Her conversation with Gavins haunted Marcia all afternoon. Gavins had basically said she was a bitch who hated men. She hate men? What a stupid idea, she thought. She loved men. So many of them wended their way through her life, making it miserable. She was just involved with the wrong men, that was the problem. Brooding on this, she looked up from her desk to see the supremely wrong man standing in front of her.

Ranier threw a bundle of papers down on her desk.

"Marcia, redo this analysis of the Hundefutter warehouse," he said briskly. "I must say, your analysis was a bit on the skimpy side; not up to your usual standards of detail. I need it by noon tomorrow." He flashed her a toothy, professional smile and strode back to his lair before she could say a word.

The Hundefutter warehouse? Which one was that, she thought, shuffling through the well-thumbed file. Ah, ha. It was the one in Elk Grove Village across Higgins Road from another warehouse she had analyzed last week. Marcia felt as if she had analyzed every warehouse deal available among the hundreds of square miles of warehouses that surrounded the airport. They bored her so much she was getting sloppy.

Well, she thought, she couldn't do much about her husband, but she sure could do something about this job.

She picked up the file, walked into Ranier's office, and sat down in one of the delicate chairs in front of his desk. He was standing in the corner, his back to her, talking on the phone. When he hung up and turned around, he gave a slight start.

"Well, Marcia. What can I do for you?" he said, but Marcia knew he wanted to drop-kick her out of his office. He hated surprise visits from his staff; he hated any visits from his staff. He wished they would all just work like little robots and leave their nasty little personalities at home.

"I have some problems I want to discuss with you," she said firmly.

"I have to leave for Atlanta in fifteen minutes," he said in his best managerial voice, "but I can give you a few minutes. Let me show you what I want on that Hundefutter deal."

"It's not the deal I want to talk about, Mr Ranier. It's me."

"I am pressed for time, Marcia. I'll be back next week. We can talk then." He smiled again.

"I want to talk about it now, if you don't mind." Her tone was flat and angry.

Suddenly, Ranier's attitude toughened. From the friendly manager, he became the impatient real estate dealer.

"Okay, shoot." He sat down behind his desk, all business.

"Look. I'm unhappy in this job. I want to get on some of the bigger deals, get more involved, and start getting promoted. I want to be a loan officer."

"Yeah."

"Well, what am I supposed to do to get that promotion?" Her voice was starting to crack with frustration. "I've worked my tail off for three years at this bank and I'm going nowhere. Baxter and the rest of the guys are working on the real big deals and I'm still stuck doing the crummy little warehouses out in the middle of nowhere."

Ranier's face remained impassive.

"I got my MBA degree. I do good work. I get along with customers—the few I get the chance to see—but I'm going nowhere. When does my big break come? When?"

Ranier stood up from his desk, put his hand to his forehead, and stared out the window.

"Marcia, this is a bank," he said with controlled impatience, as if he were talking to a small child. "Banks do not promote people quickly or easily. It takes a great deal of time to prove yourself and get on here and that's how it should be."

He turned towards her with practiced earnestness. "You have to win people's trust. It took me years to get where I am today." Ranier had been with the bank since he had graduated from college; his family had been important figures in First Midwestern since its founding in 1872.

"Are you saying it will take me years to get promoted?" she said, excited by her own audacity.

"No, Marcia, of course not," he snapped. "Those people who need to know about your work, know about it and they're keeping an eye on your progress. Trust them. They'll promote you when they feel you're ready."

Marcia thought this sounded as though she was entering some medieval religious order.

"When do you think they'll get around to promoting me?" she asked insistently.

Ranier was clearly exasperated. "Marcia, I really don't know. It's not just my decision. I will, of course, speak up for you when we do job evaluations this fall. But we do have a collegial approach to management that we must adhere to."

He cleared his throat. "Now if you'll excuse me, I've got work to do." He showed her to the door.

Marcia went to the ladies' room, cried quietly for five minutes, and resolved to find another job.

FOURTEEN

Gin's interview at Pleasantview High School was scheduled for one p.m. At ten a.m., he called in sick to Computer World and pulled out his map of the Chicago area. He had never heard of Wayland Center, but Bellicosi said it was about ten miles north of Elgin. That made it a good fifty miles from the city. He let his index finger drift over the map. There it was, the tiniest of black dots at the intersection of County Roads A and County MM.

Good Lord, Gin thought, it's halfway to the Wisconsin state line. On days when traffic was light, it would probably take over an hour to get there, and then only because it was mostly expressway to Elgin.

Take this job and live in your car, he thought. Or fight it out with the kids at the high school on the West Side. It was no contest. He would rather live in his car than die young; most suburban kids didn't carry knives.

He poured himself a cup of coffee and fingered Marcia's note, which had been propped against the pepper shaker on the kitchen table. The conciliatory tone appeased, but did not satisfy him. She was trying to play the brave, supportive wife when he knew she wanted to kick his teeth in and run off with a rich lawyer.

He sipped his coffee. Why hadn't he married a nice girl instead of an ambitious career type like Marcia? Other women wouldn't be on his case like this, constantly implying he was a failure. They would shut up, work hard at their jobs, and support their men, no matter what.

Like Rose Mary Thornberg. Now there was a real woman. Why hadn't he married her?

Because she'd turned him down.

Rose Mary had been the love of his college days. A round little woman with thick black hair, dark eyes and an amazingly clear, rosy complexion, Rose Mary acted as if she thought he walked on water. At least she did until his senior year, when he proposed.

Then she balked. She wasn't ready to marry yet, she said. She needed more time. After graduation, she went home to live with her parents in a Chicago suburb and took a teaching job at a grammar school in another, farther suburb. Gin began working at Howard High School.

It took an hour to get to Rose Mary's, a trip he took less and less often as her parents made it clear they disapproved of him. As a teacher, he would never make enough money to make their little girl "financially comfortable," as her father put it to him bluntly one evening over after-dinner drinks.

Rose Mary would never cross her parents; her love had staying power only with their approval. She cried big crystal tears when she and Gin broke up and promised to remember him in her prayers. A year later she married a lawyer who worked for a big insurance company downtown. They had three kids and a big house in some bedroom suburb. Gin was sure Rose Mary's luscious figure had gone to fat.

After Rose Mary, Gin dated widely. He went out with teachers, nurses, social workers, secretaries and a few businesswomen. The businesswomen thought he was boring because he wasn't in business; the others spurned him because he would never make enough money to support the fantasy life they were sure was their due after marriage. A few women did respond, but he found them unattractive or dull.

By the time he met Marcia, he seemed to be well on his way to a career in school administration at St Paul's. The money was bad; the potential was great. Marcia was willing to take the chance that fame and fortune would soon follow.

They didn't. Now it looked as though his chances with her were running out.

So much for women's lib, he thought bitterly. Women still want you to support them financially and be the big, tough protector.

Marcia said she wanted a marriage of equals. Except she wanted him to be a flawless equal. If he faltered, she punished him by withdrawing her love.

Gin watched a squirrel scamper along the telephone wires in the alley.

The kitchen curtains billowed in a summer breeze.

Money, money, money.

Houses, cars and clothes. Vacations in expensive resorts.

Handsome, tall men with strong jaws, big incomes and all the answers. That's what women really wanted; that's what he would never be.

Women, he thought. What a bunch of castrating vampires.

He finished his coffee and poured himself a bowl of Rice Krispies. It was conceivable that he would never be laid regularly by an attractive woman for the rest of his life.

Snap, crackle, pop—the end of his love life.

*　　*　　*

The trip to Wayland Center was as endless as Gin had guessed. The Kennedy Expressway was glutted with heavy traffic; two lanes were closed for road repair. Gin ground along behind a large semi for an hour before reaching even the city limits. And this was late morning; the horrors of the Kennedy during rush hour could hardly be imagined.

Beyond the airport, traffic opened up. Gin sped past an expanse of low-lying, boxy warehouses with corrugated metal walls: Centex Industrial Park, the source of the endless stream of warehouse deals that flowed across Marcia's desk. Warehouses gave way to office buildings, sprouting like a fairy ring of mushrooms around Woodfield Mall, the huge shopping center that was almost a town in itself. The roads around it were lined with squat apartment buildings and long rows of split-level houses.

Still he drove. The rows of houses became interspersed with farms; then there was only farmland. The road dipped into the Fox River Valley; Elgin came and went. Rural Illinois was spread out before him, flat, miles of corn and soybeans baking in the noon heat. It must have been ninety.

Five miles past Elgin, he turned off the expressway at Hickerts Road, a two-lane asphalt road; four miles later he pulled over to the side. Giant white clouds were sailing through a blue sky that seemed faded by the brilliance of the sun. The heat sank into his shoulders through his thin shirt. He was moving through an ocean of corn; enveloped by its sweet smell. The only sound was the rustling of corn tassels, stirred by a dry west wind. He rolled down all Vivian's windows; the delicious sweet smell filled the car. He felt giddy and carefree, as though he were on vacation.

He wanted to keep driving for hours, but ten minutes and two turns later he was in Wayland Center. You could see it two miles before you reached it, an island in a sea of corn, shimmering in the heat. A road sign named it: Population 1,250.

The main street was lined with white frame houses with big verandas and porch swings. The few side streets ended in corn fields. Several kids were riding bicycles down one side street. Downtown consisted of Tom's Food Store, Martha's Home Cooking Cafe, four bars and three gas stations. There were also a laundromat, a post office, a hardware store and the First State Bank of Wayland Center. A dog could be heard barking and a combine hummed in a distant field. Gin was charmed.

Pleasantview High School sat on a small knoll not far from the business district; it was surrounded by old frame houses and big trees. It was an 1890s red brick building with a pastiche of wood and brick additions on its sides and back. A cracked plastic sign on the lawn said, "Home of the Pleasantview Pirates. School Starts September 10." A crumbling sidewalk led to the main entrance, over which stone flowers and vines were entwined.

Gin thought, as he pulled Vivian into a rutted gravel parking lot behind the building, that it looked like every country high school he had ever seen. They all seemed to date from the 1890s. Their nearly bankrupt school boards struggled to patch them together so they could make it though the 1990s.

The leaves of the trees rustled in the wind which came off the cornfields visible past the few houses behind the school. In the parking lot were a new Toyota, two pick-up trucks in fair condition, a late-model Chevrolet and a 1973 Dodge Dart in its final death throes from rust. Not a soul was around.

Gin tried a back door in the old section of the school and walked into the coolness of a long corridor lined with fifty-year-old olive green lockers and floored with beige linoleum. The air smelled of musty leather and aging wood, like an antique store. I've entered a time warp, Gin thought. A tanned young woman in a flowered sundress came around the corner and gave him directions to Mr Bellicosi's office. Her long strawberry blonde hair was twisted into a bun on top of her head. Gleaming strands floated loose about her graceful neck.

"Up the stairs, turn right," she said pleasantly. "Two doors down, on your left."

Her face, glowing with health, was dominated by a pair of vivid green eyes. Gin stared after her as she disappeared through a doorway. This job could have certain benefits after all, he thought. God knows there was no one like that on the staff at St Paul's.

Her directions led him to a door in one of the newer sections. A long worn counter stretched across the center of a big room. Behind it was a row of offices with glass doors: the school nurse, the vice principal's office, the principal's office. A jowly middle-aged woman drooped over the counter, a human basset hound. Tiny curls of grey hair stuck to her forehead. She was sorting registration forms. An old window air conditioner clunked away without apparent effect; the room was hot and airless.

Yes, the woman said, Mr Bellicosi was in. The far office on the right with the open door.

In the far office, a short, fat man was fiddling with the knobs of an ancient air conditioner in the window. The machine gurgled, whirred and slurped. Finally it produced a scraping metal noise that could only be described as a death rattle. Then it was silent. The fat man swore under his breath.

Gin knocked on the door frame. "Mr Bellicosi?"

The man spun around. "Oh, good heavens, you startled me." His heavy black eyebrows, like two thick caterpillars, arched in alarm and his half-frame glasses dropped off his nose. They swung from his neck on a black cord. "You must be Mr Bernthal," he said, recovering his composure and extending his hand. "I'm Franklin Bellicosi. Please sit down."

He pointed to a grey plastic chair with metal arms. It looked like army surplus from the early 1960s; so did the grey metal desk, the other grey plastic chair, and the cracked grey plastic couch, mended with black electrical tape and piled with books and yellowing papers.

Bellicosi looked like a potato; with arms and legs like sausages. The sausage arms ended in soft fine hands, pudgy around the knuckles. He was sixty years old and short, about five foot six. His huge belly hung over his baby blue wash pants; his pale green golf shirt was darkened with damp patches under the arms.

"Can I get you something to drink? We've got diet pop, coffee and iced tea."

"Iced tea would be great," Gin said. Sweat was dripping down his back. He took off his coat and loosened his tie while Bellicosi moved with remarkable sprightliness out of the room. He returned in a few minutes with two scratched plastic glasses filled with lukewarm tea. Gin gulped his down; he felt he might faint from the heat.

"Sorry about the air conditioning. It seems to be on the fritz," Bellicosi said with a wan smile, nodding his balding head toward the dead air conditioner.

It has probably been on the fritz for the past fifteen years, Gin thought. He smiled back and wiped his forehead.

Bellicosi opened the window and turned on an oscillating fan that dated from the Industrial Revolution. Hot air heavy with the sweet smell of corn swirled through the office. The principal sank down in an old swivel chair behind his cluttered grey desk; it reminded Gin of a mothballed aircraft carrier.

"Well, Mr Bernthal, I'm glad you're here. Maria Rodriguez told me all about you." Bellicosi put his elbow on the desk and the tips of his fingers together, flexing them nervously. "You could be a real life saver for us," he said. "We're in a terrible bind."

Two weeks ago Mr Gustafson, Howard Gustafson, who had been at Pleasantview for as long as anyone could remember, had suddenly keeled over while he was cutting his lawn and died from a heart attack. Mr Gustafson had taught freshman and sophomore English, Civics, Social Studies, and Drivers' Education. In his spare time, he coached the baseball team. Gin would pick up his load.

He didn't know anything about baseball coaching, did he? Gin smiled and shook his head no. Oh well, Bellicosi continued.

Now, here he was, only two weeks before school started, with a big hole in his roster. Pleasantview had four hundred students last year; four hundred and fifty this year. Enrollment would be picking up all year as more people moved into the area.

Business was booming; the town was growing; everything was looking up, up, up. Bellicosi bounced in his chair with enthusiasm.

Gin was puzzled. Wayland Center looked like a rural nowhere. Where, he asked, was all this development?

He had missed it all because he had come down Hickerts Road from the north, Bellicosi said. He should have come in from the south. The Gorgon Cement Company had just opened a new plant three miles south of town; Horganzaller Company made disc brakes for Toyota two miles to the east; and rumors had it that a computer software company from Boston, United Techniplan, was going to relocate to a big wooded site nearby.

United Techniplan wanted to get away from all their competitors and move to an unspoiled rural area, Bellicosi said. They thought it might improve their creativity. It would certainly improve their distribution system: all their big dealers and customers were in the Chicago area.

The Chicago suburbs had marched to the edge of Wayland Center farmland and were awaiting further orders. "You go two miles east and south of here, and all you see are new houses, new offices, new shopping centers, Valdosky & Company, the big real estate company from Chicago, is building an office park just off Bloomfeld Road. Should be a biggie." Bellicosi sipped his tea; sweat drops glistened on his upper lip.

"There's big money coming in here trying to buy land, but the farmers are wise to them all. They're making a lot more money selling off their land than planting it to corn and beans.

"I tell you," Bellicosi said, wiping his mouth with a balled-up white handkerchief. "In ten years, you won't recognize this place. We'll be one of the prettiest little suburbs you've ever seen." His face glowed. Clearly, in his opinion, the prospect of Wayland Center being engulfed by Chicago's suburban sprawl was the greatest thing since the milking machine.

Wayland Center may be on its way to becoming the Houston of the prairies, but it certainly wasn't spending money on its school, Gin thought. He watched the prehistoric fan lurch back and forth.

"Well, Mr. Bellicosi," he said, "the school must have a bright future with all that money moving in."

"Oh, definitely, definitely. A very bright future," Bellicosi said. His cheeks flushed with the thought; his caterpillar eyebrows danced. "We're the only high school within a fifteen mile radius; the kids will all come here."

Gin looked at him expectantly.

"But, uh, well, our growth really won't be much until they start developing the land and putting houses on it," Bellicosi said. "In the meantime, we're just basically a rural school district—with a rural school district's budget, which, as you know. . ." He coughed into his handkerchief. "Isn't much."

"You're still offering only ten thousand for the job?" Gin said.

"Well, yes, if I can get that."

"You mean you're offering me less?" Gin was incredulous. No wonder they couldn't find anyone to take this job. This guy's nerve was incredible.

"Well, Harold did coach the baseball team and we'd have to pay someone else to do that now. I don't know if I could get the board to agree to the higher salary without it," he mumbled, looking at his fingertips which were doing rapid-fire push-ups against each other.

"You're kidding me." Gin felt his face flush. They sat silently for a few moments; sweat trickled down Gin's back. Teaching was truly slave labor, he thought. Maybe he should earn an MBA and get a job in the business world? At least they had air conditioning.

He stood up, picked up his coat, and extended his hand. "I'm afraid I'm really not interested," he said calmly. "I enjoyed meeting you. Thanks for your time."

"Now wait...wait...wait a minute here," Bellicosi sputtered, standing up and flapping his arms like an excited turkey. Gin sat down again. "Now I didn't say I couldn't get you that amount of money. I just said it might take some doing."

Gin stared at him.

"But I think I could do it," he said, looking at Gin with hope. "Yes, I think I could do it. Would you be interested in the job then?"

"Possibly. I have to think about it."

"You think and I'll get some more tea." Bellicosi hopped down the hallway with the two glasses.

Gin stretched and walked to the window, which overlooked Wayland Center's main street. A convoy of cement trucks went by, "Gorgon" stencilled on their sides in blue and white.

What was there to think about? he thought. He didn't want to sell computers, he wanted to run a school. To do that, he had to keep teaching and pushing, teaching and pushing, scouting all the school districts for a vice principalship. One day some bright superintendent of some fat suburban school district would recognize talent when he saw it and give Gin the second slot at a school, or even make him principal. With luck he could be out of this dump and be vice principal of some prosperous suburban school by next fall.

He mopped his forehead again and studied the water spots on the ceiling tile. Pleasantview would be his year in Purgatory—spent mostly in his car.

It was fifty miles, one way, from Chicago to Wayland Center. Oh, well. We all must make sacrifices. For a moment he considered moving to the suburbs—but he didn't want to live in the suburbs; he just wanted to run a suburban school. By next year he would find a job closer to home.

Bellicosi bounced back into the office with more tea. They toasted Gin's new job, at ten thousand a year. Gin didn't even ask about a raise schedule; in a year he was going to be out of this place anyway.

Bellicosi took him on a tour of the building—a miasma of peeling green paint, bad lighting and cracked linoleum. The halls were gloomy, but the classrooms were filled with light. In many of them tall old windows ran the length of one wall, affording views of trees, housetops and the Wayland Center water tower.

Bellicosi filled Gin's briefcase with tax forms, school books, teaching guides and lesson plan books. Teacher orientation was next week; he would meet the rest of the staff then. "You don't know how pleased we are to have a teacher of your calibre join us," Bellicosi said, pumping Gin's hand vigorously. Gin was embarrassed. Bellicosi was acting as if he had just saved the school from Bubonic Plague.

Going home Gin got caught in rush-hour traffic on the Kennedy; that added to his depression. What a come down. After eight years of teaching, he was back where he started—or actually farther back from where he started. Howard High was no picnic in the park, but Pleasantview was straight out of the Middle Ages. He couldn't imagine what the students would be like.

It took two hours to get home. It was horrible to think of so much wasted time. Maybe he should buy some language tapes and learn Spanish while he was driving? Lots of Latinos were moving into Chicago; a principal who spoke Spanish would be a real asset.

FIFTEEN

Marcia was sitting on the couch, working on her third Scotch and water, when Gin walked in around seven. "I thought you would be home about six," she said, sullenly. She had been counting the minutes until he came home; every minute after six p.m. was a black mark against him.

"I didn't get out of there until five and traffic was terrible," Gin said. "Don't talk to me in that tone of voice," he added irritably. "I'm not in the mood."

"What tone of voice?"

"That accusing tone, like I've done something wrong."

She shrugged. "Well, you did say you'd be home at six and it is after seven." She swished the melting ice in her glass and shifted on the couch. Gin eyed a pile of greasy chicken bones sitting on a Colonel Sanders bag on the coffee table.

"Yours is in the kitchen," she said. She got up and wobbled that way herself. "You want a drink?"

"Just a beer. I'll get it." This was strange, he thought. Marcia never drank hard liquor at home. He dumped his load of books in his office and met her at the refrigerator, where she was retrieving some ice cubes for another drink. She handed him a beer.

"Marsh, what's going on?"

"I'm getting drunk," she said tonelessly. She dropped the ice cubes into her glass and weaved toward the Scotch bottle on the counter.

Gin intercepted her in mid-kitchen. Wordlessly, she plowed into his shoulder and began to cry. The ice from her glass spilled on the floor. Gin put his arm around her tightly, feeling her body shake from her sobbing. Bellicosi, the Kennedy, and now this. What a great day.

She sniffed and sobbed for about thirty seconds before looking up from his shoulder. Her eye makeup was running down her face; her eyes were bloodshot; and her face was dappled with red blotches. She smelled of booze.

"Marsh, you look truly awful," he said gently, handing her his handkerchief. It was stiff with dried sweat. "You don't smell so hot, either."

She looked at him with one smeary eye. "Thanks, Gin, you're cute, too." She began to laugh, but the laughter turned back into tears.

So much for the humorous approach. He drew her over to the kitchen table, sat down on a chair and pulled her onto his lap. He held her with one arm, popped open his beer with the other, and took a long swig while she went on sobbing.

After about a minute, she wiped her eyes and blew her nose loudly; she sounded like a Teamster. Gin made her sit on a kitchen chair. His leg hurt from her weight.

"I've decided to leave the bank," she said.

"I thought your mother had died or something," he said, shaking out his leg.

"I would have preferred that." Marcia twisted the handkerchief in her hands. "They'll never promote me. I'll be sixty years old and still a loan analyst. That little twerp Baxter will probably be running the place."

She rested her elbows on the table and propped her head in her hands. "I want to be out of there by next spring."

"What happened? I thought you had made your peace with the place?"

"So did I, but I guess I just got fed up. Ranier waltzed me once too often around the office." She relayed her confrontation with Ranier, her breakdown in the bathroom, and the agony of the rest of the afternoon. She had seriously considered breaking up Ranier's office furniture into bite-sized pieces.

"I decided it was better to quit than kill." She smiled sweetly. "Would you get me a beer?"

He popped open a can for her.

"So much for the world of real estate high finance," she said. "What's new on the academic frontiers? How was Pleasantplot or whatever it is?"

Gin bristled. Now that he had accepted the job, he needed moral support, not wifely sarcasm. "I took the job," he said stiffly. "The place isn't so bad." He described his day, including his hope that in a year he would be a vice principal in a good district.

Marcia looked at him with bleary eyes. Gin and his jobs, she thought. What a drag. She felt tired and vindictive. "Do you seriously think that someone is going to hire you as a vice principal when you're just a crummy nobody at some nothing school?"

Gin was stunned. "Thanks, Marsh, you're a real ego builder," he said. "You want my balls on a platter or straight up?"

Marcia thought of Gavins' comment at lunch. "Sorry, Gin," she mumbled. "I didn't mean that." The trouble was, she thought, she did. She tried to work her way out. "I mean it's just going to be difficult to find a good administrative job, but I'm sure you'll do it," she mumbled, trying to smile brightly. She looked like a smiling fish.

Gin felt he knew now why some men beat their wives. He glared at her. "Why is it, Marsh, that you have no confidence in anything I do?"

"But I do," she flashed her team-player smile. "You'll do just fine."

"No, you don't. You think I'm a failure."

"Well, uh." She was tired of lying. "You don't have much of a record of achievement, now, do you?" she said, flatly.

"And you do?" he said, his voice rising in anger. "You've been sitting on your ass at that bank for three years and letting them walk all over you. Now, finally, you decide it's time to stand up for yourself. My God, Marcia, I've been telling you to get out of there for two years, but you never listen to me. I'm just your dumb husband. What do I know?

"You practically need an engraved invitation from Ranier to see the handwriting on the wall." He laughed harshly. "For such a hard-bitten career woman, you're a real pushover. You've got your nerve criticizing me for my job problems. Give me a break."

Marcia felt her face flush with anger, but her voice was cold. "Well, at least I'm not stupid enough to get myself fired before I have some other source of income lined up," she said. "I can pay my own bills, and yours too, when you're dumb enough to get canned."

She stood up, intending to head for the counter and make herself another Scotch and water, when Gin slapped her hard, across the mouth. Her face stung and she knew her lip would swell.

The blow knocked her into a higher level of rage. She hurled a string of obscenities at Gin, who stood there stunned, his rage turning to bewilderment. He had never hit a woman in his life, certainly never Marcia.

"Marcia. I'm sorry, honey. I didn't mean it. Please, forgive me." His voice was shaking. He moved to put his arms around her, but she threw them off and paced up and down the kitchen like a caged animal.

"How the hell am I supposed to go to work tomorrow with a fat lip?" she screamed. She felt hysterical; no man had ever hit her before. "You're terrific, Gin, just terrific. The argument doesn't go your way and you slug me. That's just great, just marvelous," she muttered, pacing.

She turned to her bewildered husband. "You ever hit me again and this marriage is over, kaput," she hissed. "You can find yourself some other dumb bunny to take care of you and all your little problems."

With that salvo she went into their bedroom and slammed the door. He heard her talking on the phone. When she came out, ten minutes later, she had an overnight bag. She was glad to see that Gin looked crushed.

"Where are you going?"

"To my sister's. I've had enough." She stalked out the door. Gin heard Vivian's engine start up. He went to the window and watched numbly as the car rolled down the street.

*   *   *

Camille "Dinky" Grimley was five years younger than Marcia and unmarried; she lived in a tiny studio apartment in the hot area for young career types. Dinky was her family name. When Marcia, then five years old, first saw her baby sister she asked why she was so "dinky." The name stuck. Who wanted to call anyone "Camille"? Dinky hated all her names. Sometimes, when she was trying to get picked up in a bar, she would tell men that her name was Linda and she was from Dallas.

Camille was a dental hygienist who worked for a dentist in Mount Prospect, a prosperous suburb, northwest of the city. Camille was the baby of the family, after Marcia's younger brother, Calvin, Jr. Marcia's parents, Calvin and Mary Beth-Grimley, had run out of child-raising steam with Camille; she had been an accident. She had lived on the crumbs of attention which fell from the dining room table while Marcia and Calvin, Jr were eating their fill.

As a child, Dinky was fat and morose. But when she moved to the city she took up athletics with a passion. When she wasn't cleaning teeth, she was running marathons, lifting weights, or jumping around in an aerobics dance class. Now she looked and acted like a hyperactive teenager, with a head of frizzy dark hair and a wardrobe filled with jogging clothes.

I found real estate and Dinky found her pectorals, Marcia thought as her sister buzzed her into her apartment lobby. It was a big, cheap building, with thin walls; the tenants were always moving to other cities. Dinky's apartment was on the third floor in the back, overlooking the garbage cans in the alley. Marcia heard the television and the sound of Dinky's voice.

She knocked on the door twice before her sister opened it, the phone pressed to her ear and the extension cord stretched tight.

"Hi ya, Marsh," Dinky whispered, covering the receiver. "I'll be off in a minute." She went back to making plans with the man on the phone; someone named Jerry. It sounded as if they had a big weekend ahead: they were going to a resort in Lake Geneva. Jerry was apparently a trader on the Options Exchange. It sounded as though he had lots of money and did lots of drugs. In her two days at the Lake Dinky would probably snort cocaine worth more than she earned in two months working for Dr William Hornsfield, DDS.

Marcia plopped into an old overstuffed chair, after removing a pink sweatsuit, a tennis racket and a pair of lacey blue bikini underpants. They were clearly a gift: dental hygienists couldn't afford silk underpants with French labels.

From Jerry perhaps? Marcia watched a situation comedy on Dinky's portable color television, last year's Christmas gift from Calvin, Sr and Mary Beth. What a slob her sister was. The day bed was a rumpled mess of sheets and clothes. Shoes and newspapers littered the floor. Two beer cans and a carton of cold carry-out chop suey sat on a tiny round formica table. Marcia felt as though she was sitting in a room-sized closet. She touched her lip; it was swollen.

Finally, Dinky hung up. She strode across the room with an athletic pounce and pecked Marcia on the cheek. Dinky and Marcia had never been close, but they tried to like each other. They were the only sisters they had.

"So he clubbed you, I see," Dinky said, looking at the lip with an expert eye. She had a deep rich voice. "What a drag." She pulled an ice cube out of the freezer and twisted a dish rag around it. "For the swelling," she said, handing the ice to Marcia, who dabbed her lip with it gingerly.

"You don't look too much the worse for wear," Dinky said, eyeing Marcia's pasty face and red-rimmed eyes. "The way you sounded on the phone, I thought he was killing you." She sat down on the floor against the day bed, a diet pop in one hand. She wore electric blue running shorts, a skimpy white cotton top, and expensive running shoes. She was lean and tall and tan from playing tennis outdoors all summer. Her frizzy brown hair was pinned up off her neck and framed her face like a bush. The picture of health. Marcia hated her for looking so good.

"Well, I guess I overreacted a little," Marcia said. She touched her lip again, feeling foolish about her histrionics with Gin. She had a headache from all that Scotch. She wanted to go home. Who was this strange woman staring at her with wide brown eyes just like her own?

Dinky smiled. "Well, I can't be too much an angel of mercy tonight, Marsh. Tommy's picking me up at eight-thirty for dinner." It was eight o'clock. "I won't be back until late, but you just make yourself at home. There's cold pizza in the refrigerator. You can sleep on the bed. I'll use the floor; I've got a sleeping bag."

She flashed Marcia a brilliant smile, before heading for the bathroom. "But if I'm lucky, I won't be home until tomorrow morning."

Typical Dinky behavior, Marcia thought. She went through men as if they were disposable razors. Marcia followed her into the bathroom. She felt like the handmaiden to the Queen of the Nile. The bathroom was filled with fluffy white towels, makeup mirrors, and a full line of expensive skin cream. Dinky shed her clothes and hopped gracefully into the shower, where she listened to Marcia relay the events of the evening. Marcia sat on the toilet cover and peeked at herself in Dinky's makeup mirror. Compared to her sister, she looked dead.

"Marsh," Dinky said, stepping from the shower, "I hate to say this, but you asked for it." She shook her curly head and began drying herself. "I mean really, it sounds like you torture the guy."

Marcia chewed her lower lip. "Yeah, I know. But I just couldn't stop myself, Dink. I'm so mad at him."

"Well, honey, I can see why you feel that way," Dinky said, stretching her long arms over her head. The nipples on her small, round breasts pointed perkily up. "I like Gin a lot, Marsh, he's one of the sweetest, nicest men I know. But you know, first of all, he's never going to make a dime for you."

She leaned against the sink, peered into her makeup mirror, and began brushing on eye makeup with expert speed. "Second of all, he's not satisfying you. You're too complicated for him. You overpower him." Dinky thought of Marcia as a kind of superwoman; after all, there had to be some reason why their parents worshipped Marcia and ignored her. She was glad to have a chance to give Marcia advice for a change, to see Marcia looking like a wreck.

She turned to Marcia. "Did you ever think of having an affair?" she asked. Her brown eyes glowed against a background of lavender eyeshadow.

"Oh, Dinky, of course not," Marcia said, thinking of all the times she had dreamed of running off with a rich real estate developer. But those were just dreams. In her waking hours, she had never looked seriously at another man. Well, not too seriously.

"I think you should consider it," Dinky said, working on her lipstick. "Find yourself some ambitious, exciting guy with mucho money. Play around with him. Have a good time. Then go home and get love and kisses from Gin.

"Let's face it, Marsh. Daddy is right. You're too much woman for just one man. You're getting bored."

"Dink, that's a goofy idea," Marcia said. "I love Gin. I couldn't play around behind his back."

Dinky sniffed. "Suit yourself, Marcia. You always were old-fashioned." She moved into the main room. "But frankly, I think you should try it before you knock it. A little affair on the side could really perk things up between you.

"At least you wouldn't be acting like a cat in heat, ready to scratch Gin's eyes out."

Dinky slipped on the blue silk panties that Marcia had thrown on the day bed, following them with a skirt and blouse in the loveliest lavender silk Marcia had ever seen. The skirt drifted over Dinky's long legs; her nipples stood out against the thin material of the blouse. She put on beaded sandals, hung an enameled pendant on a gold chain around her neck, and fluffed her hair, a brown halo around her face. She looked stunning.

"Dink, you look terrific," Marcia said, with jealous admiration.

"Thanks." Dinky sprayed herself with a light, spicy cologne, playfully giving Marcia a squirt from the atomizer. Marcia drank in the smell.

"Who is this guy you're going out with?" She could never keep Dinky's male friends straight. She had so many.

"Oh, Tommy? I met him at a party a couple weeks ago. He's an attorney with Kirkman and Edwards." Kirkman and Edwards was one of the most prestigious law firms in the city.

The doorbell rang and a few moments later Tommy walked in. He was in his early forties, with curly salt-and-pepper hair and a good physique under his well-cut suit. He was probably married, with three kids, a sad wife and a big mortgage on a house in an expensive suburb. Probably told the wife he was working late. Or maybe he was divorced.

Tommy's eyes lit up when he saw Dinky, but glazed over when she introduced him to Marcia. The dowdy elder sister, Marcia thought, as they exchanged small talk. They were dining at Avanzare, an elegant Italian restaurant on the Near North side; they were already late, they had to run. Dinky pecked Marcia on the cheek and grabbed up her purse and a fine wool shawl. Their warm laughter drifted down the hall.

Marcia opened the tiny refrigerator and took out the remains of a pepperoni pizza. She finished it in fifteen minutes while she watched *The Jeffersons* on TV. Then she poured herself a Diet Coke and tried to read the newspaper, but she couldn't concentrate and her headache was growing worse. She felt fat, ugly and depressed.

Maybe Dinky was right. Maybe she was old-fashioned. She probably should take a lover. If she lost ten pounds, started wearing silk dresses and hanging around at cocktail parties where there were moneyed men, maybe she would find somebody new—somebody who would be as lovable as Gin, but have money too and some direction to his life. Someone who would take care of her, for a change.

Maybe she would even divorce Gin.

She shuddered and turned off the air conditioner and opened a window. She stood watching the night hawks dive for mosquitoes in the twilight.

Maybe she shouldn't have married. Lots of career women never did. They couldn't fight their way to the top of the heap and have enough energy left to make a marriage work. You had to have one or the other: a career or a marriage. You couldn't have both. That's why her career and her marriage were both a mess. She should have settled for one or the other. Trying to do both, she was succeeding at neither.

She hugged her knees and turned off the lights. The sky glowed from the sunset; big crocodile tears rolled down her face. She couldn't help it; she loved Gin. She missed him. But after her melodramatic exit, she was ashamed to call him back and apologize. She hoped he would call her.

She found an old copy of the *National Geographic* and read about sea cows in the southern Phillipines. The night wore on. Around eleven, she curled up on the bed. She slept badly. When she woke at seven the next morning, Dinky still wasn't home.

I guess she got lucky, Marcia thought, dressing for work. Her lip was hardly swollen at all, but she had a devil of a hangover.

SIXTEEN

Gin heard Vivian's engine in front of the building. Quarter after eight, and he had been up since five. Was Marcia going to divorce him? Throw him out of his own house for battery? Sign a complaint with the police?

After Marcia had stormed out the night before, he called Harvey, who said he would have come right over, but it was opening night for *Jack and the Beanstalk* at Lakeview Elementary School, and his eldest daughter, Danielle, had a big part in it. Don't worry, he said, all married couples have these kinds of fights. He said he would have them both over for dinner soon, and hung up.

Gin spent the rest of the evening thumbing through the material Bellicosi had given him and hoping that Marcia would call. She had done most of the screaming; she should do most of the apologizing. He wondered what nonsense her nitwit sister was filling her with. Dinky gave Gin a headache; he thought of her as a semi-professional prostitute.

The lobby door creaked. He sat on the couch in his bathrobe and listened to Marcia plod up the stairs. The moment of reckoning.

The door opened. The Fury had turned into a bedraggled little girl dressed in a rumpled blue linen suit and lugging a lumpy overnight bag. There were bags under her eyes.

"Hi," she said coldly. She dropped her bag on a chair and headed for the kitchen. "Any coffee?"

"Sure. Help yourself," he said, in an equally glacial tone.

He followed her to the kitchen; he could use another cup himself. She fished a red mug from the dish rack and came up behind him as he poured his coffee. She put her arms around his waist, nuzzled her cheek against his shoulder, and murmured, "Hi there, stranger. How about a truce?"

Gin smiled in relief; he turned and pulled her into a hug. "Okay, a truce." he whispered, "Where's your white flag?"

Marcia reached behind him and grabbed a dish towel, once white but now brown with food stains. She leaned back and dangled it in his face. "Will this do?"

"Why not?" He kissed her.

"I'm sorry, Gin. I behaved like an idiot last night," she said, when she could breathe again.

"Me, too."

"You working late tonight?"

He nodded.

"See you around ten then." She ran her hand through his soft blonde hair. "I love you, Gin. I just have a strange way of showing it." She kissed him, bolted down her coffee, and started off to the bank.

When Gin got home that night, Marcia was curled up on the couch in her nightgown, with an Agatha Christie novel and Carmen asleep at her feet. She was the picture of domestic peace; her soft skin looked warm and rosy against her pink gown. The harpy was under wraps for the night.

He kissed her gently and took her hand. They held a joint pep rally: everything was going to be better soon. Marcia would leave the bank; Gin would be a vice principal. They would live happily ever after.

Gin suggested they drive out to Wayland Center on Sunday so that Marcia could see his new school. Groaning internally, Marcia agreed. It would be a pleasant ride in the country. She suggested they stop by and see her parents on the way. She hoped the old house, the familiar surroundings and the utter bland predictability of her parents would calm her down. Why did she still hope such a silly thing after all these years?

Gin made a face, but agreed to stop at his in-laws'. After all, Marcia didn't want to see the school; the least he could do in return was put in time at the Grimleys.

That's what marriage was all about, he thought. Compromise. Bending for the other guy. He wondered why anyone ever got married if it meant spending a good percentage of your time doing things you couldn't stand.

They made polite love that night, with little passion. It took Marcia a long time to come; Gin developed a bad case of blue balls. He had nearly ground her into the bed by the time he brought himself to orgasm. They collapsed in an unsatisfied heap, pleased that they hadn't argued and wondering if it was worth it.

Gin dreamt he was making love to the blonde sunflower queen he had talked to at Pleasantview High. Marcia dreamt she was romping in the surf with her handsome real estate developer; this time, she almost got him to make love to her.

The next morning, they both felt guilty; they didn't share their dreams. They kissed warmly, joked over breakfast, and went off to work, glad to get away from each other.

*   *   *

Calvin and Mary Beth Grimley lived on a cul-de-sac in the Harbor Springs subdivision in northwest suburban Palatine. There was no harbor and no spring; the houses clustered around one of those man-made lakes gouged out of the earth by the State Highway Department when it built embankments for expressways. From his in-laws' patio, Gin could see the traffic on Route 53 whiz by—eight lanes of trucks and cars surging through a sea of pastel houses.

Gin listened to the hum of the traffic and watched his father-in-law poke at the charcoal in the tottering old barbecue grill. A tall, bony man, Calvin Grimley was well-named: he was a dour Puritan with work habits to match. He had worked for the Illinois State Highway Commission as a civil engineer ever since he had gotten out of the army in 1953. In his entire life he had taken only two weeks of sick time, and then only because he had been nearly dead from pneumonia.

It was hard to believe that someone who looked so lifeless could be so tough, Gin thought, sipping his Scotch. He poured most of it on the grass when Calvin wasn't looking. Calvin bought only the cheapest Scotch and tried to avoid serving ice cubes and soda. He himself did not drink.

When Marcia had called to say they would like to stop by, Mary Beth Grimley had insisted they come for lunch. They would have a barbecue, and she would invite Calvin Jr and Dinky. Calvin Jr was a hefty replica of his father. He was twenty-eight years old, unmarried, and lived with his parents. He had brought his girlfriend, Liz, a pale, serious woman with stringy hair.

Dinky couldn't come, Mary Beth said; she was going out of town with some nice young man she met at a party. Marcia wondered if her mother realized that she had just told them that her daughter was off for a weekend of drugs and sex with a complete stranger.

The Grimleys lived in a two-story house covered with pale blue aluminum siding. The Harbor Springs subdivision dated from the early '70s. The developer had offered only four styles, so all the streets looked alike; the only variation was the color of the trim or the size of the garage. A two-car garage had been optional. The Grimley house had a two-car garage, a fireplace, and a built-in dishwasher; they were well above the average Harbor Springs luxury level. But their status was cut down by a notch because they lived across the street from the lake. The real high-rollers lived right on the water.

Calvin came from a long line of Iowan Lutheran farmers; most of his family were still in Ames, Iowa. His older brother, Martin, had inherited the family farm. That was fine with Calvin: he was the first Grimley with a college degree and a good city job. At the Highway Commission, he now headed the planning division for the west Chicago suburbs.

Mary Beth had been Calvin's childhood sweetheart, a plump, intelligent woman who had gotten fat as she grew older. She had married Calvin to escape poverty and her family. Her father had been a philandering handyman who played the ponies; her mother worked as a waitress to support her four children. The rest of the family tree was infested with a distinguished collection of drunkards and crooks.

Mary Beth reached adulthood craving money and dependability. Calvin had both. In that sense, it was a match made in heaven. He made the money; she held on to it. She was a self-taught income tax expert.

"Did you get that note I sent you on the gasoline tax deduction?" Mary Beth asked, while she and Marcia set out paper plates and bowls of potato salad on the dining room table.

Marcia tried to remember. Her mother was always sending her little notes with financial addenda. She had gotten one the other day: "Dear Marcia. Aunt Mildred passed away yesterday. Funeral on Monday. Don't forget the Investment Tax Credit on your new typewriter. Love, Mother."

"You know, the one-cent tax on gas in Cook County," Mary Beth said.

"What about it?"

"You can deduct it from your Federal income taxes, dear. But you have to save your gas receipts or keep a log of your gas purchases." She rearranged the daisies in the centerpiece.

"I know. We saved the receipts, Mom." Marcia was the equal of her mother in all things financial. But you had to get up pretty early in the morning to beat out Mary Beth on the tax code.

Mary Beth nodded her approval and went into the kitchen to fetch a relish tray filled with pickles from the refrigerator. "Did you see that ad in the *Tribune* last Sunday on certificate rates at Creighton Federal?" she called. "I clipped it out for you. It would be good for your IRA." Marcia came into the kitchen. Her mother set down the pickles and fished a newspaper clipping from a neat pile in a kitchen drawer.

"Eleven point seventy-eight percent for ten years. That's a good rate, Marcia." She squinted through her bifocals at the fine print. "I don't know about the compounding, though. I don't think you get a very effective rate."

The two women were poring over the ad when Gin came in to get the hamburgers for the grill. Marcia and her mother had the strangest mother-daughter relationship he had ever seen. Most women related to their mothers through their children, husbands or failed diets. Marcia and Mary Beth got together over the tax code.

"Mom, let me get my calculator and we can figure out the effective rate for ourselves." Marcia went off to find her purse.

"The grill's ready, Mary Beth. Where are the hamburgers?" Gin asked.

His mother-in-law handed him a plate of the world's tiniest hamburgers; she always got five patties out of every pound of cheap hamburger she bought. By the time the fat cooked out of them, they resembled big chunks of dog food, dried out and cooked to a reddish-black char. The difference was that a dog got several chunks in his bowl; the Grimleys apportioned one and a half per person.

"Do you have any Diet Coke, Mary Beth?" Gin opened the refrigerator and poked through the generic soda cans on the top shelf.

"What, dear?" She was still squinting at the fine print on the IRA ad.

"Diet Coke. You have any?"

"No, dear. No Diet Coke. But there's some nice diet ginger ale and diet cherry drink. Here, let me get you some." She elbowed her way in front of him and began fishing around in the refrigerator. She was built like a brick outhouse, short and squat. Gin towered a good foot over her. He hoped the old adage about daughters growing up to look like their mothers wasn't true.

"Never mind, Mary Beth," he said. "I'll just have some water."

"Fine, fine." She backed out of the refrigerator and closed the door. "Well, I'd better get this show on the road or we'll never eat." She flashed Gin a blank smile that reminded him of Marcia's team-player smile, all teeth and no content.

Mary Beth put out some day-old Wonder Bread buns, a jar of watery catsup and a small bowl of pickle relish. The stale potato chips would be next, Gin thought. Sure enough, here they came. "I hope these aren't stale," Mary Beth said, knowing they were. She dumped the small bag of broken chips into an old wooden bowl.

"When the hamburgers are ready, we're ready to eat," Mary Beth announced cheerfully, as if she had just single-handedly prepared a gourmet meal for twelve.

Gin took the platter of meat chunks to the patio and handed it wordlessly to Calvin. Then he went to a sunny room at the back of the house where Calvin Jr and Liz were watching the Cubs battle St Louis. They had a six-pack of Stroh's beer in an ice chest on the floor.

"Help yourself," Calvin Jr said. His arm was around Liz and his eyes were glued to the game.

Gin felt like kissing Calvin Jr; Mary Beth bought only generic beer and he had forgotten to bring his own. He settled into an uncomfortable little couch on rockers. The smell of burning grease drifted in from the patio.

The Cubs had just scored in the second inning when Mary Beth called them to lunch. They arranged themselves around the dining room table. Calvin Sr sat at the head and said grace. For what? Gin wondered. He couldn't believe that this amount of food was going to feed six adults.

They passed around two small bowls of potato salad, a plain orange jello mold and the hamburgers. Everyone took one-sixth of what was offered. Gin was doubly glad he had his Stroh's; it helped to fill him up.

Marcia sat across from him, looking overheated. A lock of brown hair fell across her flushed forehead. She laughed and talked, primarily with her father. Their conversation dominated the table. Liz and Calvin Jr looked sullen and whispered to each other. Mary Beth smiled her smile. Gin could have been part of the furniture; Marcia didn't seem to notice him.

But Marcia's father glowed, at least as much as anyone like him could glow. For him, clearly, Marcia was the only member of the family who mattered. He looked like a love-struck old fool, flirting with the belle of the ball.

Marcia regaled him with stories of her derring-do at the bank. She gave the impression that in five years she would be either running the place or heading her own real estate empire. Stupid bankers just didn't appreciate talent in women, she said, taking a big bite of hamburger.

Well, Calvin replied, looking wise, the bankers had a point. Many women deserved to be passed over for promotion.

Marcia bristled. Calvin looked pleased at having gotten a rise out of her. She tried to argue that women had a rough time in the business world, but Calvin merely smiled and repeated his assertion over and over again. It was like arguing with a dripping water faucet.

Marcia became angrier. Finally Calvin said that maybe she had a point. Maybe banks weren't the greatest places for women. He smiled benignly, as though he was just humoring her. It looked like a lover's smile, Gin thought. Calvin was teasing her because he wanted to see the fine color mount in her face. But it was also the smile of a man who hated women; she could have argued and pleaded until Doomsday and he would have refused to listen, out of pure spite.

But Marcia didn't seem to see that. She flashed her father a brilliant smile. She had always argued like this with dear old Daddy.

Gin watched the orange Jello melt on his plate. He saw himself throwing it at his wife and then stabbing Calvin with his fork. Why didn't the old bastard just grab his daughter and commit incest on the dining room table? Whenever they arrived at the Grimley's and whenever they left, Calvin always gave Marcia a bone-crushing hug and a big kiss. Once Gin could have sworn he had absently raised his hand to her breasts, but had caught himself at the last minute.

Gin twisted a piece of hamburger into a pill and gave Marcia a nasty look that said, Shut up and calm down. But she was so wound up in her love duet that she just smiled at him and chattered on. Now she and old Dad were laughing over an experience she had had at the mortgage banking firm where she had worked before she married Gin.

Mary Beth began clearing away dishes and bringing out coffee and dessert—two cream pies and a chocolate mocha cake. You could always get enough dessert at the Grimley's. Mary Beth had an incredible sweet tooth. Gin was sure she bought in bulk from the Sara Lee plant and then froze her cache. But she never planned far enough ahead: one bite of the cake showed that it was only half-defrosted. Gin discreetly pushed his aside. Everyone else ate it as if it were the most normal thing in the world to find ice crystals in your fudge frosting.

The table was momentarily quiet. Marcia and Calvin were taking a small break to refuel before continuing their dining room tryst.

"Well, dear," Mary Beth said to Gin, handing him a delicate china cup of coffee. "You're so quiet over there in the corner. How's the computer business treating you?"

"Yes, how is the computer business?" Calvin asked disdainfully. Calvin disliked Gin; he had stolen his lover.

"Not very well, I'm afraid," Gin replied, glancing at Marcia. She looked nervous. " I decided to quit computers and go back to teaching. I just got a job teaching at a small school northwest of here for ten thousand a year. It's not much, but I'm hoping to use it as a springboard to get into administration."

"Oh, really, dear? That's nice," Mary Beth said. How could her daughter have married such a zero? She had been looking forward to having a son-in-law who was a successful lawyer or businessman and who would give her good free financial advice.

"Yep. I just decided that computers were pretty boring. I couldn't take it any more," Gin said, looking straight at Marcia. She had turned red with embarrassment. She hadn't told her parents that Gin was going back to teaching.

"Well, well, young man, this is an interesting development," said Calvin Sr. He leaned back in his chair and stared at Gin. "You're not exactly going to get rich on that kind of money, are you?"

"I guess not," Gin said, laughing. No one else laughed.

"Just what kind of teacher are you anyway?" Calvin asked archly. "Are you Socrates? Are you Aristotle? Are you Mortimer Adler? What kind of teaching methods will you use in your reincarnated career?" He smiled viciously. Calvin loved to run Gin down in front of Marcia.

"I though I'd try the Howdy Doody approach to teaching, sir," Gin said politely. "You know, something like the kind of high-powered education you got." He smiled and sipped his weak coffee; Mary Beth used the grounds twice.

"I see. Well." Calvin wasn't used to resistance. He shifted in his chair and called down the table. "Mary Beth, would you cut me another slice of that cake?"

Calvin then turned to his son and asked him for his opinion of the current crop of sweet corn. The younger Grimley was assistant manager at a Jewel Food store; his father assumed he had the inside track on commodities. Cal Jr droned through his opinions on sweet corn, green pepper and lettuce prices for the next month. His father looked depressed.

Lunch lurched on. Marcia worked on the iceberg in the middle of her cake. Mary Beth helped herself to her third slice of coconut cream pie. Liz looked bored.

At two-thirty Gin stood up and announced that they would never make it out to the school and back unless they left right away. Marcia looked angry. She got him to sit down for another half hour of pointless chitchat about shasta daisies, worms in the tomatoes, and the local school referendum. At three o'clock he reasserted himself, this time successfully.

Calvin Sr gave Marcia one of his indecent hugs. In retaliation, Gin shook his hand, squeezing it so hard that Calvin winced. "So nice to see you again, sir," he said, glaring at him. Marcia looked embarrassed.

Mary Beth gave them a frozen vanilla custard cake to snack on when they got home. Smiling and waving, they backed out of the driveway.

SEVENTEEN

Within one block of the Grimleys, Gin turned the Cubs game up loud on the car radio. He hoped it would deter Marcia. It didn't.

"I couldn't believe it. I don't believe it," Marcia started in. "How can you be so rude to my family?" She turned the radio down.

"I wasn't rude; we had to go."

"Christ, I thought you were going to slug my father." She was very angry.

"The way he grabs at you, he's lucky I don't kill him."

"He's just being friendly. A little fatherly love."

"Horse manure. He's a dirty old man."

"You're overreacting."

"I'm not. You should see you two together," Gin said coldly. "It's disgusting." He turned up the radio. The Cubs were ahead, two to nothing in the bottom of the eighth.

Marcia said nothing. Hot summer air filled the car; the radio blared cheers and the prattle of the announcer. They drove onto the expressway and in a daze she watched the suburbs rush by. She was exhausted. Visiting her family always drained her. She always did her best to perk up Dad, to drag him out of the depression that constantly hung over him. And for an hour or two, she succeeded. Calvin would laugh and banter with her. But then, relentlessly, he would sink back into his private mire, unreachable. By the end of the visit, she would be frantic.

"Daddy looked especially sad today, don't you think?" she said.

"He always looks like that," Gin said distractedly. A little bit of Calvin Grimley went an awful long way.

"No, he doesn't. Sometimes I can perk him up."

"The only way you can perk him up is if you climb into bed with him."

"How can you talk like that about my father?" she said angrily.

"Sorry, sorry." Gin didn't want to start another fight; they had had enough of those recently.

"Maybe we should come out and see them more often? Maybe I could perk him up a little more," Marcia said.

Gin sighed with exasperation. "Are you crazy? We already see them at least once a month. What more could you do?"

"I don't know." She twisted a fold of her flowered skirt around her index finger. "Maybe do things with him. Go to the zoo. Take long walks. Discuss the arts. I don't know." Her voice was small and frustrated. She had gone to see her parents to be comforted; instead, she felt sucked dry.

"Marcia, you don't even have time to do those things with *me*, and I'm your husband," Gin said. The Calvin Grimley Mental Health Patrol was going to stop right here, he thought.

"You don't think it would help?"

"Marcia, your father is just naturally depressed," he said impatiently.

"You don't think I'm doing something wrong, do you? Offending him or something?"

"Of course not." St Louis pulled ahead three to two in the bottom of the ninth.

"Damn, what happened to the outfield?" Gin yelled; he slammed the steering wheel hard with one hand.

Marcia sighed deeply. She really didn't have much luck with men. A pleasant pauper for a husband and a chronic depressive for a father. God had it in for her.

Gin made the turnoff for Wayland Center and they sailed through the sea of corn. The further they drove from the Grimleys, the better they felt, as if they were escaping from hell. They were alive again, on a beautiful cloudless summer day with warm breezes stirring their hair.

Gin stopped at a farm stand and they bought a dozen ears of sweet corn, the first of the season. He kissed Marcia playfully on the cheek. She pinched his backside and he chased her around the car. When he caught her, he covered her forehead with kisses.

Marcia thought Wayland Center was charming. The school looked a bit down at the heels, but he wouldn't be there long. The building was open; they strolled through its cool, empty halls and into classrooms with big windows that overlooked the treetops.

They drove south out of town, through a strip of fast-food restaurants and gas stations. They passed the Gorgon cement works, with its huge piles of sand and limestone, and new factories that made springs, electric motors and parts for water softeners.

A housing subdivision loomed on the edge of a giant cornfield, row on row of neat white houses with scorched lawns and stick-like trees.

How she would love to own a house, Marcia thought, but not here. In Barrington—that's where she wanted to live. Near the rich and successful, like Frances Klein and her wonder-banker husband. They had an old colonial house on a wooded one-acre lot.

She suggested they drive home through Barrington. It was on the way and only ten miles from Wayland Center. They flew down a two-lane state highway, bordered with wild flowers. The subdivision gave way to forest preserves, horse breeding farms and the country estates of successful businessmen.

The land turned hilly, with ponds and small lakes set in forests of old oak and maple. The side roads weaved among the lakes and the mansions that overlooked them. Dense August foliage blocked the sight of many of them from the road; only weathered signboards gave them away: Green Acres, The Hollistons, Bank Note Thoroughbred Farm. Occasionally there was a glimpse of a tennis court or even an oblique view of the main house, with its chimneys and screened porches.

They wound their way through the roads. Marcia never tired of straining her eyes to see these houses. I wouldn't mind living here either, Gin thought. He hated the suburbs and farm life was not for him. But Barrington was neither suburb nor farmland. It was a Norman Rockwell painting of the idyllic American life—only everyone was rich. I could learn to be happy in a $500,000 house overlooking a small clear lake and surrounded by five acres of private woods, he thought. He slowed to let a red Porsche zoom by.

The village itself had a colonial motif, even to the white railings and cupola on the supermarket. Little boutiques sold sensible, expensive tweeds to the Barrington matrons and imported toys for their precocious children. The real estate offices looked prosperous.

They stopped for an ice cream cone at a cafe with hanging plants and lots of wood. They walked the streets of the village, passing old frame houses with gingerbread trim and huge oak trees spreading over well-tended lawns. Young couples worked in flower beds filled with marigolds, while their small children toddled happily through the grass.

How did they do it? Marcia wondered. How did they afford houses in such a lovely place? And if *they* could do it, why couldn't she?

They strolled through a park and watched a group of ten-year-olds hang by their knees on a jungle gym. Marcia rolled the finances over and over in her mind. Why couldn't they live here, too? They deserved part of the American Dream. If she could live here, it would make her life rosy again.

On a wooden park bench under an old elm tree, she popped the question.

"How would you like to live in Barrington?"

Gin looked at her and laughed out loud. "Are you serious? We can hardly keep body and soul together now."

"If we borrow the money from your parents and mine for the down payment, and get a good mortgage, we could do it," she said firmly.

Gin said that they had a better chance of living in Barrington by becoming indentured servants than by trying to buy a house, but Marcia waved him to silence.

"Look. You're going to be making ten thousand a year teaching. I'll be getting a small raise at the bank. Two people without kids ought to be able to afford a house on $38,000 a year. We could use your salary for mortgage payments."

It depressed Gin deeply to think that every penny he made would fly to some bank to cover his mortgage payments. "Marcia, that's like working just to pay your taxes."

"No, no," she said eagerly, "it's not like that at all." She pulled out her pocket calculator and mechanical pencil, and on the back of an old electric bill, she sketched out a financial scenario that would permit them to buy a $115,000 house, keep Vivian the Volvo, and live happily ever after, nearly tax-free, in idyllic Barrington.

How could they go from being stone broke in a third-rate city neighborhood to becoming home owners in one of the wealthiest suburbs? Only ten thousand in extra income and some intra-family loans could accomplish all this?

He listened carefully, but got lost when Marcia began explaining the benefits of an interest-rate write-off on their marginal tax bracket.

"And," she concluded, "the best part comes last." She put down her pencil and folded her hands. "If we live here, you'll be only ten miles from school, down country roads with no traffic. I can take the train in to the city. The commuter service here is great.

"So what do you say?" she said, grabbing Gin's arm in excitement and bouncing up and down on the bench. They could do it, she thought, they could do it.

"Well, I suppose so," Gin said in a bewildered voice. He hadn't seen Marcia so excited and happy in months; it lightened his heart. Could something as silly as buying a house right what was wrong between them?

But it didn't seem to hang together right: he couldn't follow her financial gymnastics. But then income taxes and mortgages had never interested him; they were Marcia's bread and butter. She worked in real estate for a living and he trusted her judgment. But still, he found her plans difficult to accept.

Marcia was staring at his face with manic fascination. If he gave the word, he knew she would sprint to the nearest real estate office. By nightfall they would be prowling through quaint Victorians.

"Marsh," he said, hesitantly. "Are you sure this would work out?"

"Of course, of course, it would," she said, tightening her grip on his arm. "Interest rates are down now. They were so high before we never could have bought, even though you were making more money at St Paul's.

"But now that's all changed. They have all sorts of crazy mortgages. I even saw one with nine and seven-eighths percent rate on the first year. We could easily swing that. Just think of it, Gin, we could be in our own house by the time the snow flies."

She gazed off into the distance and dreamed of sitting in front of a warm fireplace at night, her arm around Gin, and Carmen curled at her feet. She was reading a mystery and drinking hot buttered rum.

The idea of owning a beautiful old house in a beautiful old village tugged at Gin's heartstrings. And Marcia's excitement was becoming contagious. But nothing was ever this easy.

"There's got to be a catch to it," he said, getting up and pacing in front of the bench.

"Try me," she said.

"All right. What about borrowing money from the parents? You think we could squeeze it out of them?" Being in debt to both Calvin and Hodge frightened him. Calvin would probably want connubial rights; Hodge would demand that he start selling insurance.

"No problem," Marcia said, smiling. "I have ten thousand saved for the down payment, and Mother said they'd be happy to lend us ten thousand. I'm sure we could hit up your folks for the same amount. Alice told me she and Hodge lent Jack and Fay eighty-five hundred to buy their first house. She said they'd be happy to pitch in when our turn came."

"When was all this going on?" Gin sat back on the bench in surprise. Neither his father nor his father-in-law had ever offered him a home loan.

"Well, we ladies do have our little chitchat and secrets." Marcia was amused at his bewilderment over her financial machinations. "Don't be such a stick-in-the-mud." She cuddled playfully up to him. "Trust me. The down payment money is there; we can get a mortgage for another ninety thousand or so. Just think of it: our little dream home all to ourselves."

And he did. He saw himself kneeling in front of a glowing fireplace, with Marcia spread out before him, naked on a sheepskin rug. They were just taking a breather from hours of enraptured sex and were drinking hot buttered rum.

If they bought a house, not only would he see more of her, she would be happier. They would have more sex; he wouldn't have to live in the car. And a house in Barrington would be far more pleasant than the tired, old two-flat they lived in in the city. He would miss the city, but they could always drive in to visit friends and go to restaurants.

"Well." He put his arm around Marcia, feeling his own excitement rise. "Let's do it."

She threw her arms around him, kissed him hard, and emitted a very unbankerly yelp. Then, to Gin's amazement, she did three cartwheels across the grass. It was the most physical exercise she had had in months; she collapsed in a laughing heap. Gin began tickling her without mercy.

The kids on the jungle gym stopped swinging and stared. Their mommies couldn't do cartwheels. And mommies never rolled in confused piles with daddies on the grass in Holworth Park.

Gin and Marcia lay on their backs and watched a few puffy clouds float by. Gin dreamed on; Marcia began listing all the things they had to do. Arrange the loans with their parents, start looking for mortgages, check out the train schedule, and actually find a house they wanted to buy. They had to get moving on all this, she lectured her dreamy-eyed spouse. You never knew when interest rates would start back up again.

In response, he pulled her to him and kissed her slowly. She looked so much prettier when she was happy, he thought.

Although it was after six, Marcia insisted they stop at a real estate office before they went back to the city. A plump middle-aged woman with a face like a hamster and earrings made of tiny fruit baskets gave them some mimeographed listings, a pamphlet of other listings in the area, and her card. Mrs Juanita Fernwell.

She would call Marcia tomorrow at work, after they had gone over the listings. She could make appointments for them to see the houses they liked for the next weekend, or even during the week, if they wished. Then they could sit down and discuss specifically what they were looking for in a house, where in the village they wanted to be, and other topics.

Such as how much of a place we can afford to buy in the first place, Marcia thought.

Mrs Fernwell smiled, baring a set of long, yellowed teeth.

As they drove home, Marcia paged through the listings, ooh-ing and ahhing; every few minutes, she darted over to kiss Gin on the cheek. They spent the evening studying the listings; everything looked a bit more expensive than Marcia had ex-pected, but nevertheless, she circled five houses she wanted to see. She would have a whole list for Mrs Fernwell to line up for next weekend.

By the time they crawled into bed that night, she was ex-hausted. But not enough to discourage Gin's advances. They had the best sex they had had in months and slept like two lambs, nestled against each other in the hay.

EIGHTEEN

The week flew by.

On Monday, Marcia called her mother and mother-in-law about the loans for the down payment. Neither seemed surprised by the request. Alice Bernthal said demurely that she would have to talk to Hodge about it; being a woman, she didn't know anything about money.

Mary Beth knew. She asked what kind of collateral her daughter and son-in-law could come up with to secure the loan Marcia was asking for.

"Just our all-American faces, dear Mama," Marcia answered, astonished by the question. Her mother knew they were broke.

"Well, dear," Mary Beth had answered, "I know you're really going to make something of yourself in the real estate business. So we'll lend you the money based on your future earnings potential." Mary Beth really should have gone into banking instead of motherhood, Marcia thought, as she hung up the phone.

On Monday, Gin gave notice at Computer World. Friday would be his last day. They celebrated his re-entry into the teaching profession by having dinner with Harvey and Dominique at their favorite Mexican restaurant, Rio Brava. It was good to see the Teitelbaums again. Because of Gin's long hours at Computer World, they hadn't seen them for six weeks.

They drank Margueritas and ate piles of nachos while Harvey gave them an update on St Paul's. Nothing had changed. Dotson had hired some kid out of college to replace Gin for the coming year. Harvey's relationship with the principal was cold, and getting colder, he added, dipping a corn chip into some hot chili sauce. He had the sense that Dotson had told Gerry Fry, head of the history department, to spy on him. Fry often asked to see his lesson plans. No more trips to see *Cleopatra* and Elizabeth Taylor's cleavage.

Gin described Franklin Bellicosi and Pleasantview High. Everyone laughed at his description of the ancient school and its penguin principal. For some reason, Gin found his whole job situation outrageously funny, when only two weeks before, it had depressed him profoundly.

He attributed his good humor to the liquor and his enchanting wife, resplendent in a brilliant blue blouse and embroidered Mexican skirt. She pressed her knee against his under the table, and bubbled along in conversation, tossing her dark hair back from her face. Occasionally, she squeezed his hand and kissed him on the ear. He was in love with her all over again.

Marcia explained the Barrington house strategy in detail. Dominique was charmed. She wished she could persuade Harvey to accept the joys of country life, she said, elbowing her husband in the side.

Harvey grunted, twirled the stem of his Marguerita glass, and announced that he would never leave the civilization of the city for the bourgeois pretensions of the horsy set. As a child of a rich family, he had seen enough prancing horses on close-cropped green fields to last a lifetime. He preferred his crowded old townhouse in the city any day.

Nevertheless, he promised to come out and visit the Bernthal homestead. He toasted the crabgrass, bad plumbing and termite problems they were sure to encounter.

Marcia laughed nervously. Harvey could be a royal pain-in-the-neck, she thought. With his trust fund, he didn't have to work another day in his life. He would never understand how much owning their own house meant to them—or to her anyway. She glanced over at Gin, working his way through enchiladas mole. She didn't need Harvey's big-mouth comments to talk her husband out of it.

She steered the conversation to a safer topic, the Teitelbaum's ski vacation, coming up in December. Harvey discussed the cuisine of a half-dozen ski areas in Colorado. He had a taste for good food; Marcia and Gin drooled through his re-creation of the last five years of great meals on the ski slopes. They had never gone skiing in their lives, but they went home feeling as though they vacationed in Aspen every winter.

They would be well-to-do someday. They were upwardly mobile; they were going somewhere. One day, they would be skiing in beautiful resorts and eating fresh oysters, Marcia assured Gin as they drove home in the hot, sticky night. At long last, their ship was starting to come in. The house was the first step.

It was an early evening. They had to be at Mrs Fernwell's office at ten the next morning to see their first house.

*   *   *

Saturday traffic clogged downtown Barrington as Gin steered Vivian toward the office of Crestwood Real Estate. They waited through two traffic lights at the corner of Main Street and Barrington Roads in the center of town before pulling up in the small parking lot behind the realtor's office.

It was a small storefront that someone had "countrified" with a quaint peaked roof and carved white wooden trim around its red door. Except for Mrs Fernwell and a receptionist, the place was empty. "Everyone's out looking at property," she said, pointing to the five desks. They were strewn with paper and phone messages.

"With interest rates so low now, demand has exploded," she said, leading them to her small cluttered desk in the middle of the floor. "Everyone's out buying while the money is around." She smiled, showing her pointed yellow teeth. Gin thought she looked like a predator; he imagined her with a dead field mouse in her teeth, padding back to her den.

They sat on two metal chairs with black plastic cushions. Gin daydreamed; Mrs Fernwell reviewed their financial situation briefly with Marcia. They had $25,000 for a down payment, a $38,000 income, and no other debts but their car. With that she said, they should certainly be able to afford a $115,000 house.

But they could get something really nice if they went to the $120,000 range. Nothing outside in the horse country, mind you. Prices for the smallest shack there started at $150,000, she said. But they should be able to find something they could afford in the village.

Gin wondered if it would have indoor plumbing.

Mrs Fernwell fished out her car keys; they drove off in her new silver Cadillac to their first appointment. It was a two-story frame house, painted light blue with white trim, crammed on a small lot, with two huge pine trees overpowering its front yard. To the left was a house with peeling red paint; to the right, an ugly little brick bungalow.

"This one's a real dollhouse," Mrs Fernwell said as she led them up a cracked cement walk. The porch steps creaked; one was loose. Probably rotten, Gin thought. Through the screen door, they heard the sound of children's cartoons on the television and a woman's voice in the background.

Mrs Fernwell rang the doorbell. A dog began to bark. "Mrs Thurston?" she called through the screen door. They heard footsteps; a distracted woman in her mid-thirties came to the door. She was wiping her hands on a half-apron which she wore over baggy shorts. She was wearing running shoes and holding an excited German Shepherd by the collar.

"Come in, come in," she said. They entered a tiny vestibule cluttered with toys. "Tommy," she called into the living room, "turn that down." The TV volume dropped slightly.

"Just carry on as if we weren't here," Mrs Fernwell said, beaming. She led Gin and Marcia up the dusty staircase to the second floor. Clearly, Mrs Thurston hadn't read all the articles in newspapers about how to present your house for sale. The place was cluttered with toys, clothes and books. It was a household out of control.

Gin and Marcia trailed Mrs Fernwell through the main bedroom with its unmade bed and fussy flowered wallpaper. Mrs Fernwell pointed out the lovely view of the backyard from the main bedroom, but Gin was more interested in the woman's underwear slung over one bedpost. Marcia would look good in a black panty and bra set; he decided to get her one for her birthday.

The two other bedrooms were tiny; one had bunk beds and room for nothing else. The other faced the wall of the red house next door. It had a water-damaged ceiling. Maybe the place needed a new roof, Marcia thought.

In the bathroom, there was an old claw-foot bathtub with a do-it-yourself pipe shower on the wall and tiny white and blue tile on the floor. The entire second floor had not been renovated since the house was built, probably some time in the 1920s, Marcia guessed.

Mrs Fernwell preceded them down the creaking stairs. Gin caught Marcia's eye. She wrinkled her nose in distaste and gave him the thumbs-down signal. He smiled and nodded. The downstairs would have to look like Versailles to compensate for the cramped feeling of decay on the second floor.

It wasn't Versailles, but it was much better than the second floor. The wall had been knocked out between the living room and the dining room, Mrs Fernwell announced and the kitchen which had been remodeled only last year, was huge. Its wide new windows overlooked the backyard.

Mrs Thurston was whipping cream at the circular oak work-place in the center of the kitchen, and talking on a cordless phone. Two little girls, about five and seven years old, sat in pyjamas playing with their breakfast cereal at the table. Gin made a face at them and they giggled.

The Bernthals traipsed past the tiny bathroom off the kitchen and down the stairs to the basement. The furnace looked about twenty-five years old; there were signs of water leakage on the cement walls. There was central air conditioning, but the unit was off. Marcia wondered if it worked. At the end of the yard was a tiny wood garage, in need of massive repair.

Marcia's heart sank: this is what $110,000 would buy?

Actually, the price was $119,500, Mrs Fernwell told them as they walked to the car. But the Thurstons were anxious to sell; they had already bought another, larger house in LaGrange and they had to close on that next month. She could probably get the price down to $110,000.

Mrs Fernwell noted the fallen faces of her charges, but ignored them.

"Now that house is nice," she said. "It has potential. If you're handy, you could really fix it up. Knock out a few walls, strip off the wallpaper." She had seen more than one couple buying their first house collapse in despair and buy a "handy-man special." She beamed at Gin, the handy-man to be.

He beamed back. "I don't paint, wallpaper, or do floors," he said, cheerfully. "I'm militantly un-handy." If this was all they could get, they should stay in their cheap, comfortable apartment in the city.

"I think we want something in better condition," Marcia said, tactfully.

"Well," Mrs. Fernwell said. "You did express interest in Victorian houses. To find one well-restored and in your price range would be awfully difficult. Most of them go for $150,000 and up.

"But don't get discouraged," she rushed on. "Perhaps you'd consider something a little more modern?"

She reached into the car and retrieved her listing book. She flipped it open to a page of blonde brick bungalows from the 1950s. They were little shoeboxes with heavy cement porches and glass block windows in the front basement windows. The owners had stuck "family rooms" on the back and half-stories on top, raising their prices along with their roofs. The ugly boxes were priced between $110,000 and $120,000.

Marcia was appalled. She shook her head. "No."

"Well, cheer up," Mrs Fernwell chirped, snapping the book closed. "We have lots of other houses to see. The day is still young."

She drove through tree-lined, sun-dappled streets to their next appointment—and their next appointment—and one after that. By lunchtime, the Bernthals had seen more remodeled, old frame houses than they had ever wanted to see.

"Great potential here, kids," Mrs Fernwell would pipe as they dragged themselves out of someone's rehab nightmare.

At twelve-thirty they broke for lunch. They had two appointments in the afternoon, as well as a "surprise house" that had just been listed yesterday. Marcia looked suspicious, but Mrs Fernwell assured them it was a " real dream home." They agreed to rendezvous at Mrs Fernwell's office at one-thirty.

Gin and Marcia dined on bacon, lettuce and tomato sandwiches at Kay's Cozy Corner Cafe, washing them down with big glasses of iced tea. Marcia watched the foot traffic. In fifteen minutes, she saw no blacks and four Latinos. The Latinos got into a truck labeled "Michaelson's Landscaping."

The Bernthals despaired in silence. Gin was alarmed at the look of grim determination in Marcia's eyes. It was the look she had when she visited the dentist or left for work.

"Hey, over there," he joked. "How about perking up?"

"Yuck," she responded bitterly. "What a bunch of dumps."

"Maybe the next ones will be better."

"They've got to be better than what we've seen." She picked at her sandwich.

"Well, we don't have to buy," Gin said. "I wouldn't mind staying put."

It was the wrong thing to say. "Don't be silly," she snapped. "Of course we're going to buy. Owning your own house is the cornerstone of your financial plan." She chewed resolutely on a piece of bacon. "We'll find something."

Gin moaned to himself. He was following a female Moses to her self-described Promised Land.

*　　*　　*

The first house they saw after lunch was fifty feet from Route 59; traffic roared by the kitchen window. So much for village quiet.

The second house was bereft of trees and sat next to a gas station.

All the houses that sounded so lovely in the listing book were disappointments.

By three o'clock, only the "surprise house" was left.

"Now I'm not exactly sure what this house is," said Mrs Fernwell, turning down a road on the edge of town. "It's a little beyond your price range, $120,400, and it's a newer house, but what the heck, right?" She flashed her teeth at Marcia, who was drooping in the front seat.

"Sure, why not?" Marcia replied, too tired to resist.

Mrs Fernwell pulled up in front of a nondescript, low-slung ranch house with an attached garage, set in the middle of a lawn studded with big trees. The house was engulfed in evergreen bushes, but from what they could see, it was built of beige wood, with a bit of grey brick trim on the front. It blended into the bushes as if it were part of the foliage.

No one was home. Mrs Fernwell let them in through a heavy wood door.

The front of the house was a little forbidding, the inside was like an invitation to life. The entire interior was painted a light blue, the color of a faded summer sky. The ceilings were low, and the floors were a shimmering pale oak. Through large windows, facing south, sun flooded the main rooms.

It reminded Marcia of California houses, with light colored furniture and modern art. A tribute to perpetual summer.

On one wall of the living room a Navajo rug hung over a grey stone fireplace, before which stood a big soft sofa covered in nubby white.

Sliding glass doors opened from the dining area onto a red brick patio, shaded by a giant oak, and surrounded by flower beds and tall thick hedges. Someone here was a real gardener.

The kitchen was small but reasonably modern. The breakfast nook had a floor to ceiling window which looked out on a geranium bed and, beyond that, cornfields and a distant farm.

Marcia could see herself and Gin sitting there in the morning, drinking their coffee, eating their Rice Krispies, and watching the sunlight on their garden and the open fields beyond.

Two small bedrooms at the front of the house faced north; they were rather dark, although one was lightened by a skylight. But the master bedroom facing south, had big windows and was filled with light. It had also a sliding glass door which opened on its own diminutive red brick patio.

They peeked into closets, checked out the furnace and flushed the toilets in the two bathrooms. Their heels clicked on the shiny wood floors. The house was about twenty-five years old and in good condition. It was not large—Marcia estimated it at 1400 square feet. Was that why it was only $120,400?

She double-checked the price with Mrs Fernwell. Yes, the real estate agent said, it was $120,400. No, she didn't understand why it was so cheap. A divorce sale? Perhaps they needed to sell it fast? Lovely house though. Should go quickly at that price.

Gin was happily poking around the fireplace, wondering where he could find a white wool rug for lovemaking. Marcia caught his eye; they both smiled.

Only then did she allow herself to feel excitement. "Mrs Fernwell," she said, clasping the surprised agent by her shoulders. "We'll talk about it tonight, but I think you've got a buyer." Gin's smile grew broader.

"Oh, hell, what do we need to talk about?" she said, her arm around Gin. "I can tell you right now that we want it." She gave Gin a big hug.

Mrs Fernwell was surprised. Most young couples took weeks to find a house; this couple had pounced on one the first day.

Actually not. In her mind, Marcia had been house-hunting for at least five years.

NINETEEN

Mrs Fernwell tried to get the price down, but the owners stood firm: $120,400 and not a penny less. Marcia telephoned her mother, who agreed to lend them an additional five thousand. Within four days, the contract was signed, earnest money deposited, and a closing date set for the end of September.

Now all that remained was to find a mortgage institution that would lend them $90,000. And to try to control their anxieties. The day they decided to buy the California Dream House, they were jubilant. The next day, they were in shock. What an incredible amount of money. How would they be able to pay it off?

The day they signed the contract, Marcia's nightmares began. Gin had not slept well since they decided to buy, but he didn't dream about it.

That night Marcia dreamt they had only seven hundred dollars in their checking account. But the mortgage payment was eight hundred and fifty and it was due the next day. And they still had to pay their heat, the tax escrow money, the utility bill, the payments on Vivian the Volvo and interest to their parents on their down payment loan. The list seemed endless. She woke up in a sweat at four in the morning, just as the bill collectors were closing in and they were about to be turned out onto the street to sell rags.

She looked at Gin, asleep beside her. He trusted her, he assumed she knew what she was doing in buying this house. What if she didn't? What if she were leading them over a cliff?

She would have to stay at the bank and keep her nose to the grindstone, or find some other job that paid equally well. She had a house to support. They would need every penny they could scrape together. What if Gin did something rash and got himself fired from this job too?

She had a new goal in life. Instead of trying to find a job she liked, she had to devote herself to paying off the mortgage.

She pulled the sheet over her head and tried to go back to sleep, but her mind kept dwelling on an ever-growing collection of financial horrors that could overwhelm them.

She wanted to pour all her fears out to Gin, but she didn't dare. He might get cold feet and try to back out of the deal. She didn't want that either. Despite everything, she wanted that house. The house was a sign from God that they had made it, that she and Gin were like all the other young couples struggling to get on their feet.

She told herself that everybody had a hard time making mortgage payments; it was taken for granted that young people strained to buy a house. Everything always worked itself out in the end. They all got promotions and raises; their mortgage payments became manageable and eventually became negligible in the light of their income.

In ten years they all looked back and laughed at the number of beans and bacon suppers they had eaten in order to scrape together the mortgage payments. The American dream of home-ownership always had a happily-ever-after ending.

Only one problem. She and Gin didn't seem to be like everybody else. Nobody was giving them promotions and raises: Gin couldn't even keep a job. Maybe they would always have to struggle to make their payments.

And home values weren't climbing the way they used to. You couldn't count on selling the house for more than you paid for it. Inflation wasn't going to bail you out.

Residential mortgages were different now, too. You didn't just pay a fixed amount each month for thirty years; your mortgage payment changed. If interest rates went up, so did your payment. Sometimes, if interest rates climbed high enough, the lender started adding your increased interest onto the balance of the loan. You could pay and pay and pay and your mortgage balance would increase, not decrease. You would always be in debt up to your armpits.

She fell back into an uneasy sleep.

When the alarm went off at seven, she woke feeling better. She scolded herself for worrying about a lot of nonsense. Millions of people buy houses and take out $90,000 mortgages. If they can do it, so can we.

By the time she left for work, she was excited about the house again.

Gin was surprised she was so chipper when she looked so tired.

*   *   *

Marcia had made the mistake of telling Henrietta Rattner that they had bought a house in Barrington. By the middle of the week, the entire real estate department knew. To her face, they congratulated her. Behind her back, they all tried to figure out how she could afford it—all except Tom Gavins.

He just came out and asked her one day over lunch. When she told him, he toasted her with weak coffee: "Marcia, you are a tribute to the American way of debt. Good luck." She laughed and swore him to secrecy.

Nearly everyone in the department lived in cheaper suburbs; only Frances Klein lived in Barrington. And she was married to a bank wonder-kid with a big income. They concluded that Marcia had either big loans from her parents and in-laws or some independent source of income. Baxter suggested she might have made some money in the stock market or from some real estate deal. Gavins said nothing, but reported all the gossip back to her.

All such conjectures were in her favor: she had money from somewhere. Her status rose in the department. Even Ranier admired her for trying to live in a place that would stretch her to her financial limits.

Frances Klein asked her for her new address, now they were going to be neighbors. But she had never heard of the street. Then again, she lived out in the countryside and didn't know the village well. They would have to get together sometime. Marcia had never met Andrew, her husband, had she?

Marcia loved it all.

Today was mortgage day. Somewhere, out in the vast Chicago metropolitan area, there was a financial institution that was going to lend her an awful lot of money to buy a house she could barely afford. All she had to do was find it.

After a morning of phone calls, she was sure she had found it: a small bank in Downers Grove had run an ad in the Sunday paper advertising a nine and seven-eighths percent rate, for one year. After that it looked as if they might take your first child as collateral: the ad degenerated into a maze of small print and complicated tables.

Just get me through the first year, Marcia prayed. We can always refinance. The bank was offering the cheapest money anywhere around.

She had had a devil of a time getting through on the phone. When she did, the exhausted clerk who answered said she had better get in there quick. The money was going fast. Marcia made an appointment for the following evening.

Things were moving along swimmingly.

She wandered over to Frances Klein's desk and asked her to lunch.

Why not, Frances replied. They were neighbors now both at work and home. Had Marcia seen the Barrington train schedule yet? No? Well, she and Andrew always caught the six-fifteen a.m. express train. He liked to be at his desk before the New York currency market opened; she liked to start the day early.

And there was an excellent butcher shop in the village. Marcia would have to try it.

They lunched at an expensive little cafe near the bank. Marcia splurged on veal and a glass of good wine. They chatted about interior decorators; or, more exactly, Frances talked about her interior decorator while Marcia listened. The idea of hiring an interior decorator had never crossed her mind. Her cash flow was going into mortgage payments. But she smiled and nodded.

Near the end of the meal, Frances told Marcia that she was working on a regional shopping center deal. She had to analyze this shopping center rent roll, she said, throwing her red curls behind her shoulder. Frankly, she could use some help. Could Marcia stop by this afternoon and give her some pointers?

Could she ever. Maybe some of Frances's golden-girl aura would rub off on her.

See, she said to herself as they walked back to the bank. This house is bringing us good luck already.

*   *   *

Friday at six p.m. Marcia and Gin were sitting in the waiting area of the main office of the River Valley Bank and Trust Company in Downers Grove. They had fought their way through rush hour traffic to get to the bank; they were exhausted. They were also in shock. They had seen the house they wanted to buy only last Sunday. Now they were getting mortgage money. In less than a week, their entire world had been stood on its head.

They smiled nervously at each other.

Their mortgage loan officer was a tall, thin young man with bad acne scars on his face and a cheap suit. He was extraordinarily sincere. He explained the mortgage to them in a slow, monotonous voice, as if he were talking to people who didn't understand English well.

On a $90,000 mortgage, they would pay $841.79 a month or something like that, depending on where interest rates went. Then, in ten years, the entire mortgage would be due.

He droned on. They both listened attentively. The room was hot; Gin loosened his tie. He found it all rather confusing.

Marcia gave the officer the details of their incomes, their down payment and the price of the house. He wrote it all down in a square childish hand on the mortgage application. He said that they should have no problem getting the loan. They would hear from the bank in three weeks. Marcia wrote a check for the two hundred dollar processing fee, and they left.

"That's it?" Gin said outside in the parking lot.

"That's it," Marcia said.

"On the basis of that skimpy little interview and that application they're going to lend us $90,000?"

"Probably. You heard him. They have to look at the house—send out an appraiser, and they have to check our credit. That's why it takes three weeks. But otherwise, that's it."

"My God." It was amazing how little it took to borrow yourself into financial servitude.

"Come on," Marcia said. She slipped into Vivian's driver's seat. "Let's go celebrate. We're going to be home owners."

They drove through Downers Grove, Countryside and Westmont, looking for a restaurant, but all they saw were greasy spoons and fast-food franchises. Finally, they found a Chinese place. They toasted the California Dream House in Chinese beer while they ate beef in bean sauce.

Gin's fortune cookie said: "You will be a man of great wealth." He laughed so hard at that that Marcia became uncomfortable.

That weekend, they drove out to see their new house. They drove by it slowly. No one seemed to be home. They parked the car and prowled around the grounds, peeking into windows and admiring the garden. It was more beautiful than they remembered. The garden was in full bloom; Gin picked a souvenir marigold and presented it to Marcia.

"From the royal gardens, Your Highness," he said, bowing gracefully.

"Rise, Sir Gin of the Big Dick, and give the royal personage a big kiss," she said. They collapsed on the ground in laughter and wrestled themselves into a tangle. Marcia got grass stains on her new shorts, but she didn't care. She hadn't been so happy in months.

"It's a new beginning, Gin," she said in the car. "We're really making it; we've got our own house. I just can't believe it's finally all happening."

Gin couldn't either.

TWENTY

The first day of school for Pleasantview High School dawned stormy and dark. Gin dressed quickly, kissed Marcia and headed out for the long, lonesome ride to Wayland Center. Traffic was terrible; he was glad he wouldn't be making this drive much longer.

At the eight a.m. staff meeting, Bellicosi greeted him warmly. He introduced Gin and two other new teachers to the school's staff of twenty. Gin was struck by the spectrum of age in the group. A sure sign of a stingy school board, he thought. Only the very young and the very old will stay.

In the back row he saw the pretty woman who had given him directions the day he had first come to the school. Her strawberry-blonde hair was still piled high on her head; she wore a demure green dress. She gave him a friendly nod.

He went up to her after the meeting. Her name was Karen Gillette; she taught junior English. She had a beautiful smile. She also had the same lunch period as he. They agreed to meet for lunch.

You're a real mover, Gin, he thought, walking to his first class. Having lunch with the prettiest woman in the school within fifteen minutes of arrival. Nice maneuver.

But you're married, remember?

He felt guilty and then decided he had an overactive conscience. For Chrissakes, he'd just asked her to lunch, not to bed.

With infidelity on his mind, he stepped into the hallway and into rural Illinois. The kids were brown and muscular, even the girls. Many of the boys had white lines across their foreheads, where their caps had sheltered them from the sun while they drove their fathers' tractors. Some of them wore their caps to class: green and yellow, with " John Deere" or " DeKalb Seeds" printed above the visor. Without these identifying marks, it was difficult to tell the farmers from the suburbanites. Most of the kids wore a uniform: blue jeans, T shirts and running shoes. Here and there were boys affecting the punk look and girls wearing hot pink mini-skirts and heavy eye makeup: the punk hooker look. Those were undoubtedly from the new suburbs.

Gin found this clothing startling after the blazer and tie uniforms of St. Paul's. He found it unsettling to have girl students now anyway: many of them seemed a lot more mature than the boys, who were still shoving each other around in the corridors. His heart was in his throat as at least four Lolitas glided past him on the way to class.

First period was freshman English. They were nervous and uncertain, but they were able to emit groans when he made the first assignment: an essay on My Summer Vacation, due in two days. He expected that: nobody made kids write any more. But he did, in every class. He sat on the edge of his desk, opened the grammar book to homonyms and drilled them on the difference between "there" and "their." He smiled grimly to himself. Next month he would have them diagramming sentences on the blackboard. No one did that any more either.

Second period was sophomores, and third was study hall. Fourth period was a new experience: Drivers' Ed. The class started the next day but he had to meet with Stanley Ovronski, the gym teacher who ran the program, a beefy man with a neck that bulged over the back of his collar.

He explained that the special cars had a brake the teacher could hit if the neophyte driver got into trouble. Ovronski drove several miles with Gin playing teacher and learning how to apply the brake, which tended to stick and pull the car, a late-model Dodge, to the left.

The rain had stopped and the sun was shining on the cornfields. Gin suggested they keep driving. Maybe to Mexico?

Ovronski laughed and slapped him on the back. "Brother, don't I wish," he said. Gin liked him a lot. Ovronski was about twenty-five, lived in South Elgin with a wife and two kids, and was going to coach the junior varsity baseball team in the spring to bring in a little money. He loved baseball; he'd do it for nothing.

"But don't tell Bellicosi, that cheap SOB," he said. Gin laughed.

When they got back to the school Ovronski gave him a copy of *Rules of the Road*. Going over it, Gin was surprised to find that when he parked uphill he had been turning the wheels in and he should have been turning them out. Luckily there were few hills in Illinois.

It was time for lunch.

* * *

During fourth and fifth periods the gymnasium became the cafeteria. The janitor set up long tables; the food was displayed behind a stand of hot trays and jerry-rigged heat lamps.

Today lunch was hot dogs and beans, cole slaw, potato chips and chocolate cake for dessert. What do you want for only a dollar? Gin thought. While he stood in line for his hot dog he looked around for Karen and spotted her sitting alone at a table in a corner of the gym.

"Well, hello," she said, "how was your first morning?" Her green eyes were amused.

He pulled back a folding chair and set his tray down. "I think I like Drivers' Ed best," he said. "Do you know, I found out I've been parking uphill the wrong way for fifteen years? I could have killed somebody."

She laughed, a low warm chuckle. "With the brakes on my car, it doesn't matter how I park. Anyone behind me is doomed."

Her face was tanned; freckles were sprinkled across her wide cheek-bones. Her body under her green linen dress was compact and athletic. Gin guessed she was about thirty years old.

"You look as if you spend a lot of time outdoors," Gin said.

"In the summer, anyway," she said. "I swim a lot, run, play tennis. And I like to just lie in the sun. That is, when I get the chance."

She brushed a strand of golden hair off her forehead. "This summer, I taught summer school all morning, and worked at Sears in the afternoons. It didn't leave much time for the country-club life."

"Where you from?" Gin asked, munching on a potato chip.

"St. Louis. I taught at a private school there for four years. But when I got divorced, I decided on a change of pace and headed north. I have some family up here, some friends from school. Been here two years.

"I live in Elgin," she added, sipping her lemonade. "With my son, Tommy. He's seven. What about you?"

"I live in Chicago now, but we're buying a house in Barrington."

Karen's eyes widened.

"My wife's a banker. I think she's mortgaging my underwear to swing it."

Karen laughed. "Sounds like a talented woman."

"Oh that she is," Gin said, laughing. "She's one of the most determined creatures I know." The light played off Karen's thick blonde hair. He wanted to touch it.

Two men with trays appeared out of nowhere and asked if they could join them. Gin wanted to say no, but caught himself. Karen introduced them to him, a math teacher and a chemistry teacher; Gin immediately forgot their names. Karen and the two men chatted about their summer, the decaying state of the school building, and people Gin didn't know.

When the bell sounded, they stood up and bussed their dishes.

"See you at lunch tomorrow, if not sooner," Karen said. "This is a very small school."

The afternoon flew by, a blur of homonyms and *Silas Marner*. Gin could hardly wait for tomorrow's lunch.

*   *   *

Marcia double-checked her moving estimates once more. How could it cost a thousand dollars to move so little furniture, she thought, her fingers flying over her calculator. And how could it cost a hundred fifty a month in train fare to commute to the city? What they saved in gas on Gin's commute they would spend on hers.

Then there was the matter of the new roof. The appraiser said they needed one; his expert eye picked up water stains that hers, enraptured with the house, had missed. That was another $2,500.

She sighed and ran her hand through her hair. Everything always costs more than you think. In real estate, that was rule one. Still, she winced every time a new expense appeared. Their finances were pulled tight already; one more tug and they'd rip.

She covered her calculations with some file folders and a computer printout. No point in letting Ranier know what she was up to on bank time. For once, she was glad to be adrift in the backwaters of the department: it gave her the time to handle her personal affairs.

Things were going well, she thought, heading down to the cafeteria for a cup of coffee. The parents weren't being too picky about their loans, though her mother was still asking about her "collateral." The lender was moving fast: they could be in their new house October fifteenth at the latest. Even Gin was upbeat, despite some grousing about all the debt they were carrying. And he liked his new job.

True, her job search was on hold. But she was enjoying buying the house so much, she didn't care. She could start looking once they were settled.

She put a plastic top on her coffee cup and went back to the department. She was helping Frances Klein analyze a big loan on a forty-five million dollar regional shopping center outside Dallas. Frances would get the glory, but Marcia didn't care. She was enjoying the work.

Besides, she thought, on her way to Frances's desk, just wait until I get out of here. I'll eat you all for breakfast.

TWENTY-ONE

For two days after they moved in, they expected a phone call from the bank. Sorry, there's been some mistake. The beautiful house with the golden floors isn't yours; you'll have to move. But no one called. It really was theirs. Now, all they had to do was furnish it.

Emptied of the previous owners' furniture, the house was a huge blue desert; their meager possessions couldn't begin to fill it. The fineness of the walls and woodwork only emphasized the weariness of their own furniture.

They needed new furniture; they couldn't afford it. So, they bought one bentwood rocker and arranged their shabby throw rugs carefully over the massive floor, islands in a blonde sea.

"Just consider it the loft look," Gin said, sitting on their old sofa in front of the fireplace. "Lofts are full of space and no furniture."

Marcia sat next to him and chewed on her lower lip. Her eyes filled with tears.

"Aw, Marsh," he said, drawing her close. "Don't worry. It'll be all right."

The wind howled down the chimney. It was the first cold day of fall; under the overcast sky the house seemed desolate. It would be nice to have a fire, Gin thought. But they couldn't afford a screen and grate.

"We should have bought a smaller house," she said. "Then at least we could have afforded to put something in it."

Gin gave her his handkerchief; she blew her nose with a big honk.

"I mean, look at this," she said, looking around and waving the handkerchief over her head. "It looks like hillbillies live here."

It did, he thought. But so what? He thought their lack of furniture was kind of funny, while to Marcia, apparently, it was the end of the world.

"How about we sell all this stuff, buy some cushions, and sit on the floor?" he suggested whimsically. "Just like the Japanese. We could hang parachutes from the ceilings."

When he was a kid, one of his friends had a red parachute from the Army-Navy store hanging from his bedroom ceiling. Gin had always wanted one.

"Parachutes and floor pillows," she said. "Are you nuts? It sounds like the sixties." She stared at her hands.

In their first rush of enthusiasm, they had set a date for a housewarming party. Next Saturday, everyone they knew was coming to a buffet lunch and open house.

"We'll be humiliated," she whispered. "How could we be such idiots?"

"We could borrow some chairs and tables from my parents," Gin said.

"We'll have to."

Why hadn't he talked her out of this foolishness, she thought. This house, the party. Why hadn't he put his foot down and told her she was mad?

Instead, he just followed her lead. She had to make the big decisions alone; he was such a child.

Her dream lover would have handled the whole deal himself, presenting her with the deed to her new house over an intimate dinner at an expensive restaurant. Then he would have bought her lots of new furniture.

She sighed and stood up. "I better call Alice and see when we can pick up tables and chairs," she said. "Maybe she'll lend us their fireplace stuff, too."

*   *   *

The party was the Saturday before Halloween. They filled every naked corner in every naked room with dried cornstalks, pumpkins, and bunches of field corn. Gin even made a scarecrow out of some hay. A fire burned in the fireplace.

Thirty people sat on folding chairs or stood around orange-draped tables, the combined resources of the Bernthal-Grimley families. Toddlers and small children milled among the adults or ran into the back bedroom to watch television. The hum of conversation mixed with the music of Marvin Gaye and the Temptations.

"Marcia, what a charming house," Frances Klein said, surveying the autumnal cornfield that was now the living room. "Whatever did you do with all your furniture?"

"We just put it away to give us more room," Marcia said, hoping Frances wouldn't go looking for it. "We wanted a housewarming party with a Halloween theme."

"Well, it's really something," Frances said, gazing at the big oak near the patio. It was a blaze of yellow leaves, against a leaden sky. Several men in jackets stood around the patio holding beer cans or glasses. Gin poked at the hamburgers and hot dogs on the big Weber grill, borrowed from Calvin Grimley for the day.

Unfortunately, it came complete with Mr Grimley. He sat alone under a black paper witch in the living room, a soulful, lost look on his face. Marcia tried not to look at him; he made her feel guilty. Gin wondered if Calvin practiced being depressed. His own father certainly had no such problem. He was circulating among the young families like a fox among the chickens, selling whole life insurance.

The party broke into two groups. For the most part, the teachers talked with teachers and the bankers with bankers. There was some cross-pollination. Andrew Carton, Frances Klein's husband and whiz kid of currency trading, displayed a phenomenal knowledge of baseball. He and Stanley Ovronski, the Drivers' Ed teacher, were deep in conversation about next year's season in the National League.

Dinky, Marcia's sister, was attracting a good deal of attention from all the single males. She had come with one named Terry, a trader on the Mercantile Exchange. He made the mistake of going into the kitchen to get two beers. When he returned, she was telling a dazzled young banker about the difficulty of finding a job in dental hygiene in a world overstaffed with dentists.

"I mean the dentists can clean teeth as well as I can," she said seriously, tossing her dark curly head. Her brilliant orange sweater pulled tight against her breasts.

Marcia watched her sister from the kitchen door, shaking her head and laughing. "What's so funny?" a voice asked behind her. She turned to see a good-looking man, in his late thirties, with thick black hair. He wore a powder-blue sweater that matched his eyes and he held a beer in his hand.

"My sister. She's a stitch to watch with men," Marcia said. "They just buzz around her."

"I can see why," the man said. "She's very pretty—but then so is her sister."

Marcia blushed and laughed. "Well, thank you," she said. "I'm Marcia Bernthal. I think we met earlier, but I forgot your name."

"Rick, Rick Matthews," he said extending his hand. "I came with Frances and Andrew Carton."

"That's right. You're Andrew's friend who works for Delta Realty, in the Hancock Building." She shook his hand warmly. "You'll have to forgive me. Ordinarily, I'm good at remembering names, but all this is a bit overwhelming." She gestured toward her chattering guests.

"Well, even hostesses get some time out, don't they?" he said, motioning her to two empty chairs at a card table.

"So what brings you to such a fuddy-duddy affair as a suburban housewarming?" Marcia asked.

"Andrew and I are doing some real estate deals together on our own. I was out at his house today and they were coming over here. So, well, I just tagged along."

He sipped his beer. "Frances says you work in real estate with her at the bank. She says you're very good at picking deals apart."

"I've sure seen enough bad ones to practice on." Rick laughed, a good, deep male laugh. Marcia liked it; she liked him.

"You like the bank?" he asked.

"Are you kidding? It's the last holdout of the Middle Ages. I'm so fed up I'm ready to put up a billboard at State and Madison: 'I'm being held captive at First Midwestern National. Send help.' "

They both laughed.

"What's so funny, you two?" Frances asked from behind them.

"Just some real estate tall tales, Frances," Rick said.

Frances smiled. She had put in her required appearance at Marica's little party. Now it was time to go; Andrew had some work to do at home.

"I'll call you Monday," said Rick, shaking Marcia's hand. "We should have lunch this week. There's always room for good people at Delta Realty."

Marcia beamed and murmured a pleasantry. She was exhilarated. A job lead! With one of the biggest real estate firms in the country.

She went looking for Gin, to tell him the good news. He was deep in conversation with a tanned woman who had a long braid of strawberry-blonde hair down her back. They were annoyed when Marcia interrupted. Gin seemed politely pleased about her news; he was anxious to return to his conversation.

Who was that woman? Marcia wondered. A Karen Somebody from school. . .

She went back to clearing tables, opening beer cans and mingling with her guests.

*   *   *

Rick Matthews called on Monday; lunch was set for Wednesday at an expensive Italian restaurant just off Michigan Avenue. Wednesday morning Marcia dressed carefully in her blue wool suit and the blouse with a tiny lace collar and cuffs. She put several copies of her resume in her briefcase and rehearsed her lines. She wasn't interested in any more grunt work; she had put in her time in the trenches. She wanted to do deals, to buy properties for investors.

Delta Realty would be the perfect place. Each year they bought over a billion dollars worth of real estate on behalf of individual and institutional investors.

She arrived early and waited nervously in the foyer, watching the well-dressed clientele meeting for lunch. It was an elegant restaurant: the rugs were pastel blue and there were good prints on the wall. It had been months since she had been to a good restaurant. She felt giddily rich.

Rick bounded in ten minutes late. In his soft grey pin-striped suit, with his shiny Italian shoes and his heavy leather briefcase, he looked like someone in a magazine ad for expensive whiskey. He made Marcia feel dowdy.

The waiter led them to an intimate table. "Sorry I'm late," Rick said, throwing his dark cashmere coat over an empty chair. "We were finishing the final details on a shopping center deal and the developer wouldn't let me out of the office. I practically had to club him to escape."

"It was worth it though," he said, "you look lovely." He stared at her with his magnificent blue eyes.

"Thank you," she said, startled by the compliment and the intensity of his gaze. "You look pretty spiffy, too."

He laughed. They made some small talk about the weather and the fickle nature of interest rates. They ordered drinks and, as an appetizer, some marinated octopus. It was delicious.

"So, Mrs Bernthal," Rick said, munching on a delectable tentacle, "tell me your life story."

She did. She told him about growing up in Palatine and about going to an exclusive college full of pointy-headed intellectuals where she didn't fit in. She told him about her decision to go into real estate, so she could "get rich quick."

He nodded his head. He had gone into the business with the same idea.

"And did it work out that way?" she asked.

"Not yet. It's taking a little longer than I thought," he replied, smiling. "But I'm getting there. But go on."

She told him about her work for mortgage bankers and then spoke bitterly about her situation at the bank: Ranier, the baby loan analysts, her frustrations—it all came tumbling out. Rick listened carefully, nodding his head and making sympathetic comments.

She was delighted. It was the first time in months she had spoken to someone who understood and who was interested in her work. Gin tried, but her business bored him. He fidgeted his way out of her confessionals.

She was halfway through her pasta with clam sauce before she finished her story. Rick's story took up the second half of the meal.

He was from the New York suburbs; his father had been a successful real estate developer and Rick, following in his footsteps, had started in Real Estate Lending at Citibank, moved to Prudential Insurance, and then jumped to a big shopping center development firm in Maryland.

He bought land for them, sites for their shopping centers. Soon he was putting together land for regional centers, giant shopping centers that constitute America's new downtowns. But it was frustrating work. It took years to put together a center site; he got tired of fighting suburban zoning boards.

So about ten years ago he had gone to work for Delta Realty, in acquisitions. He flew around the country buying real estate for Delta's investors. It was fun.

"And a hell of a lot more lucrative." He poured Marcia another glass of Chianti. "Delta has a terrific incentive plan. I'm a shareholder in the company now."

Marcia was wide-eyed with admiration.

"Do you think you'd like to get into acquisitions?" he asked.

"I thought you'd never ask," she said. "I just happen to have a few resumes here."

He laughed.

She took a resume from her briefcase and handed it to him. While he was reading it she unwillingly remembered what had happened the last time she had taken a job like this, a job that required a lot of travel. A mortgage banking firm had sent her around the country, looking at deals. She was on the road three or four days a week.

They had just been married and she could not bear to be away from Gin so much. After six weeks and a night spent crying herself to sleep in the Atlanta Airport Hilton, she quit.

But she had been a newlywed then. Now she was an old married lady. And given the way the marriage was going, maybe being on the road for a while wouldn't be a bad idea. Absence makes the heart grow fonder and all that.

And Rick was dazzling. Handsome, attentive and with those blue eyes. This was more than a job interview. She fiddled with a lock of her hair. This could be an interview for an affair.

She was shocked by her own thought. It was one thing to dream about being carried away by a real estate developer; it was another to actually allow it to happen. She wondered if he was married.

"Are you married?" she asked abruptly. The wine had gone to her head.

"Divorced five years ago. No kids." He didn't seem surprised at the question.

"You're married though," he said. "A tall blonde guy, right? A teacher. And no kids."

"Well," Marcia said. "What else do you know about me?" Maybe he knew her marriage was in trouble. He wouldn't have to ask anyone about that, probably. Maybe she was sending out signals to prospective lovers.

"I know all sorts of dark secrets," he said, in a mock-ominous voice.

She smiled weakly. "Is there lots of travel in acquisitions?" she asked, changing the subject.

"Sure. We're all over the place. You have to be where the deals are—always on the prowl." He saw her face fall. "You're not big on travel?"

"Well, I wasn't once," she said. "But that was several years ago. When I was first married. I'd be willing to give it another try now."

"Good," he said, looking at her intensely again. "Situations do change."

Marcia had the sudden feeling that he wanted to hold her hand. What made it uncomfortable was that she wanted him to. She had not felt so attracted to a man since she had met Gin. But this was supposed to be a job interview.

"What kind of acquisitions' jobs do you have open?" she said, wrenching herself back to the ostensible subject of the lunch.

"Well, we create the job for the people, and we're always looking for good people," Rick said. "You'd go into our training program. We're one of the few real estate firms that have one.

"As part of it, we ship you out with one of the acquisitions guys as his assistant for a year or two. Then you get your wings and fly on your own. That's it. Very simple."

He sipped his espresso.

"We have a committee that interviews for acquisitions trainees," he continued. "I'm on it. And I'm looking for an assistant myself right now. What do you say?"

Marcia couldn't believe it. A dream job had just floated into her lap! Her face was flushed with wine. Her eyes danced and her voice turned husky.

"Just show me where I sign on the dotted line, mon capitain," she said.

Rick laughed. "Good. I knew you'd say yes." He paid the check and picked up his luxurious coat. "Just let me line up some interviews with some people and we'll be ready to roll. I'll call you."

They shook hands; Rick gave her a peck on the cheek.

Marcia was so happy and drunk that she splurged on a cab back to the bank and began cleaning out her credenza.

TWENTY-TWO

That night Marcia bought a bunch of daisies in the railway station. She read the newspaper on the train, occasionally peeking down at the flowers in her lap.

Congratulations, kid, she thought. You're going to make it after all.

The five-thirty-five arrived in Barrington right on time. Marcia joined the well-dressed commuters streaming off the platform past the neat brick station house, looking for their rides home. The new house was just far enough from the station so that Gin had to pick her up in the evening. Just another aspect of suburban living.

She spotted their car and climbed into the front seat next to Gin. He was wearing a blue striped shirt with no tie and brown corduroy pants. Compared to Rick, he looked like an aging college student.

She gave him a quick kiss and launched immediately into an exciting, bowdlerized version of her luncheon job interview.

"Marsh, that's just great," Gin said. "It's time you get out of that bank." His smile was preoccupied.

Marcia beamed at him. "I go talk to the entire group of head honchos or whatever next week. I could be out of the bank in two weeks."

"That's great, Marcia, really great." He maneuvered the car through the clotted traffic near the station.

"Only one drawback, though," she said.

"What's that?"

"Lot's of travel. I could be on the road three or four days a week." She watched his face; he didn't react.

"That didn't work out so hot last time, did it?" His voice was even. "Are you sure you want to try it again?"

"Well. . .I thought this time it could be different." She twisted the paper around her daisies. "We were just married when I was traveling before. Newlyweds—you know, kind of nervous.

"See now. . .well, it's been three years. Things are more settled, we're more settled. We have our own house, I thought it would be okay to try it again." She wondered whose marriage she was talking about.

Gin pulled into the driveway. From the hallway one small light shone over the lawn.

"Well, I suppose it's all right," he said slowly. "Why not give it a try?"

"Great, Gin. I'm so glad you see it that way." She gave him a hug. If he thought it was okay to travel, then everything had to be fine.

*   *   *

"Turn left, left, left, a hard left," Gin yelled, jamming his foot down hard on his brake. The blue Dodge with the "Student Driver" sign on top shuddered and just missed the rear end of the delivery truck double-parked in front of Johansen's Sausage and Fine Meat Shoppe. A startled Yugoslavian stared at them from the truck's rear door as the car veered into oncoming traffic.

Luckily no one was coming the other way.

"Pull over, right now," Gin said. "I mean right now. Come on. Come on."

The driver, a short freckled girl in a red sweater, blushed to the roots of her red hair. The car lurched to a halt in front of a drugstore.

"Just what the hell do you think you were doing?" Gin yelled. "You could have gotten us killed."

The driver began to cry softly. In the back seat a tall, skinny boy and a girl with hair like purple spikes sat, stunned.

"Didn't you see him?" Gin went on, his voice shaking. "How could you miss seeing a delivery truck? You nearly rear-ended him."

Tears streamed down the girl's cheeks. For thirty seconds, there was silence.

"Uh, Mr Bernthal," the boy said.

"What is it, Henley?"

"Wouldn't it have been a better idea to rear-end the truck instead of driving into oncoming traffic?"

Gin felt like strangling him. He was still quaking with fear, and already Henley was doing a post-mortem. The guy would probably grow up to become an Air Force test pilot, risking his life for some engineer's scatterbrained innovations. After the plane dropped two thousand feet in less than a mile, Henley would calmly say, "You should have put more thrust in the engine."

"Henley, in situations like that, you just go with the flow."

"Excuse me?"

"It was six of one, half a dozen of the other," Gin said, turning around to face Henley. The kid reminded him of a bony stork with glasses.

"Gail could have either run into the rear end of the truck, seriously injuring the delivery man and definitely hurting us, or she could take the chance that nothing was coming the other way and perhaps avoid an accident completely." He came up for a breath of air. "Fortunately, we lucked out and there was no one coming the other way."

"Oh." Henley seemed confused; he wanted definite rules.

"Of course," Gin went on. "We wouldn't have had to worry about any of this if someone had been paying attention to where she was going."

He glared at Gail. She rested her head on the steering wheel, her eyes closed and her hands gripping the top of the wheel.

"What in the hell was going through your mind?" Gin said.

"I don't know. I just didn't see him," she whispered.

Gin let out an exasperated sigh. "Okay. Okay. That's enough for one day. Get in the back seat. Let's give Wilma a turn at the wheel."

The freckled child with the tear-streaked face was replaced by the harpy with purple hair and black eye makeup. She looked like a raccoon.

"Okay, Wilma," Gin said. "Let's head for the edge of town and go back to school."

Wilma bit her lower lip, looked carefully back over her left shoulder, and slowly jerked the car into traffic. She was clearly terrified.

"Wilma, you can go faster than ten miles an hour," Gin said. Cars were backing up behind them.

Wilma picked it up to twenty. She managed the courage to top thirty-five on the country roads back to Pleasantview High. Gin was relieved to pull into the parking lot alive.

He would have a lot to tell Karen at lunch.

*   *   *

Karen was sitting alone at their favorite table in the back corner of the gym, the one with the view of the tumbling mats on the walls. It was like eating lunch in a padded cell, Gin thought, pulling up a chair across from her.

"Christ, what a morning." He set his tray down. No one else had arrived yet. Usually, they spent their lunches engulfed by other teachers and students. "Gail Murphy nearly killed us all in South Elgin. She almost rear-ended a delivery truck. Then I nearly got us killed in oncoming traffic."

"Good heavens," Karen said, alarmed. She wore a khaki-colored dress that set off her brown skin and pile of golden hair.

"You look lovely," Gin whispered, leaning across the table. "But then you always look lovely."

"Compliments, compliments," she said casually. But she flushed and smiled.

"Tell me about your near-brush with death," she said.

"Well, we're cruising around South Elgin with old Gail at the wheel. She's doing real well and I'm kind of daydreaming out the window when suddenly, up ahead, there's this delivery truck stopped, blocking the whole lane. Some guy in a white apron was rummaging in the back. And old Gail is about to cruise right into him at thirty-five miles an hour.

"So it was either instant death for our friend the delivery man or we take a chance on oncoming traffic." He took a deep breath. "So I took a chance at a head-on and we lucked out." A cold wave went over him as he thought of what would have happened if someone had been coming the other way.

"God, Karen, what would have happened if there had been traffic coming? The state police would be picking our pieces off the highway and Pleasantview could be gearing up for four funerals.''

He looked at her. "You know, it was probably the wrong thing to do, veering into traffic, but I didn't know what else to do."

"You did the right thing," she said quietly. "What other choices did you have?" She patted his hand lightly. The surprise of her touch distracted him.

"I mean who expects someone to drive right into the rear end of a truck?" he said, picking up his hot dog.

"Well, for what it's worth, I hear Gail Murphy has a lot on her mind these days," Karen said. "I overheard two girls in my fifth period class talking last week. Rumor has it that she's pregnant."

Gin groaned. "You mean she was either catatonic from the shock, or. . ." He stopped, finding it hard to believe. "She was trying to kill herself—and us."

Karen nodded.

"Oh, for God's sake," Gin said in disgust. "What a ridiculous situation. Doesn't she have someone to talk to here? Some sort of counselor or something? The school nurse?"

"Nobody official," Karen said. "Remember, this is a low-overhead high school. We teach them to read and write. If they kill themselves, that's their problem.

"Actually," she continued, "I'm going to try to talk to her this afternoon. She was in my English class last year; she's a quiet girl, but I think she'll talk to a woman." She pursed her lips and her green eyes widened. "Anyway it's worth a try, don't you think?"

"Absolutely," Gin said. They sat in silence for a while. Then Gin spotted Stanley Ovronski and Susan Masterson, a pear-shaped P.E. teacher, coming toward their table with their trays.

He turned to Karen. "Hey, what are you doing for dinner tonight?"

"Not much. Tommy and I were just going to have hamburgers and sit around and watch TV."

"Why don't you see if you can get a sitter and come over? Marcia's out of town and I could use the company. I'll pick up some chicken or something on the way home."

"Sounds good to me," Karen said. "I'll leave Tommy with the woman across the hall and her little boy."

"Come by around five-thirty."

She nodded her head just as Stanley and Susan set their trays down next to them. "So how's the new Drivers' Ed teacher doing?" Ovronski asked. He popped open one of his two cartons of milk.

Gin and Karen looked at each other and laughed.

TWENTY-THREE

Twice Gin rearranged Marcia's blue cloth napkins and silver on the small kitchen table. He chopped up some broccoli, ripped up lettuce for a salad and poured half a bottle of teriyaki sauce over the raw chicken as a marinade. A bottle of California Chablis was chilling in the refrigerator and there was a quart of pistachio ice cream in the freezer.

It wasn't elegant, but it would do. He turned on the radio to classical music and started a fire in the fireplace. Thank God, his mother had let them keep her old grate. She had even dug up a set of andirons for them.

When the doorbell rang at five-thirty, the lights were low and the fire was burning brightly.

"Welcome to my humble abode." He ushered Karen into the sparsely furnished living room.

She handed him a bunch of carnations. "For the chef," she said, glancing around. "My, what a lovely place this is. I hardly recognize it without all the cornstalks."

"Well, they had to go sometime or other. I wanted to keep them, but Marcia thought they were a fire hazard."

Karen laughed. He took her coat. She had changed into blue jeans and a soft green sweater that hugged her body. Wisps of blonde hair framed her face. She was soft, warm and blonde, Gin thought. Marcia was brown, severe and cold. Or efficient—maybe efficient was a better word.

"What can I get you to drink?" he said, seating her on the couch in front of the fire. "The hint is all I have is Chablis."

"A glass of Chablis would be fine," she said.

He went into the kitchen, humming the melody of a Bach Cantata that was playing on the radio, and fished the wine out of the refrigerator. As he poured a glass for Karen and one for himself, he wondered just what in the hell he was doing.

I'm a married man, he said to himself, humming and re-turning the wine to the refrigerator. And I'm happier than I've been in weeks.

Karen was sitting against one arm of the small cotton-covered couch, her legs stretched out in front of her. His heart thumped with excitement. "So, here you are," he said. He handed her her wine and sat down in the middle of the couch propping his feet on the flimsy coffee table in front of it. The fire crackled. "Well." He cleared his throat. "You like it? The wine?"

She took a small sip. "Yes, it's very good."

They sipped their wine and stared into the fire for several moments.

"How did it go with Gail Murphy this afternoon?" Gin asked.

"She wouldn't tell me a thing," Karen said. "I came right out and asked her if she was pregnant and if there was anything I could do. She denied everything. She looked at me like I had impugned her teenage honor."

"So now what happens?"

"She gets as big as a house and drops out of school in the early spring, that's what. Same old story." Karen looked tired. "It frustrates me that I can't do more." She looked at Gin squarely; her big green eyes were filling with tears.

"I didn't realize you took all this so personally," he said in surprise.

"I do. I do. I really hate to see someone so young mess up her life like this. Even when I don't know them well and they don't want my help, I still feel terrible when it happens."

She pulled a handkerchief out of a pocket in her jeans and dabbed at her eyes. "I know it's silly, but I do it anyway. You know, I cry at movies about wounded animals. I even tape the soap operas while I'm at school and watch them at night and cry. It's an addiction of mine."

Gin didn't find it silly at all. He found it endearing. Marcia would never watch a soap opera, much less cry over one. She favored *Wall Street Week*.

He scooted next to Karen, put his wine down on the table and then took hers out of her hand. "You won't be needing this for a while," he said, placing it on the table.

Then, he put his arm around her. "Let's not talk about those ungrateful kids at school," he whispered. "Let's talk about you and me."

He kissed her. She kissed him back, firmly, then eagerly, opening her mouth and flicking her tongue into his mouth.

Her hands moved on his body. He helped her slip off her sweater and they made love on the couch, the glow of the fire playing off their skin.

She was a willing lover, as soft and warm as he had expected.

Afterwards, she slipped into one of his bathrobes and helped him assemble their supper. They ate in the breakfast nook with a candle on the table, drinking a toast to Pleasantview High. He told her about his plans to become an assistant principal and get into administration. She listened intently.

Then they went back to Marcia and Gin's big bed and made love again, this time with more room and much pleasure. It was past eleven when Karen left for home.

"Tommy's going to be a crab tomorrow, with his Mommy coming in so late," she said, kissing Gin. He pulled her close to him. . .

"Oh, my," she laughed. "Start that again and I'll never get out of here."

"Sounds fine to me," he said, kissing the curve of her neck.

"My junior English class will just have to get their papers back a day late," Karen said, pulling herself free. "I'll see you at lunch tomorrow, okay?"

"Right."

He watched her get into her rusty little car and back down the long driveway to the deserted street. He went back to bed and slept soundly, the spicy smell of her cologne rising from the sheets.

The next morning, he woke alone, gripped with anxiety. My God, he thought, stripping the bed and cleaning up the dishes. I'm cheating on my wife.

*　　*　　*

Marcia had forgotten how long airport corridors could be when you're wearing high heels and carrying a suit bag, a briefcase, an overnight bag and a coat and purse. She tottered down Concourse G of the Los Angeles Airport.

Somewhere there had to be Gate 11G, United flight 403 to Phoenix, Arizona. Rick would have given her a hand, but he was toting his own luggage as well as twenty-five pounds of blueprints stuffed in a cardboard tube. The blueprints were the layout and construction specifications for the Costa Mesa Regional Shopping Center in Phoenix.

"Couldn't you just have sent them to Chicago by messenger?" Marcia gasped as they hurried down the corridor.

"I don't trust messengers," Rick said, hoisting the plans from under his right arm to his shoulder. His suitcoat bunched up under his armpits.

"These are the only copies," he said. "I lose them, the deal is dead. I once did that, you know. I'm not going to let that happen again." He picked up his pace. They were running behind schedule.

"Besides, Coop would kill me if I lost these," he said, smiling at her. Cooper "Coop" Hendron ran Delta Realty's construction and engineering department. His staff crawled over every building Delta wanted to buy, looking for dripping ceilings, neglected elevators and cracked floors—anything that could be used to negotiate a lower price from the seller.

"Rick," Marcia said good-naturedly. "If Coop wants these drawings, let him send out his own flunkies to get them."

"It's no skin off your nose, Marsh," Rick said. "I'm carrying them."

"Yeah, but if you weren't carrying them, you could carry my suit bag."

He laughed. "What happened to women's liberation?"

"Give me a break." The strap from the bag cut into her left shoulder. She was sure it was going to leave a permanent mark. They reached the gate just as the last passengers boarded the plane.

"You know, next time I go to L.A. I'm not bringing a suit at all." Marcia jammed her luggage into the tiny overhead compartment and collapsed into the seat next to Rick. "I'm going to wear a cute little sundress and sandals. I'll have hardly any luggage, my feet won't hurt, and I'll fit right in to the whole California schtick."

She turned to Rick. "You know I've never negotiated a hundred and thirty-five million dollar deal with a guy who wore sneakers, chinos and a pink T-shirt with a grease spot over his left tit."

Rick laughed. "That's just Ernie for you. When you're worth two hundred and fifty million and own thirteen regional shopping centers, you can dress any way you like."

"I'd like to start now," Marcia said, fussing with the bow around her neck. She smoothed the rumpled material of her skirt. Hard to believe the hotel had just pressed it last night. "I swear to God, Rick, if I had a pair of shorts and a T shirt I'd wear that to the negotiating session this afternoon."

"Great," Rick said. "They could look at your legs and I could squeeze extra money out of the deal." He fastened his seat belt over his trim, pin-striped middle and smiled his wide, clean smile.

"You know, Ernie really liked you," he said. "He likes women who talk to him straight. A lot of developers do. You're doing real good for four weeks on the job. I think you're a natural at this."

Marcia was flabbergasted. Rick had been supportive, but this was the first full-fledged compliment he had given her. In fact, it was the first full-fledged compliment she had gotten from any man she had ever worked for.

"I bet you say that to all the girls," she said, laughing with delight.

"I mean it," he said, looking at her with intense blue eyes.

"Really?"

"Yeah. You're good. You just don't know it. Lots of women are like that. It's a real shame."

She wanted to throw her arms around him. She settled for squeezing his hand. He looked pleasantly surprised.

"Thanks, Rick," she said softly. "That means a lot to me."

He leaned over and kissed her gently on her forehead.

"Keep it up, Marcia; you'll go far," he said. She could smell the piney scent of his aftershave.

They lay back in their seats, exhausted. Soon he was asleep, his relaxed face looking young and smooth under his black hair.

Rick was a master of the airline catnap. In the last four weeks Marcia had watched him sleep during everything from puddle-jumping flights around North Carolina to transcontinental voyages. He awoke at their destination, fresh and relaxed, while she staggered off the plane with a cramped back.

It had been one hell of a month. She counted to herself as the plane began to climb: in four weeks she had been to Los Angeles four times, North Carolina three times, Phoenix twice. Or was it three times?

She couldn't remember. But she believed she had been on the road at least four out of every five working days. She had visited regional shopping centers in San Jose, Phoenix and North Carolina. She had plodded through an office building in Houston and a collection of apartment houses south of L.A.

They were all potential deals for Rick. He was in tight with several big developers. Unfortunately, these guys lived at either end of the continent and built their properties anywhere in between. So she and Rick flew around a lot.

Too much, she thought. She watched the stewardesses running up and down the aisles with drinks, pillows and magazines.

Maybe the travel would die down soon. To get her off to a good start, Rick had introduced her to all his major contacts. Now that she knew all of them maybe she could stay home for a while and take a breather? No, that was unlikely. This was only the beginning.

Yet it was heady stuff. She was now on a first-name basis with some of the country's major developers. She had seen more regional shopping centers in four weeks than she had in three years at First Midwestern. She was learning an incredible amount. And Rick was a great mentor: kind, patient, making sure she made good connections, and working her like a dog.

But no harder than he worked himself. He could be really funny, but his humor was always about real estate and deals. Deals, deals, deals. He was always doing deals. No wonder he was one of the top acquisitions men at Delta Realty and a millionaire at thirty-nine. The way Rick worked, his next million should take him only another five years.

He had no compunction about spreading the wealth around. He had gone to bat for her with top management. Consequently, Delta was paying her $35,000 a year. Not bad for a trainee salary.

In a few years, when she started doing her own deals, she could be making $150,000–$200,000 a year, plus stock options. She shook her head: she still couldn't believe it had all happened to her. She loved it.

She thought again of how Ranier had turned purple when she quit. Stonily, he wished her good luck. The EEOC was bearing down hard on the bank to increase the number of women in management. Ranier had to explain to his boss why another one had left. It didn't look good for him.

Serves him right, Marcia thought, the creepy bastard.

Everyone else responded predictably. Baxter and the baby real estate analysts were green with envy. Baxter slipped her his resume; she burned it in her fireplace. Henrietta Rattner, the idiot, probably didn't even know Marcia had left. Frances Klein played dumb.

Two days before she left, the department took her out for a farewell lunch at an overpriced German restaurant with bad food. The next day, Tom Gavins, her homosexual friend, took her to lunch at Chez Paul. Over her Bibb lettuce salad au vinaigrette, he presented her with a package of paper doilies. For her coffee cups, he said.

She stared out the airplane window at the blue, cloudless sky of the desert. Hard to believe it was the first week of December. Chicago had already seen its first light snow.

Gin had told her that last night when she called home. Gin, Gin. How she missed him. She was used to seeing him every night. Now she slept in broad empty beds in look-alike hotels. She tried to keep up on their life together over the telephone and on week-ends, but it was impossible. She was living with a stranger, or a half-stranger. Their relationship was on hold until she got off airplanes for awhile.

But at least she was making some money. It would be easier to pay all those bills that flooded her desk. She wondered how

bad off they really were financially. Since she had started working at Delta, she hadn't had the time to look, but her financial
radar was sending her overload signals. She shuddered.

Maybe things would calm down. She could straighten out
their finances. She and Gin could pick up where they had left
off. Yeah, she thought sardonically, we could pick up our fights
where we left off.

She sighed, flipped down her seat tray, and tried to review
the numbers on the Costa Mesa deal. The final negotiations were
set for that afternoon. She and Rick were to meet Ernie and
Harry, his lawyer, at Harry's office in Phoenix.

The numbers blurred before her eyes. She leaned back in
her seat and the noise around her faded into a gentle buzz.
When she awoke, the plane was landing in Phoenix. She felt
stiff, but refreshed.

"Sleeping Beauty awakes," Rick said, looking at her tend-
erly as she stretched. She flushed. He smiled his handsome grin
and squeezed her hand.

"Come on," he said. "It's time to go at it again." He retrieved his tube of blueprints from the overhead compartment.
He was the third person off the plane.

TWENTY-FOUR

From three in the afternoon until midnight, they sat in Harry's office and negotiated: Ernie, Harry, Rick and Marcia. Or rather the three men haggled and Marcia played handmaiden to Rick, handing him computer printouts of her analyses, taking notes, and just watching.

Rick paced around the office, peering out the window, sitting down and getting up from various couches and chairs around the room. Ernie sat in the swivel chair behind Harry's big teak desk. Harry and Marcia sat on a big leather couch against the wall. Ernie and Harry were both in their late fifties, tanned, balding men with small paunches.

They complained that Marcia's analysis of the center's cash flow was all wrong. Costa Mesa was throwing off more cash than she showed.

Rick retorted that their rental income had been "overstated"; the department store tenants were also deadbeats. They weren't paying their share of expenses for maintaining the center's common areas.

In response, Ernie lectured them on the battle of Guadalcanal. His combat experience had taught him how to lease shopping centers, he said. "You've got to go at them with all guns blazing," he said, punching the air with his pen.

He pulled out *his* computer analyses of the center's cash flow.

"See, these guys are paying through the nose on common area expenses, Rick," he said, jabbing at the printout.

"Not so I can see, Ernie. You should have taken a refresher course after World War Two," Rick said. "This center isn't as tight as Preston." Preston Mall was a center outside Kansas City, which he had bought from Ernie two years ago.

Ernie looked angry. "Come on, give me a break on this expense stuff," he said.

"No breaks, Ernie," Rick said. "Marcia and I took the leases apart; it's no go without a cut. I got forty-five million cash on the table and I can cut this deal right now if you'll give where you know you've got to."

Ernie looked at Harry. Harry shrugged.

Ernie stood up and walked over to the window. He had changed his pink T shirt for a rugby shirt with red stripes. He looked as though he were dressed to watch his grandson play Little League baseball.

"Okay, cut it by two hundred thousand."

"Five hundred thousand," Rick said.

Ernie groaned. "Are you crazy?"

"Look at the numbers, Ern. Just look at the numbers." Rick waved a copy of Marcia's lease analysis. She felt really proud.

"Three hundred and fifty thousand, and that's tops," Ernie said. Marcia gasped. He had just dropped the price of the center by three point five million.

It wasn't enough for Rick. "Okay," he said. "But you gotta take back fifteen million in paper at ten percent."

"What do you want, my first-born son?" Ernie yelled. "No paper. Period."

So it went. Back and forth, back and forth. Rick paced; Ernie yelled. At nine o'clock they sent out for pizzas and coke. Rick dropped a slice of cheese and sausage on paragraph four of the joint-venture agreement. Everyone laughed.

At ten, Harry stretched out on the leather couch; he had a thyroid condition. He said they should wake him up at Part Three, Paragraph three (e).

By midnight, they had a deal, subject to Coop finding anything physically wrong with the center that they didn't already know about.

Everyone shook hands and they toasted the deal with a bottle of champagne that just happened to be in the office refrigerator.

"I thought we might do some business tonight, so I took precautions," Ernie said ingenuously.

Rick howled and slapped Ernie on the back. "That's center number five I've bought from you, you old buzzard. And you always take precautions."

They drank and laughed for fifteen minutes. Then Marcia and Rick drove back to their hotel.

It was an expensive resort in Scottsdale, at the foot of Camelback Mountain. Each guest had a small adobe cottage, set apart from its neighbors and surrounded with pine trees and flowers.

She and Rick were tired, but so excited neither felt like sleeping.

"How about a late night snack?" he said, cupping her elbow. "I think the cafe here is still open."

It was a warm, clear night with stars and a gentle dry breeze off the desert. They strolled through the resort's garden, chatting about the deal. Rick felt he had gotten an excellent price on Costa Mesa.

"I'm sure Ernie doesn't even know half the things he agreed to in that joint-venture agreement," he said, laughing. "But he'll make out all right."

The candles on the tables lit the cafe with a soft, diffused light. Navajo blankets covered the adobe walls; flower baskets hung from the timbers in the ceiling. A wall consisted of glass doors, now wide open to the gardens and the desert night.

They sat in a secluded corner and listened to the fountain in the garden. Marcia was enchanted.

"This is beautiful, Rick," she said. "I feel like I'm in Mexico." On my honeymoon, she nearly added, thinking of her bargain-basement honeymoon to Madison, Wisconsin.

"I can't stand the downtown hotels here," Rick said. "I travel so much that I need some sort of break. This place really does it for me." The light played off his hair, making it look inky, emphasizing the blue of his eyes. After nine hours of negotiating, he looked tired.

"You look tired," Marcia said.

"You don't. You look terrific," came the reply from the extraordinarily attractive man sitting across from her.

"Tell me more," she said playfully.

"I will," he said, looking her in the eye. "Let's make love."

Marcia blushed furiously. She was speechless.

A tall, gawky teen-ager with a pony tail came by for their order.

"I think we changed our minds, Miss," Rick said, not missing a beat. "We're leaving."

The waitress shrugged and walked off. Rick rose and picked up their briefcases in one hand, taking Marcia's hand in the other.

"What do you think they have room service for, my dear?" he whispered in her ear as they strolled toward her cottage.

At the door, she found her tongue. "Are you serious?" she said. She couldn't believe this handsome, successful man was propositioning her, a mere female foot soldier in the real estate trenches.

"Marcia," he groaned. "How can you ask a man a question like that?"

She felt hot and uncomfortable. Yet she wanted him so much that she just blushed some more and opened the door. What about Gin, she thought. He could wait until tomorrow.

"Marcia, this is the first time I've seen you so quiet," he said. He ruffled her hair. Her face flushed. "You act like you've never been propositioned before."

She took a deep breath to steady her nerves. "Never by someone I've wanted this badly," she said quietly. She threw her arms around his neck and kissed him passionately.

After about five minutes, they tossed their clothing on the floor and slid under the covers. Rick was as glorious in the nude as he was in his clothes. He was a tender and affectionate lover; she responded to him almost too quickly. A good real estate deal and a great lover, all in twenty-four hours. This must be a dream, Marcia thought.

But when she woke at six-thirty, he was still there, next to her, his dark, hairy arm curved over his head on the pillow. She watched him sleeping and wondered how she could do this to Gin.

Rick woke up and smiled at her. They made love again, with as much passion as the night before. Gin would never know, she thought. Rick would be her private treat; he would provide the pleasure that would make her marriage bearable, at least until she could figure out what to do next.

They barely made the nine o'clock flight back to Chicago. For the first fifteen minutes on the plane they held hands and occasionally kissed. Then Rick started to talk about the deal. Marcia wanted to talk about the two of them, but Rick was now all business.

He kissed her on the forehead. "Enough fun and games," he said and took some papers out of his briefcase. "Back to the salt mines."

For the rest of the flight, he was absorbed in the joint-venture agreement. She stared at a page of *Time* magazine without reading a word.

Gin would find out. Husbands could pick up that kind of thing. He would suspect. Was she ready to throw him over for another man? Was Rick the other man? Was she ready to give up on her marriage?

The questions spun round and round her head. Finally, she tapped Rick on the shoulder.

"Hmm?" he said, still reading.

"What am I going to tell my husband?" she said.

"Nothing. Why should you tell him anything?" Rick said without looking up. He flipped the document to the next page.

"He'll find out," Marcia said in a whisper. She felt the entire plane was listening.

"So what? So let him find out," Rick said, setting down the agreement. "Really, Marcia, if you were happily married you wouldn't be fooling around anyway. So why worry what he thinks now?"

She was shocked at his bluntness.

"Well, I'm very confused right now," she said, pursing her lips. "I really don't know what to do. I've never done anything like this before, you know, I mean being married."

Rick smiled. "Don't worry," he said. "There's a first time for everyone. It will sort itself out, okay?" He smoothed out his papers in front of him and turned back to his work.

She stared at her magazine again. Five minutes later, she tapped him on the shoulder again.

"Now what?" he said, annoyed. "You know, I have to digest this document for an acquisitions committee meeting this afternoon. If I don't do it now, I don't know when I'll have a chance." He sounded as if he were talking to a bothersome child. "We sort of took up a lot of time with our little toss in the hay remember?"

Marcia ignored the jab.

"You're not married," she said in a witchy tone. "You're divorced. You don't have to worry about hurting a third party. I do."

"Marcia, believe me, he's a big boy," Rick said, intently. "If your marriage was meant to break up, then it will. If it wasn't, it won't."

Marcia puzzled over that one for a few moments.

"Don't worry about it," he continued. "Getting divorced is no big deal. I've been through it. You survive.

"Besides," he said, "you get a hell of a lot more time for your work. . ." He chucked her under the chin, ". . . and for playing around with some very pleasant people of the opposite sex, with no strings attached."

He laughed. Marcia laughed too, nervously. He turned back to his document and she continued to stare sightlessly at her *Time* magazine. She turned the page every now and then to make it look like she was reading, but her insides were churning.

By the time they reached Chicago, she was a puddle of anxiety. Rick was relaxed and ready for his meeting.

"Why don't you take the afternoon off?" he said, looking at her white face. "I think all that travel has done you in."

He helped her into a cab. "I'll see you tomorrow, early," he said, closing the door. "Get in by seven-thirty. We have lots to do." He flashed his bright smile.

Then he picked up his tube of blueprints and loped down the line of cabs waiting for fares.

*   *   *

Gin was sitting in front of the fire, stroking Karen's neck with one hand and her left breast with the other, when he heard the key in the front door.

They were stark naked; their clothes littered the floor. "Oh, my God," he gasped, springing off the couch and looking at the clock on the mantelpiece. It said four-forty-five.

"That cretin boss of hers must have let her off early."

Karen stared at him in disbelief.

"We got to get you out of here," he whispered in panic.

Karen pulled on her black lace panties, skirt and sweater; Gin stuffed her bra and stockings into her briefcase. Then he rushed their two wine goblets back to the kitchen and plumped up the sofa. Marcia pounded on the door.

He thanked his lucky stars: from some primitive instinct of the unfaithful husband, he had double-locked the door from inside.

"Gin, Gin honey, it's me," Marcia called, rattling the door. The curtains were drawn over the front window; she couldn't see a thing.

Gin and Karen raced to the bedroom. Karen ran like a half-hobbled horse: she was trying to put her snow boots on while she ran.

Marcia continued to pound on the door. "Gin, open up, it's me," she called loudly. "Are you all right in there?" she yelled. She was too tired to care what the neighbors thought.

"I'm coming, Marcia, I'm coming," he yelled back from the bedroom. "Just let me get my bathrobe on."

The pounding stopped. Either she had heard him, Gin thought, or she was coming around the back to get in. Oh, well, he had to take the chance.

He slid open the glass door in the bedroom. Karen kissed him and slipped out the door. She ran across the back yard and pushed through the hedge, leaving foot-steps in the light snow.

Thank God she had parked on the next street, Gin thought, yanking the drapes over the door. To think that he had made fun of her precautions. What if she hadn't. . . ?

He hurried to the front door, took two deep breaths and opened it. There stood Marcia, a bedraggled brown-haired woman in a rumpled suit, holding a briefcase and surrounded by luggage.

"Hi there, stranger; I'm home from the wars," she said, dragging her suitbag inside. "Christ, I thought you were never going to open the door." She noticed his bathrobe. "What's the matter? You sick?"

His heart thudded, but he tried to look sick and sleepy. "I think I have the flu," he said. He coughed a dry little cough. "So I came home and crawled into bed."

She looked at the fire, blazing in the grate.

"Well, first I made a little fire to cheer me up," he said. "I felt chills. Then I felt so bad I went to bed anyway. I was asleep when you knocked."

He glanced at her to see if she believed him. She looked concerned.

"Poor thing," she said, kissing him on the cheek. "You need some chicken soup or something. Maybe there's a can of it. . ." She began to walk toward the kitchen.

The kitchen! The wine glasses were still there, one with lipstick on it.

"No, no, no," he whispered urgently. "I'm not hungry at all. I just want to go back to bed."

Marcia stopped and turned back to him. "Must have been some dream you were having," she said playfully.

"Yeah," he said, "she was gorgeous."

She looked at him wistfully.

"In fact, I was dreaming about you," he said, helplessly. Anything to keep her out of that kitchen.

Marcia laughed weakly. Gin was coming on to her, even with the flu. And the last thing she wanted to do was make love to him. She felt sick with guilt.

"Well, I'm kind of tired myself, too," she said, sinking onto the couch in front of the fire.

"Let me get you a glass of wine and you can tell me about your trip," Gin said eagerly.

"Oh, I'll get it—you're not feeling well."

"No, no. No problem at all, no problem at all," he said, hurrying into the kitchen. "In fact, I just might have some my-self," he called back to her. The way his nerves were twanging, he could use it. He wiped the lipstick off Karen's wine glass, still filled with Burgundy. No use throwing out good wine, he thought. He brought it out to Marcia.

They sat a respectful foot apart on the sofa. Gin felt as though he were on a date with a painfully correct spinster.

Her trip had been uneventful, even boring, she said.

So were his three days alone at home, he said.

They spent the evening as polite strangers would in a crowded boarding house, carefully asking permission to turn on the television or change a radio station. They dined on grilled cheese sandwiches and canned tomato soup, each reading a section of the paper.

Gin went to bed early to avoid Marcia, but he couldn't fall asleep. When she came to bed about eleven-thirty, he pretended to be asleep.

Each tossed all night in an agony of self-doubt, wanting to flee to opposite ends of the house. Instead, they stayed anchored in bed.

The next morning, they looked haggard. They said little over breakfast, though Gin grumbled when he had to drive Marcia to catch the six-thirty a.m. train for the city.

"You're right," Marcia said, as he drove her through the dark streets to the station. "We should get another car." How could she carry on her affair with Rick if she didn't have the freedom of her own set of wheels?

Gin was surprised, but pleased. If they had another car, he would have more freedom to see Karen. He agreed, pecked Marcia on the cheek, and waved to her as she walked to the platform.

What had he ever seen in that woman?

How long could this comedy continue?

TWENTY-FIVE

They were both relieved when Marcia left for Houston two days later. "I'll be gone four days, but I'll call," she told Gin when he dropped her off at the airport on Sunday night.

"Okay. Sure," he said, coughing into his handkerchief.

"Take care of that flu or cold or whatever it is."

"I will."

They stood self-consciously on the sidewalk outside the United terminal. Gin pecked her on the cheek.

"Have a good trip. I'll see you late Thursday, then?"

"Yeah, right," she said. "I get in late; I'll get a cab home. I should be home about ten."

"Sounds good." He fidgeted with his keys. "You sure you don't want me to help you carry your stuff to the gate?"

"Oh no. No. That won't be necessary," she said, quickly. "You'd have to park the car and everything. It's too much bother." She was meeting Rick at the gate.

"Okay, then. I'll see you Thursday night," Gin said.

She picked up her suitbag and headed off for her flight.

Gin waved solemnly until she was out of view. Then he jumped in the car and drove to Karen's. Four nights without Marcia meant four nights with Karen. He could hardly contain his joy.

*   *   *

Karen lived over a dry cleaner's shop off the main street of South Elgin, a dying old town just beyond Chicago's furthest suburbs. She had a two-bedroom apartment with a claw-footed bathtub and windows that leaked streams of cold air in the winter. None of the doorways stood square, and the old woodwork was gouged and covered with many layers of pastel paint. The place lacked central heating: an ancient space heater took up a corner of the tiny living room.

"I would love to move," Karen had said when Gin had first seen her place—and blanched. "But where can I go on ninety-five hundred a year?" Tommy's father, a musician and department store clerk in St Louis was way behind on his two hundred dollar monthly child support payments. Besides, he had re-married; he had two children by his second wife.

"If I get money from him once every six months, I'm doing great," Karen had said bitterly. "Tommy and I get by, but not by much."

She could live in a tent in the park, for all he cared, Gin thought, bounding up the steep stairs to her flat. He knocked on the door hard. Tommy had the volume on the TV turned up high; the sound of canned laughter filled the hall. He knocked again.

Karen came to the door, clad in a pair of jeans, a worn flannel shirt and a stained apron; a heavy plait of blonde hair hung over one shoulder. The smell of hamburger cooking filled the apartment.

"Four days, Karen, four days," he said, opening his arms and lifting her.

"My God," Karen said, kissing him on the nose. "What a honeymoon."

"When can I carry you off? The car's downstairs."

"Don't be silly," she said. "I can't just run off with you now; I've got Tommy to take care of."

"What?" He dropped her. For the month they had been lovers, Karen had gone to Gin's house, parking Tommy with a baby-sitter or a neighbor.

"Oh, come on in," she said, leading him by the hand into her living room. "We can stay here. It's not that bad."

Tommy lay in front of the old TV, his head propped up on his hand. He was a skinny little seven-year-old with his mother's heavy blonde hair and his father's flat moon face.

"How you doin', Tom," Gin said jovially.

Tommy ignored him.

"Thomas," his mother hissed.

"I'm fine, yeah, I'm fine," he said, without looking away from the TV. He was watching a rerun of *The Jeffersons*. Occasionally, he let out a tinny laugh.

Gin wanted to ring his scrawny little neck. In the four weeks he had been sleeping with Karen, Tommy had never been anything but sullen toward him.

Karen drew Gin into the kitchen.

"He has a hard time, you know, without a father," she said. She looked at Gin with her wide green eyes. In the bright fluorescent light, she looked tired, "I really worry about him a lot. He really needs a father," she said sadly.

"Is that an invitation?" he said, a touch of irritation in his voice.

"Of course not," she snapped, turning her back on him and returning to the stove. A pot of sauce for sloppy joes bubbled and splattered on the back burner. She covered it and started slicing up Wonder Bread hamburger buns on her tiny kitchen counter.

"It's just that you have to realize that I'm not some young single chickie," she said, slicing and piling buns. "I can't go running off whenever I want with whomever I wish and not have to worry about anything. It's hard when you're a single mother." There was a note of bitterness in her voice that Gin didn't like.

"Hey, I'm sorry," he said, nuzzling behind her ear. "I didn't mean to be nasty, it's just that. . ."

"It's just that what?" she said, turning around and looking at him angrily.

"It's just that the kid makes me mad. He doesn't like me at all and he doesn't even try to hide it."

"Well, if your parents had divorced when you were five and you were living just above the poverty line with your mother in some slum, you wouldn't be too happy about it either," Karen said. "Besides, you've got to make an effort to know him."

"Karen, I'm civil to him. What more do you want?"

"Well you should be nicer to him."

"I am nice to him," Gin said. He put his arms on her shoulders. "But I'm interested in his mother, not him."

It was definitely the wrong thing to say. Karen's mouth took on a distinctly unfriendly expression.

"Uhh . . . I mean I can get to know him later," Gin back-pedaled.

Karen pulled herself up to her full five foot four inches. She pushed Gin's hands off her shoulders. "You take me, you take my kid," she said stiffly.

She reminded Gin of a Roman matron, throwing her cape around her children while the barbarians moved in to rape her. He was apparently cast as a barbarian.

"For God's sake," he said angrily. " What's gotten into you?"

Suddenly, the bitter woman disappeared. In her place, the laid-back California girl with the musical laugh and sun-golden hair returned.

"Oh," she said lightly, "I just get kind of nuts about my kid every now and then. We mothers do that." And she looked at him with her warm eyes and laughed her musical laugh.

Gin felt a little dizzy at the transformation. He kissed her on the neck. Soon he was ready to make love to her right on the kitchen floor, but she insisted on feeding him and Tommy supper: sloppy joes, potato chips and Coca-Cola.

Tommy refused to talk to him all through dinner; Karen refused to let Gin make love to her until Tommy went to bed at eight-thirty. They sat all evening on the couch, holding hands and watching the bad situation comedies Tommy selected on TV. Gin wondered if you could die from blue balls.

When Tommy went to bed, Gin immediately drew Karen into her bedroom. They made love on her thin mattress. Then they did it again, and again.

The next morning, they awoke, tired and late. They dressed quickly; Karen got Tommy ready for school. She was tucking in his shirt just as Gin came out of the bathroom. Tommy looked sullen; his mother looked drawn and weary. She zipped him into his jacket and whispered something in his ear, but his belligerent expression remained unchanged.

When she saw Gin looking at them, she smiled her happy smile.

To Gin, it seemed out of place. For the first time in a month, he wondered who the real Karen Gillette was.

*   *   *

That night and the next, Karen refused Gin's advances while her son was still awake. It drove Gin wild.

Karen and Tommy sat before the television set, Karen grading multiple-choice grammar tests and reading student themes, Tommy watching TV. Gin wondered how she could concentrate. He did his grading in the kitchen.

Karen didn't talk much to her son. It looked to Gin as though she just enjoyed breathing the same air as Tommy.

Gin said that the kid wouldn't care if they disappeared into the bedroom for a while or went out to eat. But Karen refused.

"I'm a working mother," she said firmly. "My son needs to have me around even if we don't even talk. He needs me just to be there for him."

The two of them sat together for hours. Occasionally Karen put aside her papers and picked up her knitting. Gin was furious. Four days alone with her lover and she was knitting!

Tommy was beginning to perk up. A smirk replaced his sullen stare. He even mumbled hello to Gin and volunteered a sentence or two about what had gone on in school that day.

"I'm so glad you two are getting along better," Karen said, after dinner on Wednesday. Tommy had described, in excruciating detail, the Christmas decorations at school. Karen listened attentively; Gin played with his peas.

After Tommy went to bed that night, Gin decided it was time for a little talk with his mother.

"Karen," he said, drawing her close to him on the couch, "don't you sometimes feel the urge to just break out of this rut?"

"What rut?" She set aside her fifth period essays.

"I mean, don't you get bored sitting around here with Tommy, watching TV and grading papers?"

"Sometimes," she replied, "but not usually." She laughed. "To tell you the truth, I kind of like it. I'm really a homebody at heart." She smiled happily and tickled him under the ribs.

He squirmed, looking at her pathetic little apartment. It would really take dedicated domesticity to want to stay home in this dump, he thought.

"When are we going to spend the night at my place?" he asked.

"Oh, now and then," she said lightly, tickling him again.

"Stop that," he said, pushing her hands away. "How about spending the night the next time Marcia's out of town? Probably next week sometime."

"Oh, we'll see," Karen replied.

"Karen," Gin said, sternly. "I don't want to sit around here watching TV with you and your son every night."

She turned on him suddenly. "Well, what do you suggest?" she said acidly. "Burying him in the backyard like an old bone? He's my son. He needs his mother."

"I know that, " Gin said. "But I need his mother, too. I can't stand sitting around here all night watching soapy TV shows and waiting for him to go to bed.

"We're adults, Karen," he continued. "We can't talk with a seven-year-old all night. I mean things were going great for the first month. Now we have to be chained to Tommy with everything we do."

"Don't be ridiculous," she said angrily. "We're not chained to Tommy. And that first month at your house was just our honeymoon. We can't live our whole lives like that, in some fancy-dancy house, climbing in and out of bed all the time."

Gin thought it was a great idea, but he was silent.

"We've got responsibilities," Karen continued. "Mine is my son."

"I understand, but I think you're overdoing it."

She sighed, pulled back from him, and spoke softly. "Look, Gin, I like you a lot. But you have to get used to Tommy. He comes with me. If we get married or something, you would be his stepfather."

It was the first time either of them had spoken of marriage. There was an embarrassed silence.

"You'd get used to him," Karen said. "Really you would."

"He doesn't like me."

"You'll grow on each other."

"No, we won't," Gin said. "Each of us wants you all to himself." He paused. "You know," he said slowly, "if you were pressed, I'd think you'd choose him."

Karen's light laugh returned. "Don't be so melodramatic, my dear," she said.

"I'm not," he said. "I'm being realistic."

She just laughed again. "I have something to tell you," she said playfully. She whispered an obscene limerick in his ear. It involved four farm animals, a tractor and a milkmaid with an insatiable sexual appetite.

"Where'd you hear that?" Gin gasped.

"In a note I confiscated from some kid in senior English."

"My God," he laughed. He reached up and switched off the reading light. They made love on the living room couch.

That night, Karen slept soundly, but Gin was restless. He dreamed that three little boys with freckles and red hair had crawled into Karen's womb. Her body blew up to the size of a house and she waddled off.

The next morning he tried to convince her to come to his place after school. But she had a drama club meeting.

After Karen's cramped apartment, his own house was a relief. Its wide, clean floors and open spaces soothed his eyes. No stale cooking odors here.

He sorted through the mail piled on the kitchen table. In four days, he had been home only to change clothes and feed the cat.

Today's mail brought the usual pile of bills and a letter from the Brookfield school board, asking him to interview next week for a vice principal's job at Brookfield High.

He was pleased; he had answered their ad four months ago and this was the first he had heard from them. Some glaciers move faster, he thought.

How many glaciers would he have to traverse before he found his dream job?

How many women would he have to bed before he found his dream girl?

What if neither dream job nor dream girl existed?

What a profoundly depressing thought.

He made a fire in the fireplace, stacked some classical records on the stereo, and stretched out on the couch.

What a mess. He was half in love with two women, and bored out of his mind at a dead-end job.

He rolled over on the couch and buried his face in a bolster. He hadn't even thought of marrying Karen, yet that would be inevitable if he went on seeing her.

He was a monogamist. He wanted one woman, and just one. But which one? He had to choose.

He couldn't. Not now. Not yet.

He stared at the fire. Then he dragged himself into his office in the back bedroom and looked at the pile of job leads and ads he had been meaning to follow up on. One thing he did know: he had to get out of Pleasantview High and classroom teaching. Karen had been a welcome distraction. Now it was time to pick up the rope and start pulling again, although it felt anchored to bedrock at the other end.

Thirty-one years old this month and he still wasn't settled. Maybe his father was right. He was a failure. They never talked about it any more; they had tired of open warfare. And Marcia was out of town so much, he hadn't talked to her about anything substantial in days. Even Harvey was probably bored with his complaints.

Harvey. He hadn't seen him for a month, an eternity. They had had dinner at a Mexican restaurant in the city. Gin walked out of his office into the kitchen and dialed Harvey's phone number.

"Long time no see, stranger," he said when Harvey picked up the phone.

"Hey there, goofball. I was just thinking of you."

"How about tipping a few?"

"Tonight?"

"Why not? I'm lonely and blue in the suburbs. And it's only six p.m."

"Tsk, tsk. Let me check with the social secretary." Harvey cupped his hand over the phone and called to Dominique. "Okay," he said. "The troops are quiet tonight."

They agreed to rendezvous at the Dog Run Inn in forty-five minutes. Gin hung up the phone and went out to the car.

TWENTY-SIX

When Gin walked in, Harvey was sitting at a corner table, drinking a beer. It had been almost a year since Gin had seen the place, but nothing had changed. The Dog Run was as dirty and tired as ever. Only Harvey looked different. He was getting fat, even fatter than he had been a month ago. Harvey shook Gin's hand firmly.

"You're late. I thought you stood me up for another girl," he said in a falsetto.

"How you been, you little fairy?"

"Comme ci, comme ça. A draft for my buddy here," Harvey called to the barmaid, a plump young woman in tight jeans and a shirt that said "Eat me."

"Harvey, this is truly a dump. What did we ever see in this place?" Gin said, looking around. The cheap paneling was peeling off the walls.

"It's the closest bar to that Jesuit insane asylum where I now toil alone," Harvey said. He plunged his hand into a bowl of pretzels. "I miss you pal. The place is no laughs anymore."

"Sorry, Harve, I'm not exactly yukking it up where I am either."

"Eat Me" waddled over with Gin's beer. He ordered a hamburger and belted down half his beer. "So," he said, "what's new on the frontiers of Catholic education?"

"The usual crap," Harvey said. He ran his hand over his balding head. "Oh, wait, there is something new. We now have mandatory daily mass for all students."

"Good God! That's medieval."

"Faculty too," Harvey said. "We're all there at seven-thirty a.m. to get right with God."

"How can Dotson get away with it? Half the kids aren't even Catholic. The faculty is almost pagan."

Harvey shrugged. "I think he's trying to win points with the new Cardinal."

"How's everyone taking it?"

"Badly. The kids complain, but so what, right? The staff's enraged. But what can we do?" He shrugged again and swirled the beer in its glass.

"You know," he said softly. "I've just about had it there. Dotson has been hard on my ass this last month. He wants me to use a new textbook for European history, written by some deranged Jesuit.

"I can understand if the book had a Jesuit point of view; the one I use now has that. But this guy misrepresents facts. It's awful."

Harvey's face flushed. "You should see the cover-up he does on Huguenot persecutions in France. And that's just for starters. It's galling. I can't teach from that book, I just can't do it."

"So what does Dotson say?"

"What do you think?"

" 'Bugger off,' in Church Latin?"

"In so many words," Harvey said, crunching on a pretzel. "He told me the book contained the latest historical discoveries. I told him it was a disgrace to Catholic historians."

"And?"

"And he told me if I thought that way I could teach somewhere else next year." Harvey looked at Gin with anguished eyes.

"That little SOB," Gin said. He polluted the air over the table with a string of epithets. Then he slammed his fist on the table.

"God, I hate that," he said. "You work your ass off on a course. You pour yourself into your kids. You try to get the best books and materials you can. And then the administration blows you out of the water with crap like this." Gin's eyes were flashing.

"You're the best damn teacher they have at that school, Harve," he said. "And Dotson treats you like you're the janitor. If I ever get a chance to run my own school, shit like that would never happen. Never. Teachers would be treated like professionals."

He slammed his fist down on the table once more. It scared the barmaid who had just arrived with his hamburger. They ordered another round of beer.

The barmaid picked up their empty glasses. Harvey pursed his lips and played with a pretzel and Gin poured catsup on his hamburger. They felt deflated.

For about five minutes, they watched the hockey game on the TV over the bar. A Canadian gorilla on the Edmonton team ground one of the Chicago Blackhawks into the boards. "I'd like to do that to Dotson," Gin said.

"You and me both," Harvey cleared his throat. "Say Gin, I've got an idea I wanted to bounce off you."

"Yeah?" The referee penalized the gorilla. While the fans booed, he skated off into the penalty box.

"How'd you like to run your own school?"

"Yeah, sure. Very funny. Maybe in my next life." A Chrysler commercial came on. The barmaid returned with their beers and Gin took a deep draught of his.

"I mean how'd you like to run you own private high school? You could be chief administrator."

"What are you talking about, Harve?" Gin said with irritation, turning to him. " Are you on drugs?"

Harvey laughed nervously. "I was talking to my Uncle Walter last week, telling him about my run-in with Dotson. I like Uncle Walter; always have. He's an investment banker here in Chicago, knows people with money. Plus he's got a pile of his own and he handles mine.

"So anyway, Walter appreciates education. He reads history a lot. So, we were having a great talk about the *Memoirs of the Duc de Saint Simon* when I told him about Dotson and me. He thinks about it for a while and then he says, 'Why don't you start your own school, Harve? I think there's a market for it. And I think I can get you the money.' "

Gin's jaw dropped. The televised screams of the hockey fans faded into the background. He moved to speak, but Harvey shushed him.

"Wait, there's more," he said softly. Gin felt as though they were part of some conspiracy. "So Walter tells me that rich people in Chicago are fed up with Latin and Parker and the other couple private high schools. They've got long waiting lists. And lots of parents don't even like the schools. Too stuffy and full of themselves. Latin is cut-throat competitive. Parker is for the touchy-feely crowd. Learn to spell by finding yourself.

"The public schools are out of the question, even the magnet schools. 'Factories for idiots,' Walter calls them.

"People don't want to send their kids to prep schools way out East. Besides the prep school is so inbred. Who wants to turn out clones of the Kennedys?"

Harvey paused to take a sip of his beer.

"So, I told Uncle Walter, 'Look, I don't want to run a school; I just want to teach in peace to bright kids who want to learn. But I have this friend. . .' " He smiled at Gin.

"Harve, this is a joke, right?" Gin said.

Harvey shook his head no.

Gin sat speechless for thirty seconds. Then he jumped up from the table, grabbed Harvey's hand and pumped it wildly. The entire bar turned and stared at them. "Christ Almighty, what news! Why didn't you tell me sooner?"

"Well, it's pretty pie-in-the-sky. I can't really believe it myself. And I did try calling you last week. But you were never home."

Gin thought of Karen. She was immediately displaced by visions of ivy-covered buildings, contented teachers, happy students and a glowing parent association raising money to buy computers for the school. His school.

A cloud floated by.

"Harve, I don't have enough experience," Gin said. "I'm only thirty-one years old. The investors would never stand for me."

"If Walter likes you, they will," he said. "And Walter will like you."

"Jesus H. Christ," Gin whistled. "This calls for a celebration." He called the barmaid and ordered another round of beer—the expensive imported kind.

Then he pelted Harvey with questions. Who was this Uncle Walter? What was he like? Who would the investors be? How much would it all cost? How do they get certified? Who would be on the board of directors?

"Gin, stop it," Harvey said. "This is all stuff we've got to talk to Walter about. I don't know anything about this stuff."

"When can I meet him?"

"Saturday night? He's coming to dinner."

"We'll be there with rings on our fingers and bells on our toes," Gin said. He took a pile of bar napkins and pulled a pen from his pocket. "Now look, Harve, I have a few ideas already about how we should go about this. . ." He began making lists on the napkins, sketching out the buildings and facilities they would need, his ideas for curricula and, among other things, the teachers they could hire.

They talked and talked. Gin would have talked all night, but Harvey remembered that he had a wife and kids at home, and tomorrow was a school day. At midnight they shook hands and Gin floated back to Barrington in a daze.

Marcia was already asleep, her luggage thrown open loosely on the floor next to her dresser. She was normally neat and orderly; Gin thought she must have been exhausted to leave her things in a mess. He tiptoed to the bed: she looked so innocent, curled up on her side of the bed, breathing softly. Sort of the way sleeping lions resemble big house cats, Gin thought. Until they wake up.

He washed and undressed quickly and slipped in beside her. She stirred, rolled toward him in her sleep and looped her arm around his neck. He kissed her forehead. She murmured and then turned over with her back toward him. He curled himself around her and fell asleep.

TWENTY-SEVEN

Marcia was exhausted; she slept badly that night. She dreamed she was standing in a giant airport, booked on four flights at once. But she didn't know which one she was supposed to take.

Men who looked like Rick strode purposefully past, going to their planes. They wore expensive dark suits and carried small luggage made of imported leather. She lugged a dented Samsonite suitcase and an ironing board.

She woke with a start, her heart pounding. Where was she? Atlanta? Houston? Raleigh-Durham?

No. She was home. She exhaled in relief. The clock on her night table said five-fifty-five; the alarm would go off in five minutes. She turned it off and looked at Gin. His sandy head was buried in his pillow. Leaning over, she kissed him on his warm cheek; he smelled of sleep.

Four days of airports, hotels, rented cars and heavy meals had dampened her enthusiasm for Rick and real estate. Maybe absence does make the heart grow fonder: Gin looked better than ever. At least he stood still for a while.

She ran her hand lightly down his back. He shifted in his sleep. She lay back against the pillows and stared into the wintry gloom of the bedroom.

She had shared Rick's bed on this trip. Every morning he jogged for forty-five minutes. He was shaved and dressed before she even opened an eye.

"Come on, kid," he said, his handsome face flushed from the exercise. "Time to hit the road." She rolled obediently out of bed and into the shower while he ordered breakfast from room service and reviewed the day's itinerary.

He was a good traveling companion, friendly and good-humored. But their relationship was more like brother and sister than lovers. They should have slept in bunk beds, she thought, baseball pennants on the wall over his and a stuffed doll on hers. The first night, they had sex, with a pleasant passion. From then on, it was all business.

They spent all day looking at shopping centers and office buildings and all evening dining out with the people who were trying to sell them to Delta. They ate rich food and talked real estate until midnight or later. By the time they went to bed, they had only enough energy left for an affectionate kiss.

Rick needed five hours' sleep; Marcia needed eight. Unfortunately, they worked on Rick's schedule. To catch up, she slept on airplanes and catnapped in the back seats of cars. In Atlanta, she fell asleep on the couch in the ladies' room of an expensive restaurant. After she'd been gone twenty minutes "powdering her nose," Rick sent the waitress to find her. When she returned to the table, sheepish and disoriented, Rick laughed good-naturedly.

Marcia sighed. Time to get moving again. Rick expected her at the office at seven-thirty to go over the numbers on the Raleigh-Durham shopping center. Next week they were off to the West Coast for three days.

Thank God it was Friday. If she slept all day Saturday, she might shake her exhaustion.

She pulled herself out of bed, eyeing her rumpled clothing and suitcase with distaste. She would clean it up tomorrow, along with her marriage.

She dressed quickly, called the Barrington Cab Company and scribbled a note to Gin: "See you for dinner at 7? Love, M." She grabbed her briefcase and just made the six-fifty train.

She watched a sleepy-eyed commuter settle into the seat in front of her and thought of her phone calls home. She had called Gin all three nights, around eleven. She had felt virtuous, calling in to show her wifely concern. To her annoyance, he hadn't been home any night. Where had he been? Where had he been last night?

Out with friends? With Harvey? Harvey wouldn't party four nights in a row; Gin didn't have any casual drinking friends. At least he hadn't had any in the past.

All sorts of things were probably happening to him that she knew nothing about. Important things. But he would tell her the important things, wouldn't he?

If she was ever home he might.

She stared at the leaden sky, tinted yellow by the train window. She was destroying her marriage, she thought. The traveling, the long hours, and the exhaustion were doing it. Rick was just a pleasant side show.

Is this what she wanted? She leaned wearily against the train window.

She awoke in the downtown station, shook the sleep from her head, and jammed herself on a shuttle bus for North Michigan Avenue.

Delta's offices, on the forty-fifth floor of the Hancock Building, were still dark. She let herself in with her magnetic pass card and walked across a thick Oriental carpet in the reception area.

Solitary lights gleamed from several offices on the floor. Some worker bees were at it already, she thought, heading for the light shining out of Rick's office.

She walked in, dropped her briefcase, and gave him her best Girl Scout salute.

"Private Bernthal, reporting for duty, sir," she said. "Permission to collapse on the carpet?"

Rick looked up from his desk, the white walls of his office setting off his black hair and blue shirt. He radiated crisp energy and good health.

"Why not try the couch, Bernthal?" he said. "It's a lot more comfortable. How you doin' this morning?"

"I'm dead on my feet, thank you."

Rick chuckled.

Marcia saluted again, threw her coat on the couch, and plopped down after it. The couch was made of exquisite pearl-grey leather. From it, she could look out the windows of Rick's office, all the way north up the lakefront. The lake was a grey frozen expanse blending into a grey frozen sky.

"Well, I got the rent rolls for you on the Osceola Green Center," Rick said, sorting through some piles on his desk. "And

I've got a pro forma on the Ashforth Court deal. If we can finish these today, we can go over those West Coast deals on Monday.

"Henderson promised me an engineer's report on that San Jose project, so we can take the numbers from that. . ." His voice droned on, Marcia half-listening as she stared blankly at the grey lake. "Hey, wake up over there," he said, annoyed.

"What? Oh, I'm sorry," she said, trying to shake her lethargy. She just didn't like talking real estate at seven-thirty in the morning. "I need some coffee. I haven't had my fix yet."

"Ah, ha. No wonder," he said, standing up behind his desk. "Come on, then. Let's go wake you up."

As she stood up, he moved up behind her, slipped his hand in the front of her blouse, and kissed her behind the ear. "After all," he said, "you're no good to me asleep."

She laughed nervously. They went down to the building's main floor and crossed the street to a coffee shop. They ordered coffee; Marcia ordered some toast and juice for breakfast.

"You don't look so great, Marcia," Rick said with concern, eyeing her closely.

"I'm afraid I'm not holding up too great under all this travel," she said, rubbing her forehead with one hand. "Do we always go at this pace?"

"For the time being. It's a buyer's market. We have to pick up what we can before the market turns again." He sipped his coffee. "When you're hot, you're hot. You know how that is."

Marcia nodded wearily, blowing the steam off her coffee before hazarding a sip. She burned her tongue anyway.

"Frankly, Rick, I don't know how much longer I can take this," she said. "I'm learning a ton of stuff; I love working with you."

She lowered her voice and smiled. ". . .and doing other things with you, but I'm not made to keep going like this."

"This pace will probably only keep up for a few more weeks," he said. "You can hang on until then, can't you?"

"Probably. How much travel would we be down to then?"

"Maybe a day or two a week?"

Marcia groaned.

"Sweetheart, this is acquisitions work," he said, sounding annoyed again. "You want to do deals, you got to get out and talk to the dealmakers."

"I know, I know," she said, waving her hand at him lightly. She took a big bite of toast.

"Besides, you're good at this stuff, damn good at it," Rick said, looking at her intently. "I think it would be a shame for you to get out of it just because of the travel. You'll get used to it. It's only your second month here. And things are a bit hectic right now."

Marcia washed down the toast with a slug of orange juice.

"I mean don't throw it all away because of the travel. Let things simmer a bit," he said. Marcia was surprised to see that he was really upset.

"Well," she said, gingerly. "I have another little problem."

He cocked his head.

"My marriage. The travel is ruining my marriage."

He looked surprised. "I thought sleeping with me was doing that," he said, softly. "In fact, I thought your marriage was over."

"You said that. I didn't," she replied quickly. He looked hurt.

She toyed with the crumbs on her plate. "I'm sorry. Maybe it is over. I don't know, I don't know how I feel about Gin. But I do know that if I keep traveling and sleeping with you, my marriage is finished. I don't know if I want that."

She looked up into his eyes. The intensity in them surprised her. He looked the way he did when he was negotiating a big real estate deal; they had just reached the crucial issue, the one that would make or break the deal. She almost expected him to jump up and start pacing.

"Well, maybe I can help you make up your mind," he said. "I like you a great deal, Marcia. A great deal. It might even be love, I don't know. These aren't feelings I have a lot of practice in.

"But I want you around me all the time. I want to be with you. I want you to live with me." He toyed with a teaspoon. "Leave your husband and move in with me, Marcia." He looked at her intently, his blue eyes drilling through her.

Her mind blurred.

"We're a great team, Marcia, a great team," he said quickly. "We work so well together. And we have such a good time, both in and out of bed. I don't want it to stop. I want to be real partners with you." He looked at her expectantly. "What do you say?"

"Oh, my God." Her stomach flopped over. "Forgive me. I'm in shock," she said, her hand at her mouth. "I don't know what to say."

"How about yes?" He grinned from ear to ear. What a beautiful smile, she thought. What a handsome, successful man. What a handsome, successful, rich pleasant man.

What a workaholic.

She saw her life with Rick spread out ahead of her, years of doing real estate deals and living on planes. They might marry; they might not. In any event, she would be very, very rich.

The only things she would have to give up were free time and the lunatic she was married to.

"No," she said abruptly. "I can't do it. You're a wonderful man, but I can't do it. This whole affair has to stop." She couldn't believe the words coming out of her mouth. "I'm sorry," she said softly.

He sighed and reached for her hand.

"Are you sure you won't change your mind?"

"I don't know, but I don't think so."

They sipped their coffee in silence for a few moments. Then she withdrew her hand and and wiped her lips with a napkin.

"Come on, Super Man," she said. "Back to the salt mines."

He laughed, paid the bill, and they headed back to the office.

*   *   *

Rick was friendly and polite the rest of the day; they finished all they had to do. They could still work together. She would still be his trainee; he would still be professional and easy to work with. But without the sexual play, it wasn't going to be half as much fun getting rich at Delta Realty.

He didn't seem to mind; she minded a lot.

She watched him all day. He was his usual handsome, attractive self, self-confident with property sellers, careful in his review of her analysis of the Osceola Green Shopping Center. He didn't act as though the woman sitting across from him over a computer printout that afternoon had just derailed his emotional life that morning.

How could he be so composed? She could hardly concentrate. It wasn't every day a rich, attractive man asked her to leave Gin and move in with him—and she had turned him down.

Late that afternoon, she went back to her computer terminal and called up a shopping center cost analysis program. Green numbers danced across the computer screen, fading in and out as she typed in the program commands.

Maybe who Rick lived with wasn't that big a deal to him, she thought. It would be nice to have an emotional life with a member of the opposite sex, but it wasn't crucial.

For her, it was.

That was the big difference between them, she thought, staring blankly at her green screen. That's why she had turned him down: she needed a man who needed her. Rick didn't need anyone.

The revelation of the month, she thought wryly. Fortune throws a rich man in her lap; she finds out she was built for love.

Why couldn't she be built for money?

She typed in several commands on the computer keyboard and pushed the "return" bar. The printer chunked out four pages of charts and tables. She pulled them off in a piece and took them in to Rick.

He flashed his dazzling smile at her; she wondered if he practiced in front of a mirror. Then they began reviewing her analysis.

He was friendly and witty.

She felt fat, ugly and unloved. She was married to a bankrupt school teacher who couldn't walk and chew gum at the same time. All they did was fight. She was up to her neck in debt. She was exhausted. Her period was about to start.

And she wouldn't have traded any of it for a life with Rick Matthews.

He looked up from the computer printouts and asked her opinion of the anchor tenants' expense stops.

She smiled broadly. "I haven't the foggiest," she said.

She looked at her watch. It was four-forty-five "Quitting time," she said. "Tune in Monday morning at nine and I'll let you know." She laughed lightly, gathered up her notes, and swung out of his office.

Rick looked perplexed. "Have a good week-end," he called after her.

"I will. You too," came the reply from down the hall.

Then he smiled to himself, shook his head, and went back to his analysis. If he worked hard he could probably finish before his racquetball match at seven with Harry Shwartz.

By six-thirty, the numbers were done. He walked to the wall, flipped off the lights, and sat on the pearl-grey couch, staring at the lights of the city. For fifteen minutes, he cried quietly. Then he wiped his eyes, blew his nose, and headed for the health club.

Harry Shwartz beat the pants off him that night.

TWENTY-EIGHT

When she got off the train at Barrington, Marcia was singing to herself under her breath.

"Camp town races sing dem songs, do-da, do-da," she hummed, scanning the parking lot for Gin and their car. It was already dark and hard to see.

Finally, she spotted the car in the back corner of the parking lot. Gin leaned against the steering wheel, resting his head on his arms.

"Nap time's over. The real estate baroness is home," she said brightly, opening the door and slipping into the passenger seat.

He awoke with a start and stared at her, as if it was the first time he had ever seen her.

"Remember me?" she said, "I'm your wife." She leaned over and kissed him on the cheek.

He rubbed his eyes with his left hand. "Hi," he said.

"Well don't overwhelm me with affection." She slid back to her side of the car. "After all, we haven't seen or talked to each other for about a week. And all you can say is 'Hi'?"

"How about 'How are you?' " he said, looking at her sleepily.

"How about a kiss?" she said.

He leaned over and planted a perfunctory peck on her cheek. "You still sick?"

"No, just tired." He yawned.

"You depressed or something?"

Her animation irritated him. He grasped the steering wheel in both hands and looked straight ahead. Then he turned to her. "Yeah, I'm depressed," he said. "I'm real depressed. I'm depressed about this fucking marriage." He spoke in a low angry voice.

"You're gone for days at a time. I never see you. We never screw. We can't talk without a fistfight. I've just about had it up to my eyeballs with you.

"Then you get off the train, slip into the car, and act like everything's just sweetness and light. 'How are you sweetie? How about a little kiss?' " He mimicked her voice in a high falsetto. "I mean give me a break."

Marcia pressed herself up against the passenger-side door.

"Well, excuse me," she said.

"We've got to talk about this marriage, Marcia. This just isn't working."

Marcia rubbed her forehead with a gloved hand. She rejects Mr Perfect for this guy and he comes out and bites her.

"Right. Well, what do you want me to do?" she said petulantly. "Wave a magic wand and make us happy and millionaires?"

"I don't know. I don't know if I want you to do anything."

"What's that mean?"

"That I've been seeing somebody else."

She caught her breath. Then she looked at his face intently, as if by examining every pore she could discover what was going on. The car was dark, but the lights of the cars leaving the parking lot reflected off his face. She wondered who the hell he was.

"Are you telling me you're having an affair?" she said.

"Yes."

"Oh." She folded her hands on her lap and sat straight up. This was not happening to her. While she was fooling around with Rick, Gin was fooling around with someone else.

"Who is it?"

"Karen Gillette, from school."

"The blonde Nature Girl?"

"Yeah."

"Jesus. Is it over?" She asked icily.

"I don't know."

"You want a divorce?"

"I don't know."

"Shit." She leaned her head against the door, stunned. Then her eyes filled with tears. No Rick, no Gin. She had lost two men in one day. That had to be some kind of record. She sobbed into the door for a minute or two, a dirge to the stream of commuter-filled cars leaving the parking lot.

Gin hardened himself to her crying. He hadn't planned to tell her about Karen like this. In fact, he hadn't planned to tell her anything at all. But when she came hopping into the car with all that phony wifely concern, something had snapped.

He hadn't had a real wife in a month—make that nine months, if you counted the time they were fighting—and he had just had enough. He was getting table scraps from two women. He needed regular meals from just one.

"Oh for Christ sakes, Marcia," he said sharply. "Pull yourself together."

She looked at him, her eyes filled with anger. "Pull myself together? You fucking bastard!" she screamed. "You're cheating on me and I'm supposed to be Miss Cool, Calm and Collected? I'm not supposed to have the nerve to get upset!" Her mascara had smeared under her eyes; she looked like a vision from hell.

"I'm busting my ass to make enough money to keep this whole fucking circus afloat and you're off screwing the Corn Queen. Jesus H. Christ!"

She began to pound his shoulder with both fists. He gripped the steering wheel and stared straight ahead, his body rocking from her blows, his face twitching.

"How could you do this to me?" She screamed. "You bastard! How could you? How could you? How could you?" Then she leaned against the door again. She felt sick.

Gin was shaken. How could he do this to Marcia? How could he let her down like this? Cheating on your wife was really a low-life stunt.

"I'm sorry, Marcia. I really am," he said quietly.

She stared out her window.

"I'm sorry," he said, this time with impatience in his voice. "Shit, what the hell do you want me to say?"

She said nothing. The parking lot was nearly empty. The harsh light from the street lights formed pools on the dirty white snow. She imagined little squirrels with microphones and top hats singing in the spotlights.

Funny what you think about when your life is falling apart.

The noise of the car starting brought her back from the land of animal entertainment.

He shifted into gear and the rear wheels spun on ice as he headed for the parking lot exit.

"Jesus Christ, why did I ever marry a bitch like you?" he mumbled angrily under his breath.

"Why did I ever marry a loser like you?" came the calm reply.

He turned into traffic on the dimly-lit village street.

"Maybe we should just can the whole mess," he said numbly. "Get a divorce."

"Sounds like a good idea to me," she said, retrieving her handkerchief from her purse and blowing her nose.

They wound their way wordlessly home through Barrington's quiet streets.

*   *   *

The five-minute ride home felt like five years, the idea of divorce hanging over their heads like a shroud. When Marcia got out to lift the garage door, she felt so exhausted she could hardly move it.

Imagine being free of Gin forever, she thought, struggling with the door. She could go back to Rick and tell him she had changed her mind. Sure, she'd move in with him. She could go in the house right now, call him, pack a bag, walk out, and never talk to Gin again except through her lawyer.

Leave him with all the bills, she thought viciously. Let him figure out how to pay them for a change. He and the Corn Queen. What in God's name was he doing sleeping with a wimpy woman like that?

That's what she was going to do. Just walk out.

She pushed the garage door up, walked through the garage, and let herself into the house. She threw her briefcase on the sofa and went to the phone. She dialled Rick's home number. It rang ten times, but no one answered. She tried his office line; no luck there either.

She hung up with relief.

Damn it, she wasn't supposed to feel relieved. If she was going to leave Gin, she should feel free, light-footed. She was finally dumping her loser.

She could take up a hobby. Oil painting, perhaps? She would spend long nights alone in front of the fire, feeling self-sufficient and reading good books. The new, independent woman.

Christ, it sounded terrible.

Why couldn't she just cut him out of her life like a kind of cancer?

Because if she didn't, she was going to have to tell him about Rick. She moaned. Couldn't they just get divorced without her saying anything about Rick?

As she sat by the phone pondering this question, Gin walked in slowly, his jaw set square. He hang up his coat on their coat rack and walked by her without a word, heading for the kitchen. She heard him rummaging in the freezer. He was probably looking for a TV dinner, she thought.

"Throw one of those things in for me, would you?" She called to the kitchen.

"Sure."

Without thinking, she sighed deeply, picked herself up, and walked slowly toward the kitchen. It was a magnet drawing her in. She felt drained, as though she was running on her last battery.

Gin was elbow-deep in the freezer compartment of the refrigerator.

"You want chicken or lasagne?" he asked.

"Lasagne."

She shuffled over to the cabinet where they kept their wine and retrieved an unopened bottle of Gallo Hearty Red Burgundy and two wine glasses. Then she sat down heavily at their tiny kitchen table, poured herself a big glass, and put her head in her hands.

Gin flipped on the oven and took the dinners out of their boxes. Maybe he could live without women? He sure couldn't live with them. He could move in to the Elgin YMCA. Oh God.

Well, maybe he really could make it with Karen. He could learn to be a stepfather. Tommy would eventually accept him in a couple years. Karen would probably want another kid by him. He shuddered.

The thought of fatherhood repelled him, not because he disliked children but because he disliked what having children did to women. It pulled them away from their husbands.

All he wanted was one woman, a real partner, all to himself. What the hell was so difficult about finding someone like that?

Maybe he could find a woman like Karen, but without a kid attached?

Yeah, special-order one from Sears, he thought, sliding the TV dinners into the oven. Even if they didn't come with a kid they would want one eventually.

Well, what about Marcia?

He felt sick. What about Marcia. Boy, he had really blown that one. He had cheated on her. She'd never forgive him for that. The marriage was over; she would never trust him again.

Can't blame her, he thought grimly, fishing through a cabinet for a bag of Fritos. If the tables were turned, I'd feel the same way. Shit, what a fool he was.

He poured the Fritos in a bowl, but he didn't feel like eating anything. He left the bowl on the counter and started walking toward the living room. He just wanted to sprawl out on the couch and sleep.

He heard Marcia's voice behind him. "We should talk," she said quietly.

"About what?" he said, not turning around. "You can have the house. I just want the car and the TV." He looked down at the floor, his eyes filling with tears. "I'm sorry about everything. I'm sorry to hurt you like this. I'm sorry it had to end this way. I just can't seem to do anything right."

And he went into the living room. Marcia followed him, two glasses of wine in her hands.

She tapped him on the shoulder. When he turned around, she handed him a glass.

"Here, drink this," she said. Her voice sounded tired and mechanical. "I have something to tell you."

"What is it?" he said, alarmed. Christ Almighty, maybe she was pregnant, on top of everything else.

"Drink first."

He took a big swig of wine.

"Okay, what is it?"

"I've been sleeping with my boss."

He stared at her. The image of a dark-haired man doing unspeakably personal things to his wife's body flashed through his mind. He felt raped and robbed.

He threw his wine in her face.

Then he set the glass carefully down on a table, and slapped her hard across the mouth. "You bitch," he screamed. "You stupid cunt! How could you cheat on me! You're lucky I married you in the first place."

He turned on his heel, grabbed his coat and car keys, and went out the front door. Marcia heard the car start. She sat down in a crumpled pile on the floor, the wine dripping off her face, and her mouth stinging.

She heard the wind rattle the branches of the big oak in their yard.

"Here's to married bliss," she mumbled, toasting herself with her wine.

Then she poured it over the top of her head and cried.

TWENTY-NINE

Gin stopped at the stop sign at the end of their block. His heart pounded and his head hurt. All he could see in his mind was Marcia, naked in bed, making love to a strange man. Over and over again the tape played, their bodies entwined in ecstasy.

It made him sick. He rested his head on the steering wheel.

How could she do it? Was it the money this guy made or what? Maybe this guy was a better lover?

He felt sicker.

The lights of a car coming up behind him reflected in the rear view mirror. Gin turned left and pulled the car off to the curb.

Where did he want to go?

He could go to Karen's. He saw himself sitting on her lumpy couch and trying to pour out his soul while she knitted and Tommy watched *Mash* re-runs on TV.

She would pat his hand and listen uncritically. He could see her warm, comforting smile. She would invite him to spend the night—after she put Tommy to bed, of course.

He should have strangled that kid the first time he met him.

Besides, maybe he wouldn't get a warm welcome. After their fight over Tommy, things had been definitely cooling down. She had been friendly enough the last few days but he had noticed a certain distance in her demeanor. He was being cut out of the running in the great race to be Tommy's stepfather.

Another replay of Marcia and Rick flashed through his head. Now they were running naked through some surf before falling into each other's arms on a white sand beach.

He gritted his teeth.

He could go to Harvey's. No, Harvey and Dominique would be out with friends. It was Friday night. Besides, he and Marcia were supposed to go there tomorrow night for dinner and talk about the school with Uncle Walter.

The school. His big chance and his wife was sabotaging it. How could he put his best foot forward when he wanted to kill her over the main course?

He clenched his fists and pounded them on the dashboard. Shit, shit, shit.

He needed to do something physical. Other than strangle Marcia.

So he did a U-turn and headed for the Triple Crown Bowling Alley out on Northwest Highway.

*　　*　　*

It was a big League night at the Triple Crown, but they kept two lanes open for strays. Gin was lucky. The alley against the far wall was open. He rented shoes, a bright red bowling ball, and bought himself a bag of Fritos and a beer. The dull sound of rolling balls filled the air.

Five young women in team shirts were squealing and bowling with abandon in the alley next to his. Their pink shirts advertised their sponsor: The Paddle-Home Bar, Cary, Illinois. Two of the women hung over the seats at the end of their alley, beers in hand. They gave him wide, warm smiles as he walked by.

"Howdy, stranger," said one of them, a thin blonde in tight jeans.

"Yeah, hi," he mumbled. He hoped they would shut up and leave him alone.

The blonde rolled her eyes to the ceiling and stuck her tongue out. Then she turned to her friend and murmured something. They snickered.

Gin cringed. Goddamn women were laughing at him everywhere he went.

He set down his beer and Fritos, put the ball in the return gutter, and spread out the scorecard on the tiny formica desk. He hadn't bowled since high school and had forgotten the scoring system.

Strikes were X's, spares were slashes, and what did you do with the tiny little boxes in the corner?

"Oh for God's sake, who the hell cares," he said loudly, ripping up the scorecard. All he wanted to do was throw some bowling balls.

He looked up to see three of the pink ladies staring at him in alarm. He smiled broadly. Slowly they returned to their game.

He picked up his ball. It was fire red with gold glitter. A formidable weapon, Gin thought, stepping into his approach. He imagined he was pouring a cauldron of red-hot lava down Marcia's vagina.

With a powerful swing, he released the ball. It bounced on the boards, crossed over to the left, and rolled into the gutter.

The blonde next door laughed loudly.

He glared at her. She stopped abruptly.

His ball popped up in the ball return. With its flame-red color, it stood out easily among the pastel blue and green balls of the Paddle-Home team. He picked up his ball and sent it down the alley with the same powerful roll. This time he picked off the two pins on the far left.

It felt so good watching them fall. Like he'd just knocked out Rick Matthews' two front teeth. He smiled wickedly.

The next time, he swung into his approach with a flourish. The ball rolled smoothly. All the pins tumbled.

"Bingo!" he yelled, jumping into the air and punching his fist into the palm of his other hand; that was all of Marcia's teeth.

He swung and released, swung and released. His balls stopped rolling into the gutter. Each time pins fell, he imagined that he had ripped off some body part of the lovers. There went Rick's penis. Whoops, that was Marcia's breasts. On a strike, he bashed in her head.

Eventually, he tired of his ghoulish game. He began bowling for the fun of it, to see how many pins he could topple. He lost track of time.

Swing and release, swing and release. The fire-red ball popped up in the ball return; he grabbed it and sent it off again. He was getting good at this. His shoulders and arms were warmed up, his hips loose.

Just the way he felt after making love.

He felt sick.

Another videotape of the lovers played in his mind. The body parts he had torn off had grown back. The lovers looked better than ever. Their unblemished bodies writhed on a background of white sheets.

He sat down at the little formica desk and stared vacantly at the other alleys and bowlers.

She was the only woman he had ever really loved—and looked what she was doing to him.

Look what they were doing to each other.

This was insanity. He couldn't live like this. It all had to stop.

He rested his elbows on the desk and buried his face in his hands. A vision of Marcia dancing on their wedding day flashed through his mind. She was lovely, a crown of summer flowers in her hair, her face flushed with happiness and excitement.

Then he saw her on a trip they had taken to Minneapolis two years ago. They had walked through a park with pine trees and a lake and talked about all the things they were going to do with their lives. Her smile, her confidence in him, the way she squeezed his hand and kissed him on the ear, it could have been yesterday.

He felt a lump in his throat.

He saw her in bed at home, curled up against him. Her creamy complexion in the soft morning light, her dark hair against the pillow. A sleeping beauty.

Then he saw her as he had left her only two hours ago: Her face puffy from crying, her eye makeup smeared, and wine dripping off her chin.

They had gone from heaven to hell in a little over three years.

How could they ever set it right again?

When he looked up, the palms of his hands were wet with tears. He turned around. A family of five were waiting stolidly for his alley. The two boys and their younger sister, a little girl of about nine, were eating pizza slices and wandering listlessly in the aisle behind his alley. Their parents sat in plastic chairs and looked bored.

Gin pulled his handkerchief out, blew his nose, and wiped his eyes. He retrieved the flaming ball from the ball return and his half-empty beer bottle from the holder on the formica desk.

"It's all yours, folks," he said, watching the children scramble over each other to get the chair near the desk.

The young women of the Paddle-Home Bar were gone. In their place were four middle-aged men with beer bellies. Their shirts proclaimed them "The Lockhart Tool and Die Lucky Rollers."

Gin wondered if they were happily married.

He wondered if anyone was.

Then he turned in his shoes at the main desk and tried to decide what to do next.

He was tired, but not tired enough to sleep. It was only eight-thirty. Besides, he couldn't face Marcia yet.

He picked up a newspaper lying on a chair and read through the movie listings. If he hustled, he could make the nine-ten showing of *Testament* at the Woodfield Mall Cineplex.

The movie was about people waiting to die from radiation sickness after a nuclear war. The movie had a strange, comforting effect on him. Compared to nuclear holocaust, what's an unfaithful wife and a wretched marriage?

He returned home around midnight, exhausted. The house was dark. He flicked on the hall light and tiptoed into the bedroom.

Marcia was asleep on her back, one pale arm flung over her head. The top buttons of her nightgown had come undone. Her breasts slowly rose and fell with her breathing. She looked so fragile. His heart ached.

Tomorrow. They would deal with it all tomorrow.

He fished his pyjamas out of his bureau drawer and gently slipped off the extra blanket bunched up at the foot of the bed. Then he picked up his pillow and padded back to the living room.

He stretched out on the couch and fell into a deep sleep.

*   *   *

Friday night was as close to hell as Marcia ever wanted to get.

After Gin left, she cried for five minutes, the wine matting her hair into a sticky mess. Then she took a shower, sat down to her lasagne TV dinner, and contemplated her fate.

Gin would probably divorce her and marry the Corn Queen. He was probably at her apartment right now.

Karen gets Gin; Marcia gets no one.

She saw her whole life before her: She would be alone, very, very alone, for a very, very long time.

She had no women friends and no interests besides Gin, her job, and her mortgage payments. If Gin left, no one would care whether she lived or died.

She poured herself a big glass of Gallo Hearty Burgundy.

She saw herself alone at the breakfast table, alone in bed, alone through her whole life, unable to connect souls with a man. She would date; she would have affairs.

But she wouldn't love, with that aching animal need that made you come back, come back, come back as long as there was any chance at all that you could work things out.

She ached for Gin; she didn't ache for Rick Matthews.

What were her chances of finding another man to ache for in this life? Ten to one? Twenty to one? She could be dead by the time she found him.

And, what if, after she found him, she still couldn't make it work?

What if there was something terribly wrong with her?

She set her wine glass down abruptly on the table and stared at her reflection in the kitchen window.

She was a cripple. She needed Gin desperately; she could feel it. But she couldn't make it work. She would never be able to make it work, with any man, anywhere.

She was doomed to a string of continuous, half-hearted affairs that ended badly.

Lord God Almighty. What did she do now?

She comforted herself with a box of Maurice Lenell's mixed assortment cookies.

Maybe she should talk to her mother?

She laughed bitterly; Mary Beth would quote her the tax code on divorce settlements.

A priest? She laughed even harder; he would advise her to get pregnant and pray.

A psychiatrist? She pictured a pinched-looking man asking her about her childhood dreams. What could he know about her real agony today?

Well, what about a marriage counselor?

She popped three chocolate-chip cookies into her mouth, washed them down with wine, and thought about this option.

She envisioned an eager, middle-aged woman with a ceramic duck pinned on her sweater and a practiced, intense look. Probably a social worker. "You've got to try to love each other more," the woman was saying seriously, as if that were any help at all.

Marcia shuddered.

Besides, who needed a marriage counselor if Gin was going to leave her anyway? All she would need would be a padded cell.

She picked up her cookies, walked into the living room, and began watching a documentary on TV about safaris in Kenya. Apparently, the volume of tourists was so great that it traumatized the animals.

She couldn't feel sorry for lions and giraffes; she switched to a Charles Bronson movie on Channel 9. He was bashing someone's head in with a revolver butt.

That's more like it, Marcia thought. He should try it on me; I'd like to be dead.

She finished off her cookies instead.

It was a windy night. Every time the wind rattled the front door or the house creaked, she jumped up from the couch and ran to the window, hoping it was Gin coming home.

It never was.

Eventually, exhaustion caught up with her; she fell asleep on the couch.

At eleven-thirty she woke up and turned off the TV.

This was the first lonely night of her new, lonely life without Gin.

She stumbled into the bedroom and cried herself to sleep.

*　　*　　*

Marcia awoke at noon Saturday, tired from her fitful sleep. Gin wasn't next to her. She hadn't expected him to be, but had hoped anyway. His pillow was gone; he must have slept in the house.

Or else he had taken his pillow and all his clothes and left her.

Her heart pounded. She jumped out of bed and flung open the closet.

All his chinos and button-down shirts were still there.

At least he hadn't run off with the Corn Queen yet.

Marcia picked up her bathrobe and went looking for him. Sunlight flooded the living room, jarring her eyes. It had snowed last night; it was a brilliant, clear day. The light reflected off the snow and through the sliding doors in the dining room.

A folded blanket and Gin's pillow lay on the couch, but he was gone.

She went into the kitchen, and the two other bedrooms, but he was not in the house.

Alarmed, she ran to the front window and pulled the drapes. Maybe she could see car tracks in the snow on the driveway? Then she would know he was gone.

There were no car tracks in the snow on the driveway because there was no snow on the driveway. Gin had already shoveled it.

Now he was working on the far corner of the sidewalk that crossed their property. He looked up, a tall, healthy-looking man in a bright blue ski parka and no hat. His hair was golden in the bright light.

He saw her standing in the living room window, a dark-haired woman in a white bathrobe.

She waved at him.

He waved back.

Her heart leapt.

She glanced around frantically for something to put on her feet. Gin's old rubber boots lay on the boot rug by the front door. She slipped them on her feet, flung open the front door, and ran outside. The boots clip-clopped on the driveway, the loose buckles jangling. The cold air went right through the thin material of her robe.

Gin just stood there, leaning against his shovel.

She clip-clopped down the sidewalk toward him, nearly slipping on a patch of ice. She threw her arms around his neck and buried her head in his chest.

"I'm so sorry; I'm so sorry. I'm really sorry," she mumbled into his parka, her voice choking. "Don't leave me. Please don't leave me. Please don't."

She looked up into his soft blue eyes, her own filling with tears. "I couldn't bear to lose you," she whispered. "I just couldn't bear it."

Then she buried her head into his parka again and wept quietly.

He stood motionless for a moment, feeling her body heaving against his.

He lifted one hand and stroked her hair.

Then he threw his arms around her and hugged her fiercely. He kissed her wildly on her hair, her eyes, her mouth. He could taste her tears.

"Don't worry, Marsh," he whispered hoarsely in her ear. "I'm not going anywhere."

She hugged him even harder.

They stood for about a minute on the sidewalk, just holding each other.

Gin stroked her hair; her crying subsided. She was shivering.

"Come on," she said, wiping her nose on her sleeve. "Let's go inside. My feet are freezing."

They walked up the driveway, their arms around each other's waist. Her boots jangled and scuffed.

The neighbors across the street turned their snowblower back on.

THIRTY

They walked into the house and sat on the couch, their arms still entwined around each other's waist. Marcia leaned her head on Gin's shoulder. The snow from their boots melted into grey puddles on the white throw rug.

They stared into the empty fire grate and said nothing for several moments. Marcia wiped her nose on her sleeve again.

She turned to him suddenly. "Do you really still love me?" she asked, her voice low.

He looked at the woman sitting next to him. Her eyes were red from exhaustion and tears; her tired face was washed-out in the bright sunlight.

"Yes I do, Marsh," he said quietly, stroking her hair again. "God help me, but I still love you."

"I love you, too," she said quickly, her mouth twisting. She looked down and hugged him tightly again. "I love you, Gin. I do love you," she mumbled.

They were quiet a few more moments.

"You're not going to leave me then?" she asked abruptly, looking up again. She looked frightened.

He shook his head no and smiled. He thought of Karen, but her picture faded. She seemed lifeless compared to the woman next to him, squeezing the air out of him with her desperate hugs.

"You're sure?" Marcia whispered.

"Yeah, I'm sure," he said, nodding and looking at her intently.

Her face was expressionless, her eyes huge.

Then she smiled.

"Thank God," she whispered. "I thought I'd lost you for good." She released her tight hug and leaned limply against his shoulder, her eyes closed.

He felt tired.

"Come on, Marsh," he whispered. "Lie down with me."

She sat up in slow motion, slipping her feet out of her oversize boots. Gin took off his parka and boots. He lay down on the couch, pulling her down on top of him.

It felt so good to have her warm weight on him. He ran his hand down her back, down the curve of her buttocks. She sighed; he could feel her breathing slow down into a regular pattern.

They dozed for about ten minutes. The sounds of their neighbors' snowblowers and shovels droned in the background.

Marcia began tracing the outline of his shirt pocket with a finger.

"Gin?"

"Hmmm?"

"Why Karen?"

He sighed deeply. He moved to sit up.

They sat up in a jumble; two couch pillows slipped to the floor.

"It was was actually pretty simple," he said. " Karen was warm, affectionate and available. I really needed a woman and you were never around."

He reached down to the floor and picked up a pillow. "Frankly, Marsh, you've turned into a harpy on me."

Marcia's face flushed.

"If I'm such a bitch, why stay married to me?" she said hoarsely.

"Because I think you deserve another chance."

"*I* deserve another chance?"

"This marriage deserves another chance." He threw the pillow behind his back. "I don't think you're really a bitch at heart. Under all that tough-guy shit you carry around is the woman I'm still in love with.

"I think she would come back if you let her. If you did, I think we could make our marriage work."

Marcia chewed on a fingernail. "Yeah, well," she mumbled.

"You know you're not exactly a prize winner yourself, either," she burst out. "You know why I went off with Rick?"

Gin shrugged.

"Because he took care of himself, made money and he didn't whine. I didn't feel like his damn mother, picking up his life after him wherever he went. He took care of *me* for a change."

"For God's sake, Marsh," Gin said. "You don't take care of me. I'm not your stupid kid."

"Oh yes you are," she replied crisply.

"What do you want?" he hissed. "My balls on a platter?"

"Just a decent-sized paycheck would be a nice start."

"I'm working on it."

He stood up abruptly and went to the kitchen. Frightened, she padded after him in her bare feet.

He put the kettle on the stove and began making coffee. She leaned against a kitchen cabinet.

"Why Mr Real Estate Hot Shot?" he said, measuring coffee beans into the grinder. "You like all the toys he could buy you?"

"That had nothing to do with it."

"Oh really? I don't see you falling for another poor teacher."

Gin turned on the coffee grinder; its noise filled the kitchen. "It seems to me that 'taking care of you' means making lots of money and then giving a big chunk of it to you. That's just high-class whoring."

He turned to her abruptly.

"What do you want to be, Marsh? My wife or Rick's whore?"

She lowered her eyes and said nothing. The question bewildered her.

He plopped a filter into the coffee pot.

"You know," he said, "I think you'd chase after him if he were Bozo the Clown, just so long as he had money and a big important job. I mean who wants to be married to some half-cocked school teacher when you can hop in the sack with a guy with real net worth?"

"That's not fair."

He ignored her.

"The way you follow him around and worship his every word, like he's some sort of God. You practically drool on his feet: all that money right within your reach."

He grabbed her shoulders.

"Just tell me one thing," he said quietly. "How was the sex?"

She pursed her lips. "It's none of your business."

"I'm your husband; it's all of my business."

She shrugged. "It was okay."

He shook her hard.

"All right, it was terrific."

He released his grip and turned away. He lifted the kettle and poured boiling water over the ground coffee. For a moment, she thought he was going to pour it on her.

They listened to the water gurgle through the grounds.

"I don't suppose you and Karen had any problems in the sack?" she said.

"No, not really."

He turned in exasperation and looked at her.

"I don't get it," he said, his voice rising. "First you tell me to stay; you love me. Then you insult the hell out of me. I start to leave and you come begging after me not to go.

"Just what the fuck do you want me to do?" he yelled.

She bit her lip; she felt totally alone and totally humiliated. But the thought of him walking out again was unbearable.

"I'm sorry about those things I said," she said. "I don't know why I say them. They just seem so real to me that I blurt them out."

She stared at the floor.

"I do want to be your wife," she whispered. "But I'm afraid I'm not very good at it. Help me."

She looked up. He stood in the doorway, shaking his head and glaring at her. Then he unzipped his parka and threw it on the couch.

She exhaled in relief.

He walked past her, back into the kitchen, and poured two cups of coffee. When she came in after him, he handed her one.

His face was impassive; she felt lost again.

"Marcia," he said simply. "I can't live like this. You either get off my case and let me live my life or I'm going to leave you. I have absolutely had enough."

She felt her heart sink. "I said I was sorry," she said.

"That's not enough. Stop it or I'm leaving." He glared at her. "And I mean it."

He turned on his heel, went into the living room, and flipped on the football game of the week on TV. The Bears were losing to Detroit, seven to nothing. He lay down on the couch, and began watching the game between his socked feet.

"I bet she was a hell of a lay, long blonde hair spread out across the bed, beautiful long legs. It must have been like screwing Christie Brinkley."

"Marcia, stop it."

"I mean who'd want to come back to a fat little brunette after that," she said icily. "Especially one who was out trying to make a buck and was never around to meet your tender little needs.

"Did she kick you out? Is that why you came back to me, because Karen kicked you out? Because you had no place else to go?"

She took a deep breath. "If that's why you came back I don't want you. I'd rather live alone." The words frightened her the moment they left her mouth.

Gin leaned his head against the overhead cabinet and whistled through his teeth.

"You never miss a beat, Marsh, do you?" he said bitterly. "You're always ready to believe the worst about me. Do you really think that I would come back to you just to take advantage of your paycheck?"

She said nothing.

"Why do you think such a stupid thing?"

She shrugged. It seemed true to her.

"Marcia, if I really wanted a woman with money, I could sure do a hell of a lot better than you."

He went into the living room and headed toward the coat closet.

Marcia followed in a panic. "Where are you going?"

"Out. I've had enough abuse for one afternoon."

She tried to remain cool and aloof, but panic set in as he zipped up his parka. She really *was* going to live alone.

"Don't go," she said, all sense of pride disappearing. "Please don't go."

He looked unapproachable.

She wanted to have a talk with him, but it was clear that he was so angry with her that it was impossible right now. She would have to try later.

She sighed, set down her coffee, and went into the bedroom. On the way, she passed Gin's office. A neat pile of unopened bills rested on his desk. She had insisted on handling their finances; he had gladly agreed. She shuddered. Tomorrow. She would do battle with the creditors tomorrow. She was so tired, she could sleep for two days.

She feel asleep quickly. About five o'clock, Gin came in and clicked on the closet light. She opened one eye. "What are you doing?"

"Changing my clothes. We're invited to Harvey's for dinner."

"What? Now you tell me." She groaned. The last thing in the world she wanted to do was go to a dinner party. But she didn't want to let Gin out of her sight. She moved to get up.

"You don't have to go," he said.

"Well, you're going," she said, sitting up. She felt dizzy. "Don't you want me to go?"

"No, not especially."

She looked startled.

"We're going to be discussing some school matters tonight. I'm sure they'd bore you."

He was right about that, she thought, stretching. Listening to teachers complain about their lot in life was not her idea of entertaining conversation. "But I'd like to be with you anyway," she said. She began to get up again.

"No, Marsh," he said, pushing her gently back down on the bed by her shoulders. "I'd rather go by myself." He didn't want her monitoring his conversation with Uncle Walter, second-guessing him at every turn. He wanted her to leave him alone right now.

He looked at her surprised face. "I need some time off right now. We'll be together tomorrow."

"You're going back to Karen, aren't you?" she said, her voice strained.

The thought struck him as so ludicrous that he laughed out loud.

A look of total confusion spread across Marcia's face.

He laughed even harder.

Her confused look turned to one of vulnerability and pain. He watched her sitting there in her pink nightgown, one strap falling off a pale shoulder, and looking ready to cry. Her dark hair set off the pale length of her back, the graceful whiteness of her arms.

Her nipples stood erect under the filmy material of the gown. She did have beautiful breasts, he thought.

Suddenly, he had an intense desire to make love to her.

He began taking off his clothes.

"What are you doing?" she asked in a bewildered voice.

"Proving to you that my heart belongs to Marcia," he said.

He pulled off his briefs and climbed on the bed next to her.

As she sat there, he stripped her nightgown easily down to her waist. He ran his hands over her breasts, over the arch of her back, over her neck and through her dark, tousled hair.

She sat motionless, watching him with her soft brown eyes, a slight smile on her face. He could feel her body shudder under his touch.

Then she put her arms around his neck and kissed him hard. She pulled him down on top of her.

The weight of his body pushed her into the bed. She slipped her hand down the powerful muscles of his back and buttocks.

"How I've missed this body," she whispered into his ear. "How I've missed it."

He smiled and kissed her again.

They made love intensely, the sheets tangled in a wad at the end of the bed, their bodies hot and wet.

They were at least half an hour late for dinner at Harvey's.

THIRTY-ONE

Marcia had wanted to cancel, but Gin had insisted they go. He couldn't wait to meet Uncle Walter.

In the car he told her about the plans for a private school. She liked the idea, but she thought it was a long shot. Her lack of enthusiasm irritated him. By the time they got to Harvey's, they were barely speaking.

Uncle Walter was a charming, well-educated man, one of the leading investment bankers in the city. In his sixties, he looked like an older, fatter version of his nephew.

Talk about the new high school dominated the dinner conversation.

Walter listened and asked intelligent questions. But when the conversation turned to money, he hesitated. He was interested in the school, yes, but it would be difficult to find investors for such a risky project, especially when they could make nine percent on Treasury bills, risk-free.

Nevertheless, there were philanthropists who would look at it as their civic duty to support a school.

Unfortunately, they would probably want someone as headmaster who was an experienced administrator, which Gin was not.

Gin had expected this: he launched into his sales pitch. He talked about the program of English as a Second Language which he had started at Howard High. He had gotten the money from the school board, designed the program, and chosen the texts. His program was now being copied by other schools.

Then St Paul's had hired him to be assistant principal. He had left them only because they had failed to keep their promise.

Walter gave him a kindly smile. He would see what he could do, but they shouldn't get their hopes up. He could probably get an answer from his investors in about six months.

He asked if they would consider bringing in an older, more experienced administrator to run the school; they would have an easier time raising money with someone like that heading the project. Gin and Harvey bristled; the answer was a definite "no."

They discussed raising money from several foundations where Walter knew the directors or the administrator. They discussed government grants; Walter was on the board of directors of a theatre company that had gotten government money. Would the government give money to a private school?

By the end of the evening, Gin had a list of budgets and proposal materials he needed to prepare and government agencies he needed to contact. He felt exhausted just looking at it.

He wondered if he had the incredible drive necessary to get this school off the ground.

He left with the distinct feeling that he didn't. The school was a pie-in-the-sky proposition, another good idea that would die for lack of funds.

He looked so sad in the car that Marcia instinctively put her hand on his thigh.

He sighed.

"Walter's probably right," he said, pulling into traffic. "The school is a real long shot."

She looked at him, pale and unhappy in the gloom of the car.

"That doesn't mean you shouldn't give it a try," she said.

He looked at her in surprise.

"I thought you thought this whole idea was crazy?" he said.

She patted his thigh. "Just because of the money problems, not because you couldn't run a school."

She gave him a half-smile. "Christ Almighty, don't you give me credit for anything?"

He laughed, and put his arm around her. "Come here, you goofy broad," he said.

She learned up against him and closed her eyes.

Maybe this school would work out after all, he thought. He began running numbers through his head again. But the more he thought of it, the more impractical it seemed. It would be too much work for too little gratification.

At the entrance ramp to the expressway, he glanced down at Marcia. She was asleep. He felt the warmth of her body; her slow, regular breathing moved against his side. All the way home, he concentrated on staying awake.

That night, they slept the deep sleep of the truly exhausted.

*   *   *

The next day dawned dark and overcast.

Marcia awoke around ten; she lay in bed half-asleep, thinking of the day ahead. Within thirty seconds, a picture of the bills on Gin's desk floated into her mind. After a month of neglect, today was the day of battle.

Her chest tightened; her heart began to pound. She had no sense of where they stood financially. She knew more about Delta's damn shopping centers than about whether she had enough money to make her mortgage payment that month.

She snorted in disgust and jumped out of bed. Startled, Gin awoke. He watched her whirl out the bedroom door.

He threw on his bathrobe and followed her to the kitchen.

He tried to calm her, but she bolted her breakfast and went to the desk immediately. When he brought her a cup of coffee, she was hunched over the desk, her bathrobe drawn around her against the morning cold. A stack of bills sat in front of her, an enemy army bivouacked in their own house.

He was unnerved to see her so upset about money; he relied on her expertise. He left quickly and dressed, to drive into the village to get the Sunday paper. When he returned, he tried to read for an hour, but he couldn't concentrate. He glanced through the want ads under "Teaching," but all he found were ads for grammar school teachers.

He decided to work on his job search. He would answer a few ads he had clipped from teachers' newsletters. He also had to write the District 305 High School Board. They wanted to interview him in two weeks for the assistant principal's job at a high school in Brookfield, a suburb just southwest of the city.

He sighed. He needed his typewriter. He could work on the kitchen table.

He got up from the living room couch and walked to the office. The door was closed. He knocked lightly, and pushed it open.

The room was dark; only a high-intensity desk lamp threw a pool of light on the desk.

Marcia rested her head in one hand. Wadded-up balls of paper encircled her. A calculator and sheets of yellow paper, covered with numbers, were spread out before her.

She looked up.

"Guess what?" she said tonelessly.

"What?"

"We're broke."

He laughed. "We're always broke," he said. "What else is new?"

She didn't smile. "This time," she said, "we're *really* broke."

She paused.

"We have to sell the house," she said. " We can't afford to live here. I'm sorry."

Gin sank down in the chair next to the desk.

"This is all a joke, right?" he said.

She shook her head.

"Marcia, you just got a new job where you're making more money," he said. "How could we be under water?"

"Because I'm a financial idiot," she said flatly. "I've got us in way over our heads."

"But do we really have to sell the house?" he said.

"Either that or the bank will kick us out."

Gin thought of the pale young man who had given them their mortgage so easily two months ago. Now he would come and evict them just as effortlessly.

"Show me," Gin croaked. "Show me the numbers."

He pulled his chair up to the desk. Marcia spread out a yellow paper covered with numbers in smudged pencil. They were bringing in $45,000 a year in income; that was $3750 a month before taxes. It seemed like an immense amount of money.

But expenses were eating them alive. The mortgage cost them $842 a month, the heat another $135. Real estate taxes and insurance ran $385 a month: Barrington was an expensive place to live.

Even with the tax writeoffs on the house, income taxes and Social Security took another $937.50 out each month. Then there were the $350 a month car payments on Vivian.

That left them $1100.50 a month.

But then they had to pay $600 a month to their parents for the loans they had received for their down payment. Marcia's mother got most of it. Mary Beth Grimley had insisted on getting back her principal with interest within two and a half years.

That left them $550.50. Marcia needed $150 for her monthly train ticket downtown. Then there were gas and insurance on Vivian, Marcia's school loan payments on her M.B.A., and the phone and electric bills, not to mention food, clothing and an occasional night at the movies.

Adding those in left them in the hole $249.65 every month.

No wonder the checking account had only $26.74 left in it.

They leaned back in their chairs and looked at each other in shock.

"How could the bank be so stupid as to give us a mortgage when we were so broke?" Gin asked. "You were making even less money then than you are now."

"I didn't tell them about the loans we got from our parents," she said. "And I underestimated everything. I thought Vivian was going to be paid off this year. I didn't know we spent so much on food. I low-balled the real estate taxes."

She looked at him. Her eyes were glassy. "Basically, I just fucked up," she said.

Gin chewed his lower lip. "Can we cut what we pay our parents on the loans?" he said.

They thought of what might happen. Hodge would lecture Gin on his profligacy and stupidity. Mary Beth would knot up her mouth and disinherit Marcia for financial ineptitude. Marcia's marriage could sour, but not her loans from her mother.

They looked at each other wordlessly: forget about financial mercy from the parents.

Gin sighed.

"So where do we start?" he said.

"We call up Juanita the Realtor and tell her to get her ass over here," said Marcia. "This house is on the market again."

She smiled crookedly at her husband.

Then she began crying. She was supposed to be the whiz at finance. She had dug them into a hole it would take them months to get out of it.

"I'm really sorry, Gin," she sobbed. "I don't know how I could have been so stupid."

He stared at her.

"I don't either," he said.

He looked at the smudged papers all over the desk. So this was finance, he thought. What comes in must equal what goes out. Some mystery that was.

All he wanted to do was live within his means. It was this idiot he was married to who insisted on stretching them to the limit.

He was about to say something sharp when he remembered that he had stood by and let her do it. He had signed all the papers; he had let her railroad him.

He was as spineless as she was crazy. What a fool he had been.

He learned over in his chair and stared at his hands, opening and closing his fist. He swore to himself under his breath.

Marcia cried softly.

He resolved to get more involved in their finances.

He stood up numbly.

"You got Juanita's number?" he said. Marcia rummaged through a manila folder and fished out a slip of paper with a number on it.

He went to the kitchen phone and dialed the number.

He caught Juanita just as she was going out the door.

*   *   *

Juanita said the earliest she could come was Wednesday night. But Gin was so insistent, and she so surprised to hear from him, that she agreed to come Tuesday evening.

"The realtor's coming Tuesday," he announced to Marcia as he walked back into the office. He threw the real estate section of the paper down on the desk in front of her and pulled up his chair next to hers.

"Time to find a place to live," he said, opening the paper.

"We can't start looking yet," she said. "It could take months to sell the house."

"We can't afford months."

"But people don't buy houses in December."

"You can sell anything if the price is right."

Marcia's heart sank. Despite their financial mess, she had secretly hoped to hold on to the house.

"Well, at least I won't have to be here when you price it," she said. "I couldn't bear it."

Gin looked up in surprise.

"Where are you going to be?"

"California. I've got a three-day business trip to the West Coast. Rick and I leave Tuesday morning."

For several moments, Rick's name hung in the air between him.

"The trips have got to stop, Marsh," Gin said deliberately. "Quit, get another job, refuse to go. I don't know what to tell you. But our marriage can't take all this travel."

Marcia turned away. She stared vacantly at the newspaper on the desk.

"Yeah, I know," she said.

She traced a pattern with her finger on the newspaper. The Dream House and the Dream Job, gone in one day. What Dream Job? Traveling four days out of five, working yourself into exhaustion—was that what she wanted? Rick thought it was fun; she didn't.

She traced the "D" in the Dominick's Finer Foods ad over and over with her finger.

"So what are you going to do?" Gin asked.

She shrugged. "I don't know. Ask to be transferred, I suppose." She looked at him. "He might fire me."

"I don't think he'll fire you. Why should he? Pure spite?"

She shrugged again.

He stood up and stepped behind her chair. He leaned over and whispered into her ear, "Besides, you've got a great set of knockers. He'll want to keep you around just for the view."

One thing led to another and they ended up back in the bedroom again, the house dark and quiet around them in the gloom of the winter afternoon.

Afterward, she slept for several hours. Gin went back into the office, set up his typewriter and typed job queries.

Later they looked at the apartment rental ads in the newspapers and got depressed. Everything in Barrington was too expensive. They would have to try a cheaper suburb.

In the early evening they went into town, stopping at the bank cash machine to withdraw the last $26.74 in their checking account.

They spent every cent on a big meal at an Italian restaurant at the edge of town. With a bottle of cheap wine, they toasted their marriage and then their disastrous finances.

They came home late, tipsy and content, and tumbled into bed.

THIRTY-TWO

Monday morning, Marcia was irritable. Sure, she would ask Rick for a transfer. He would tell her to take a hike. She would be out of a job, out of money, and they would be in an even worse mess than they were in now.

Dressing for work, she wondered if she wasn't making a big mistake staying with Gin. Maybe she should move in with Rick. She thought of his handsome face and beautiful suits. Besides, what if Gin didn't really break with Karen? And he was such a dunce about money. True, she had been the one chiefly responsible for pulling them in over theirs heads, but why hadn't he stopped her?

For five minutes over breakfast she contemplated life in the fast lane with Rick. Gin was sitting at the table grading some multiple-choice tests he had neglected over the weekend.

He looked up and smiled at her, all freckles and blue eyes, a number two pencil behind one ear.

Okay, she thought. I'll stay.

But why didn't he get a better job?

Maybe this Brookfield thing would work out. Then maybe again it wouldn't.

She glared at him over her orange juice.

"Why weren't you born rich?" she said.

"Why weren't you?" he said, not even looking up. "Then I wouldn't have to do this shit."

He laced a string of red check marks down the side of the page. "Imagine, a multiple-choice test on *Hamlet* and *Macbeth*. What genius at the textbook company came up with this? This is the last time I follow their lesson guide.

"It's back to the old essays, kids," he muttered, sliding the sheet he had been working on to the bottom of the pile. He started another.

"You could at least get a better job," Marcia said.

He looked up.

"What do you think I was doing yesterday? Sending love letters to school boards?"

"Yeah, but I wish you'd get a better job sooner than later."

Gin contemplated his wife. In her navy blue suit, starched blouse, and silk scarf she looked like an airline stewardess. A nervous airline stewardess.

"Marcia, he's not going to fire you."

"How do you know?"

"I know."

He shuffled his papers into an orderly pile. "Come on. I'll give you a ride to the train."

Vivian didn't start up right away. Marcia envisioned hundreds of dollars of car repair bills. They would be broke with a dead car, stranded in a house they couldn't afford. They wouldn't even be able to drive into town to buy a box of Cheerios for dinner.

"What if the car broke down and we didn't have the money to fix it?" she said.

"You're getting morbid, Marsh," he said.

"We'd have to steal a dog and a kid's sled just to mush into town to get food."

"Maybe your mother would send us some food."

"Not on your life; we'd starve."

They drove into the train station parking lot.

"We could live in an igloo," she said. "Low rent, no maintenance. It would melt every summer. You wouldn't have to take down any storm windows. In the summer, we could live in a tent."

He parked the car. Then he took her hand and looked her in the eye.

"He's not going to fire you," he said.

She nodded without conviction.

The signal lights started blinking; the crossing gates came down.

She pursed her lips and picked up her handbag and briefcase. "Train's coming," she said."Bye."

"He's not going to fire you," Gin said firmly.

He put his hand on her arm. She sighed.

"You don't think so?"

"Nope."

She reached for her briefcase, but he wouldn't let her go.

"Come on, I've got to catch a train." The commuters were bunching up on the platform where they knew the train would open its doors.

"Tell me you love me first. I won't let you go until you do."

She looked at him.

"I love you," she said.

He smiled, and gave her a long, lingering kiss.

"He's not going to can you," he whispered.

"I know," She whispered back.

He kissed her again.

The train pulled into the station.

Under her skirt her pantyhose frustrated exploration. Her entire lower body was encased in a man-proof layer of nylon.

"Bring back the garter belt," he whispered into her ear. "We could go home. It's only six-forty-five. My first class isn't 'til nine-thirty."

She ran over the train schedule in her mind. If she caught the eight-five, she could be at the office by nine-fifteen.

"All right," she said.

Gin swung Vivian into gear.

They romped through their love-making like two children playing hooky.

* * *

Marcia walked into Delta at nine-eighteen, her cheeks glowing.

Fifteen minutes later, she walked into Rick's office and closed the door.

She sat down in one of the chairs in front of his desk. He stood behind it in his shirtsleeves, sorting through a pile of blueprints.

He gave her a beautiful smile and kept sorting.

"Good morning," he said. "Do you know where the working drawings are for Casa Fortuna? I know I did something with them, but I'm damned if I can find them."

He started to rummage through a collection of tubed blueprints in a corner.

"Mario in Coop's group has them," Marcia said. "Hey, look, can we talk for a moment?"

"Yeah, sure. What's up?" He stood up and smoothed back a lock of black hair that had fallen over his forehead.

"I want a transfer," she said quickly. "I can't take this travel any more. It's too much. My marriage can't take it; I can't take it."

She took a breath. "I'd like to move to a different part of the company."

He sat down, his face expressionless.

Her heart pounded; this was the end.

He leaned across his desk.

"Marcia, I sort of hoped that you would change your mind about travel—and about us," he said softly. "I still think we would make a great team in everything. I wish you would reconsider."

She was speechless. He wasn't going to fire her. In fact, this attractive man with a French silk tie was making another play for her.

She sighed, smiled and shook her head slowly.

"I'm sorry, but I've decided to stay with my husband."

He smiled at her sadly.

She felt like a rat. How could she let Rick down?

The office was quiet. They could hear the faint tapping of typewriters outside. Rick's phone rang.

He got up quickly and opened the door. "Jeanette, pick up my phone for a few minutes, would you?" he called.

She admired the way his wool pants hung over his wellmuscled rear end. She thought of the curly black hair that covered his chest.

He shut the door behind him, and sat down in the other chair in front of his desk.

"Well," he said. "I'm not going anywhere. So if you ever change your mind. . ."

"Well, I . . ." she began.

"Well, no," she said abruptly. "I'm not going to change my mind."

She stared at her hands in her lap. "I'm sorry."

Silence hung between them. Suddenly, Rick's phone was a board of twinkling lights. Monday morning and the entire world was calling him. Jeanette must be scribbling furiously.

She looked at him, the picture of calm professionalism.

"So now what do we do?" she blurted. She would never make it as a calm professional.

"I don't know," he said, surprised. "What do you want to do?"

"Anything that doesn't involve me traveling around in airplanes three and four days a week. Some back office job, I guess."

After all, her life as a wheeler dealer was over. Who cared what she did now?

"You know you can't stay in acquisitions" he said. "We all travel nationally. I couldn't just let you stay in Chicago. That's not the way we're organized."

"I know," she said.

"Anything else I gave you in this department would be back-room number-crunching. You wouldn't enjoy that."

"That's for sure," she said numbly.

He paused a few moments and stared out at the leaden sky hanging over the city.

"How about property management in Chicago?"

She felt as though he had punched her in the stomach.

How about street-sweeping in Istanbul?

Property management was the lowest rung in the Delta pecking order. Instead of sparring with millionaire real estate developers, she could fight with tradesmen with B.O.

"Whose side are you on, Matthews?" she asked.

"It would be good for you," he said. "See how the bucks are really made out there in the trenches, not with all our exotic running around, buying property."

"Oh, God."

"It's invaluable experience, believe me. You could work on properties in just the suburban area," he said. "You could drive around to see them and work with the managers."

She ran her hands through her hair.

"Did you ever do it?" she asked.

"Yeah, at Citibank for a couple weeks, as part of the real estate training program."

He leaned back in his chair. "It was really worthwhile," he said.

"Yeah, so worthwhile you don't do it anymore," she said. "After I do my three weeks worth, what happens then?"

She watched his body go rigid with anger.

"Sorry," she mumbled, staring at her hands. "I'm just upset. I realize you have no obligation to do anything for me."

"Damn straight," he said stiffly.

He let out an exasperated sigh. He stood up and began pacing.

"I just wish you'd stay in acquisitions," he said. He lowered his voice. "Despite what goes on between us personally. You're good at it. If you could only get used to the travel."

He put his hands in his pockets.

"You could make yourself and Delta a lot of money. Maybe in a couple years we could just base you in Chicago. Couldn't you and your husband hang on a couple years? Just a couple years?"

He turned and gave her an appraising look.

He's telling me he'll wait for me, she thought. Just like he waited four years to get the Ridgetown Shopping Center in Tennessee. He waited until the developer changed his mind. He knew he would.

He'll wait until I change my mind and leave Gin.

She shuddered. He must know I will leave Gin.

She felt gooseflesh crawl up her arms.

No. I will not leave Gin.

No. I will not travel anymore.

"My marriage couldn't stand one month of travel," she said softly. "Several years would be out of the question."

"Well, I don't know what else to say then," he said.

Her heart sank. The best job she had ever had, with the best boss she had ever had. And she had just tossed it all out the window for Gin. God Almighty, this goddamn marriage better work now.

She cleared her throat. "Well, why don't you fix me up with the property management guy, Wilbur or Filbertson, isn't it?" she said.

"John Filbert. I'll talk to him this afternoon."

"Thanks," she said. "Thanks for everything you've done for me. You're a great guy. I'm sorry I couldn't hack it. I'm going to miss you."

She stood up and straightened her skirt. "Well, let's get this show on the road then," she said, clearing her throat. "We've got a lot of work to do for our trip tomorrow."

Rick looked pained.

She smiled again, then extended her hand.

"Thanks, Rick," she said, looking him in the eye and shaking his hand. "I wish it had worked out better, but at least I'll still be at Delta."

He shook her hand and said nothing. But he returned her look with an intensity that startled her. He did care. A great deal.

Stunned, she went back to her cubicle and leaned her head against one of its fabric-covered walls, She sat for five minutes. A handsome man who cared for her. Wealth, excitement, success. All out the window. And she was going to have to travel with this guy for the next three days. Sit next to him on planes; talk to him over dinner. She moaned.

She wanted to call Gin and tell him everything, but it was impossible to reach him during the day. He had to call her.

She buried herself in a computer printout. Around eleven, Gin called. He had a five-minute break between classes.

"I told you he wouldn't fire you," he said, breathless. He had had to run to the pay phone in the main lobby from the far end of the school.

"Property management isn't the greatest," she said.

"Worry about that later. At least you've got a job."

"Yeah, I suppose." She lowered her voice. "He asked me to move in with him again."

She felt her voice break. "Gin, he really cares for me. I feel terrible. And I've got to travel with this guy until I get into a new position here."

There was silence at the other end of the line.

"Gin?"

"I love you, Marcia," he said quietly. "Don't forget it."

He paused. "You're not changing your mind on me, are you?" he said.

"No," she said, surprised. "Of course not."

"Good. Then I don't have to break his kneecaps and your neck."

She smiled. Over the line, she could hear the sound of children's voices and lockers slamming.

"Cheer up. I'll give you a special back rub tonight," he said.

She groaned. "Gin, this is more sex than I've had in months. I'm starting to get sore."

"Who said anything about sex?"

She smiled again.

"Look, the bell's about to ring," he said. "I gotta run. See you at the train at five-fifty-eight. Love ya."

"Yeah, 'bye," she said.

She went back to her work; she passed the afternoon in a depressed daze. At five, she piled what she needed for her trip into a huge briefcase and struggled through the crowds to the train.

Gin was waiting to meet her at the Barrington station. She opened the car door and threw her briefcase into the back seat with a tremendous thud.

"Well, I did it," she said, sliding in next to him.

"Yeah, you sure did," he said.

He put his arm around her and leaned over to kiss her. It was like kissing a dead fish. He sat up abruptly.

"Marcia, it will be all right," he said.

"No, it won't," she said, her voice peevish. " Property management will be terrible."

"Maybe it will lead to better things. A better job somewhere else."

"How do you know? This was the best job I ever had."

"There's got to be something in real estate you would enjoy doing that doesn't entail you running your ass all over the county." His voice began to rise.

"Shit," she said, glaring at him. "I've got to give up my job, the only one I've ever enjoyed, just to keep this marriage together. And all you can tell me is to look on the bright side of things."

His face hardened. He stared straight ahead.

"Well, if you would rather not keep this marriage together, you're free to keep any fucking job you like."

He threw the car into gear and drove through the parking lot traffic.

Halfway home and not even a friendly look out of him, Marcia began to weaken.

"I'm sorry," she said. "I didn't mean it."

"Okay, don't worry about it." His voice was cold.

When they got home, she tried to cuddle up against him on the couch, but he wouldn't respond. About eight-thirty, she reminded him of her backrub.

"Find a spot," he said, annoyed.

She lay down on the rug in front of the fireplace. He rubbed her back, distracted by a Creole cooking program on the educational TV station.

She watched him out of the corner of her eye. When he looked lost in the mysteries of making blackened pan fish, she rolled over on her back, reached up, and grabbed him by the shirt. She pulled him down to her and kissed him hard on the lips. She could feel his teeth collide with hers.

"Knock it off, Bernthal," she whispered. "I don't deserve this."

He smiled.

She punched him in the back. He hit her on the shoulder. They wrestled on the rug, nearly overturning the coffee table, and collapsed into a panting heap.

They watched the old Creole make a gumbo, and went to bed early. Though she hadn't packed a thing for her trip, Marcia fell asleep peacefully in the crook of Gin's arm.

THIRTY-THREE

Marcia was up at five to pack for her trip. At seven-fifteen, Gin helped her into a cab. He gave her an obscenely long kiss and stood waving goodbye until the cab turned the corner.

Thursday night—and Marcia's return—seemed an eternity away.

He turned back into the big, empty house, the monster that ate up money they didn't have. Thank God he was putting it on the market that night.

He poured himself another cup of coffee.

Juanita tonight.

And Karen today.

He groaned. Karen hadn't been at school yesterday; Tommy had probably been sick. He hadn't seen her since last Thursday. It was the longest they had gone without talking to each other since their affair had started.

He would have to break it off with her today, over heaping plates of spaghetti-o's at fourth period lunch. Great moments in great love affairs.

He considered asking her out for a drink, and then telling her. No, that wouldn't work. Why drag it out? At least in the cafeteria she could give him a hateful look and go finish her lunch with someone else.

He could mail her her apartment keys in inter-office mail.

He dressed and headed for school.

All morning, he was short-tempered. The kids in his first two classes were listless and uninterested. Dickens' *Great Expectations* wasn't his favorite either, but he worked his way through the discussion. As penance, he assigned an essay on the book.

Third-period Drivers' Ed went by in a fog. He daydreamed while the kids weaved in and out of side streets in a housing subdivision east of school.

By twelve-ten, he was standing at the end of the cafeteria line, a mound of tuna casserole on his plate, looking for Karen. She waved at him from their usual table, where she sat waiting, in a blue sweater and skirt, a long braid of blonde hair over one shoulder.

She was alone.

He walked quickly to the table.

"Hello, Gin. It's good to see you." She gave him a brilliant smile.

"I've missed you," she said, dropping her voice to an intimate whisper. "Where have you been?"

"I thought we could use a little breathing room," he said. "I just spent a quiet week-end around the house."

She was such a pretty woman. He watched her toy with the end of her braid with one slender hand.

"Look Karen, I have something to tell you," he said in a low voice. "I know this isn't the greatest place to discuss this, but I have to get it out."

She looked alarmed.

"You're a good woman, a good mother," he said. "You'd make someone a great wife, but well . . . I've decided to stay with my wife."

"What?"

"I've got to break it off with you. I'm staying with Marcia."

She set her jaw.

"One little fight with me over Tommy and you're going to run back to your wife?" she whispered. " You've got to be kidding."

"I'm not kidding."

With one motion, she threw her braid behind her back.

Two teachers approached, carrying lunch trays. Gin stood up.

"Come on. We can talk outside," he said.

The halls were empty. They walked down the corridor and ducked into the first empty classroom. She leaned against the teacher's desk and looked at him with cold, angry eyes.

"What's this about?" she said. "I thought we got along so well."

He thought of their lovemaking.

"Well, we had a great sex life," he said. "But we didn't agree on much else. For one thing, I don't want to be Tommy's father."

"We could work around him. He won't always be seven years old."

"No matter what age he is, he'll still hate me."

"Don't be ridiculous. He'll get used to you."

"I don't think so. Besides, Tommy's not really the issue. I want to work things out with Marcia. I still love her."

"How touching. And you don't love me?"

His eyes wandered to a map of South America hung on a far wall.

"No, I'm afraid I don't," he said. "I'm sorry."

"I see." She unzipped her purse.

"You can give me back my keys then," she said, extending one hand.

He was surprised at her abruptness. She must have had practice at this.

He glanced at her while he worked the keys off the ring. Her eyes had a lost, hurt look. Another one that got away.

He wondered what she felt for him.

He handed her two brass keys.

"Karen," he said, watching her drop them into her purse."Did you ever love me?"

She studied him for a moment.

"I don't know," she said. "I suppose so."

"I am sorry," he said. "I didn't mean to hurt you."

She zipped up her purse, and sighed.

"Well, I suppose it's all for the best. I need someone more stable than you and with a better income. You have to pay attention to things like that when you're a single mother. You just can't hook up with any pretty face."

She flashed him another brilliant smile.

"It was fun." She kissed him lightly on the cheek and swung her purse over one shoulder. "I'll see you around, Gin."

She turned and walked out of the room, her high heels clicking on the linoleum.

He leaned against the desk. Only last week she had talked about marrying him. Now she was saying he was too poor to be her husband.

He wondered if she fell in love with men or their incomes.

Maybe she was just angry?

Maybe she was just crazy?

He decided he didn't care.

He stared at the map of South America again, tracing the Amazon with his eyes.

He chuckled. He had never thought of himself as "just another pretty face" before.

* * *

Juanita the Realtor was right on time.

At seven-thirty that night, she stood in Gin's living room, shaking the slush from her boots on the rag rug by the door.

"Well, well, well," she said, dropping her coat on a chair. "It's time to move on to bigger and better things. A bigger house perhaps?" She eyed the half-empty living room.

"Actually, we want to sell this place and rent a cheap apartment somewhere," said Gin. "We need the money."

"Oh." That took the wind out of her sails.

"This isn't a divorce sale, is it?" she asked hopefully.

"No, we're just broke," said Gin.

She frowned.

"Can I get you a cup of coffee?" he asked.

"Oh. Certainly. Thank you."

He walked into the kitchen and poured the coffee, smiling to himself. Clearly, only the upwardly mobile bought houses in Barrington. Every few years they bought bigger ones. The only acceptable reason to move down the ladder was divorce. Sliding down because you were broke was a definite faux pas.

It was not the American way.

God, would he be glad to get out of here.

He returned to the living room with the coffee. Juanita was perched on the edge of the couch, filling in a printed form on a clipboard. She pressed buttons on her tiny calculator, pursed her lips, then filled in the form with a small gold pen.

On her tiny pointed ears she wore little Santa Claus earrings, which quivered when she talked.

"The market has changed since I sold you this house," she said, taking her coffee from him. "Interest rates are up, prices are down. And people don't buy houses in December, it's too close to Christmas.

"I'd wait until January or February, if you could. The market might pick up a little by then."

"We can't wait," Gin said. "We can't afford to. What could we get for this place?"

"About five thousand less than you paid for it," she said. She was anxious to get out of the house. Distress sales made her nervous.

"I thought houses only appreciated in value?"

"Not when you live in them two months and sell at Christmas."

How long would it take to sell?"

"Next week, next month, next year. I really don't know. I've got some prospects I can think of, but like I said, people don't have househunting on their minds right now." Her earrings quivered.

"Well, see what you can do."

"Certainly." She slid her clipboard back into a cheap vinyl briefcase and set her untouched coffee on the coffee table.

She stood up and retrieved her coat from the sofa.

"Well, I've got to run. I'll call you soon."

"The sooner the better. We really want to move on this."

"Yes. Certainly."

She smiled mechanically and tromped out into the night.

Gin crumpled on the sofa. They were going to lose five thousand on this deal, plus the cost of moving again, the security deposit on the new apartment, the cost of another lawyer, and God knew what else.

Marcia had invested their life savings of ten thousand dollars in this place. They would be lucky to have five hundred left when they sold.

They couldn't wait for the market to improve. They either sold the house within the next month or two, or they started defaulting on their water bills. Every dime they had was tied up in the house.

He stared malevolently at the ceiling. Why wouldn't it just collapse? Then they could collect the insurance. Maybe they could arrange a fire?

With his luck, he would get caught.

He went into the kitchen and dumped out his coffee. He washed out the cup and refilled it with scotch and water. Then he went into his office.

What we need is income.

He pulled out a list of all the high school boards in the Chicago metropolitan area and stuck a sheet of his personal stationery in his typewriter.

He began with the first on the list, Arlington Heights school district 211.

"Dear Mr Hallenzeim," he typed. "I am seeking a position as a principal or assistant principal at a high school in your district. Enclosed is my resume. You can see that I have had experience in administration with the English as a Second Language program at Howard High School in Chicago."

By twelve-thirty, he had written a dozen letters, stuffing them into envelopes with his resume.

Next week, he would write the Catholic and private high schools.

Next week was his big interview at Brookfield High. His luck had to change. Somebody must need him somewhere.

He flipped off the lights. Exhausted, he fell into bed.

*   *   *

Wednesday and Thursday passed in a blur of loneliness, work, and depression. He was far behind on his grading. He had papers from last week that he still hadn't looked at, and he had to give a series of grammar and spelling quizzes before Christmas break. The kids would do badly on them, he would get mad, and he would end up giving them pages of grammar exercises to do over the holidays.

It happened every year, no matter where he taught. It had turned into a Christmas tradition.

He graded papers in study hall, over breakfast, and during his one free period a day. Over lunch on Wednesday, he sat by himself at a table in a corner of the cafeteria and graded some more. He saw Karen, with several other teachers, sitting at the table they usually shared.

They all waved. After they had eaten, they stopped by to commiserate with him. Karen smiled sadly and said nothing. Gin felt guilty.

Wednesday evening, while he was reading essays on *Macbeth,* Marcia called. The trip was going as well as could be expected. It was awkward at times, but not too bad.

She was tired. She missed him.

Despite her protests, he insisted on picking her up at the airport Thursday night. What did he care what Rick Matthews thought?

On Thursday night, he watched her come off the plane, a small figure with a huge briefcase, followed by a handsome, dark-haired man with a huge briefcase.

She introduced him to Rick. They shook hands and smiled woodenly at each other. While waiting for the luggage, the two men made small talk about the Bears, the Steelers, the Oilers, the Packers, the Dolphins, the Rams and every other football team they could think of.

Marcia felt sick.

She and Gin walked Rick to the cab stand. The two men exchanged another wooden handshake and mouthed friendly goodbyes. Gin and Marcia headed toward the parking garage.

Just as they turned the corner out of Rick's sight, Gin dropped the luggage. He caught Marcia by the shoulder and pulled her into his arms.

"I win, he loses," he whispered. "How about celebrating my victory?"

She smiled and kissed him.

THIRTY-FOUR

They spent a pleasant weekend together. Gin wrote letters to another dozen high schools and typed up his grammar quizzes. Marcia cleaned out her briefcase, did her expense account, and washed clothes.

Sunday, they looked through the paper for apartments. Compared to their mortgage payments, even five hundred dollars a month rent looked cheap. They could actually afford to live somewhere; the thought cheered them.

They couldn't decide where to move. It depended on where Gin would work next year and when they could sell the house. But they marked dozens of listings anyway, making big red circles with a felt-tip pen.

Late Sunday afternoon, Juanita brought over an accountant and his wife to look at the house. John and Carol Farley appeared to be in their late thirties. He was a homely man with a hooked nose, she a plump blonde with bad skin. They brought their son, a sallow four-year-old with an unfortunate resemblance to his father.

The Farleys trooped through the house, the little boy whining and dragging his feet. The man asked the age of the furnace, the roof, and the hot water heater. Then all three Farleys smiled politely and left, Juanita bustling behind them and already prattling about the next house on her list.

Monday night, Juanita appeared with some other prospects: a pair of fortyish lawyers. In their expensive navy wool suits they looked like a matched set: one male, one female. The pair spent a long time in the master bedroom alone, whispering. They left without speaking a word to either Gin or Marcia.

*　　*　　*

On Tuesday, Marcia met with John Filbert, head of property management at Delta Realty.

Filbert was a small man in his early forties; his face was pitted with acne scars. He had colorless eyes, limp brown hair and thin, greyish lips. The ashtray and stale air in his office proclaimed him a chain smoker. Marcia thought he looked like walking death.

Filbert's office was two floors under Rick's and in the opposite corner of the building. The beige walls were covered with drawings and photos of office buildings and shopping centers managed by Delta. Filbert had run out of wall space; framed photos of warehouses lay stacked on his sofa, along with piles of computer printouts.

Behind his desk, a dusty golf trophy stood on the credenza, next to a photo of a tiny, red-haired woman and a freckled boy of about ten—a pixie and her son.

Filbert welcomed Marcia with a clammy handshake. She sat down in one of the beige chairs in front of his desk.

"Rick has told me a lot about you," he said in a deep voice. Marcia was surprised such a big voice lived in such a small body.

"Oh, really?" She laughed nervously.

"Yes. He's quite impressed with your abilities." Filbert paused to light a cigarette.

"Rick told me you were tired of traveling," he said. He drew his first puff, and expelled it in a cloud.

"Yes. I am."

"Well, to be honest with you, I'm not sure what we can do for you here," he said. "We travel just as much as you do in acquisitions, if not more. Once you get good at management, you're on the road all the time, looking at properties, meeting managers, working on leases."

Marcia felt sick.

"I also rotate my junior managers," said Filbert. They work two years in one city, then I move them to another. It gives them a chance to run property in completely different markets. It's valuable experience.

"If I took you on, I'd want to do the same with you."

He took another drag on his cigarette, sucking in his thin cheeks. When he exhaled, the smoke streamed out his nostrils.

"No one just stays in the Chicago office and doesn't travel?" Marcia asked.

"No, I'm afraid not. I move everyone. I don't hire people who won't move. Otherwise, it makes no sense to train them in the first place."

He smiled thinly. "Sorry," he said.

He flicked an ash in the ashtray.

"Not everyone runs property the way I do," he said. "You could try some of the other big managers in the city. They might not move you around so much."

"Yes, I see," she said. "Well, thank you."

Fifteen minutes after she had gone to see Filbert, Marcia was back in her own cubicle, her head in her hands.

Filbert had just signed her death warrant at Delta.

Rick would probably let her stay a while. She could putter around the office, running computer analyses of deals for him.

But eventually she would have to go.

Besides, sitting in the office hunched over a computer would drive her crazy. She wanted to buy buildings.

She would have to find another job.

She toyed with a paper clip, and stared at a snapshot of Gin thumbtacked to her cubicle wall. He stood in front of their house, smiling and leaning against a lawnmower. The suburban lawn chariot, he had called it.

She sighed.

In the real estate world, she was on the slide. She would probably end up working for some small company that just bought property in Chicago or northern Illinois. The only travel would be day trips to Rockford, a voyage of two hours out the interstate and into the cornfields.

She would make less money; she would have less prestige. She would work with a sleazier crowd of people.

But her life would be her own. She'd get enough sleep; she could eat dinner at home nearly every night.

She could stay married to that nice young man leaning against the old hand lawnmower her father had lent them.

She sighed again, then pulled a mirror from her handbag and checked her makeup. She stood up, straightened her skirt, and walked to Rick's office. He was on the phone, but he waved her in.

She sat in front of his desk, twisted herself around, and stared out his windows. A wide bank of dark clouds was moving down on the city from the north. It will snow tomorrow, she thought.

Rick hung up the phone.

"So what's up?" he said.

"Bad news," she said. "I've got to go."

"I'm sorry to hear that," he said. His face was expressionless, his voice polite, but cool.

"Filbert says they really fly around down there," she said.

"I didn't realize that."

"Yeah, well they're jet-setters all right."

She twisted her hands on her lap. "Look, could you put me in the back office for six months or so until I find something else?" she asked.

He smiled.

"Sure," he said. "I'll see what I can do." Then he began shuffling papers on his desk.

She was a dead woman to him now, Marcia thought.

"I'll have to replace you, you know," he said. "I need help on the road."

"I know. I'll pitch in as much as I can."

"That would be very helpful," he said, smoothing out a long paper filled with numbers in front of him. The audience on her future was over.

"How about going over the Los Noces deal with me?" he said. He pointed to a long column of numbers on the paper. "Where did you get these rent roll figures? They look different from the ones Crawford gave me."

She walked to his side and started at the sheet. For all she knew, the numbers came from Mars.

"I don't remember," she said. "Let me get the file." She walked out of his office. It seemed ten degrees cooler outside. Her blouse was wet under the arms. As she sorted through the files on her desk, she realized she had not asked for, and Rick had not volunteered, any help in finding a new job. No ideas, no leads, no names of friends to call. Nothing.

That was a bad sign. She was on her own.

He had just agreed to subsidize her job search for six months, but how long could his largesse last? Delta didn't need her now. Rick could be overruled by upper management. They wouldn't want to set a precedent: keeping your mistress on the payroll when she had nothing to do.

She wasn't even his mistress any more. How long would he be willing to fight for her just to keep her off the streets?

She rolled her eyes to the ceiling and prayed for guidance; the acoustic ceiling tiles said nothing.

One thing was certain: she had better be Miss Congeniality. She could be selling pencils on the street tomorrow.

They had to find a cheap apartment; they could end up living on Gin's miserable pay for several months.

She picked up the Los Noces file and squelched the urge to rip it in half and leave. Instead, she forced a smile and walked quickly back to Rick's office.

For the rest of the day, they spoke only about business.

That night she stayed late; she typed up her resume on one of Delta's expensive IBM electronic typewriters.

* * *

The offices of High School District 432 were in a squat brick building next to a McDonald's in LaGrange. At nine-thirty Friday morning, Gin sat on a blue-green chair in the reception area, awaiting his first interview for the job of assistant principal at Brookfield High School. He had an appointment with the assistant superintendant, Harold Lerner.

When Gin walked into his office, Lerner shook his hand warmly. He was a balding man of about fifty-five with a slight stoop, a substantial paunch, and bifocals.

After a few pleasantries, Lerner plunged right in. "You're the fellow who did that English as a Second Language program at Howard, aren't you?" he said.

"Yes, I am," Gin said, surprised.

"Well, we could certainly use something like that in this district," Lerner said. "We used to be an all-white district, but now we have lots of Hispanics and Koreans moving in. They have terrible problems with the language."

They spent the next forty-five minutes discussing the Howard program, Gin's teaching philosophy, his goals as an administrator, and his run-in with Father Dotson at St Paul's.

They could have talked all morning, but Lerner had a meeting. "The curriculum committee," he said, shaking his head. "We fight like dogs and then run the same programs we ran last year." He laughed as he telephoned Ron Binkofski, the principal at Brookfield, to let him know Gin was on his way over.

"You'll like Ron," Lerner said. "He's a little on the reserved side, but he's a good guy."

They shook hands warmly again. "We'll be in touch," said Lerner.

Gin left feeling that he'd gotten the job. He was euphoric.

The ten-minute drive to the high school passed like a dream.

He parked in front, found the principal's office, and was escorted in. Binkofski had just gone down the hall for a moment, one of the clerks said. She brought Gin a cup of coffee in a styrofoam cup.

He sipped his coffee and stared at the walls, beige cinder block decorated with landscapes of a European countryside. The thin beige carpet was clean, but worn along the main walkways.

Why are schools built like bomb shelters, he wondered. All brick and cement block. You'd think teachers spent their time bouncing students off the walls.

He stood up and walked to the window, which looked out over the school's front lawn.

Brookfield High School was next door to Chicago's largest zoo, or rather its main parking lot. To reach the zoo, visitors had to drive by the school.

In mid-December, only an occasional car of biologists or mothers with young children would come by.

But in fall and spring there must be a constant parade of school buses and cars.

Gin sipped his coffee and smiled to himself. He pictured blacks from the city driving through these quiet streets on their way to the zoo. They must terrify the locals.

A lone station-wagon drove by. A mailman walked his route among the bungalows across the street. No black gangsters were cruising today.

Maybe they were out doing their Christmas shopping?

Hearing footsteps behind him, he turned from the window; a tall man in a tweedy, three-piece suit entered the room.

Ronald Binkofski resembled a middle-aged Abraham Lincoln. His cheek bones stuck out from the sides of his pale face like withers on a thin cow. His black hair was slicked back from a receding hairline. He smiled, revealing a collection of yellow teeth.

"You must be Hodgkins Bernthal," he said in a quiet voice. "I'm Ron Binkofski." He extended a big bony hand. Gin shook it. It was like shaking a bag of knuckle bones.

Binkofski motioned Gin to sit down in front of his desk, an old wooden thing that seemed as big as an aircraft carrier. Its surface was stained with rings from coffee cups, set down without coasters through the years.

Binkofski folded himself into the black upholstered chair behind his desk and blinked.

"So, you're interested in being the assistant principal here?" he said, glancing over Gin's resume.

"Yes I am."

Binkofski smiled his yellow smile. Then he began studying Gin's resume, line by line. For three full minutes, he pored over it, saying nothing.

Gin fidgeted and listened to the noises of the children outside in the hall.

Finally, Binkofski set the resume aside and folded his hands on the desk.

"Why do you want to be an assistant principal?" he asked.

This guy isn't much on small talk, Gin thought. He cleared his throat. "Well, I've wanted to go into administration for the last five years," he began.

He unrolled his standard history: Howard High School, his English as a Second Language program, his attempts to become assistant principal at St Paul's.

Binkofski stared at him with blank brown eyes. Gin was sure the man was sleeping with his eyes open, but he pressed on.

When he finished, Binkofski blinked several times. "Why did you make your students write so many essays in your English classes?" he asked.

Gin was so surprised that the man was awake that he blurted out an answer, "Because they're functionally illiterate and that drives me crazy."

Binkofski pursed his lips; his mouth turned up at the corners. A dry, bony rattle came out of his throat. He was laughing!

"I couldn't agree with you more," he said quietly.

"Excuse me?"

"I said I couldn't agree with you more. The students really need to write more than they do."

"Yes, well," Gin said. He decided to plunge ahead. "The kids complain a lot, but I tell them they'll love me for it in ten years."

"They don't believe you," Binkofski said.

"Of course not. But when they leave my class they can at least tell the nouns from the verbs." Gin sipped his coffee. "You know sometimes I go wild and make them diagram sentences. That really sends them up the walls."

He heard Binkofski's dry rattle again.

"You must have taught English at one time," Gin said.

"Fifteen years, in this very school," Binkofski said. He lowered his soft voice to a nearly inaudible whisper. "But I was always too chicken to make them diagram sentences."

Gin laughed, a deep rolling laugh from the pit of his stomach.

"I never thought I'd find another defender of the language in administration," he said.

"Even principals have to come from somewhere," Binkofski said. "How would you like to see the rest of the school, Mr Bernthal?"

"I'd love to. And call me Gin. It's short for Hodgkins."

"All right, Gin. Please call me Ron." He stood up from behind his desk. "We can end our tour at the cafeteria for lunch. Do you like beef sludge?"

"What's that?"

"It's what our students have aptly named the barbecue beef sandwiches the cafeteria serves."

"Why not? I had tuna sludge yesterday."

Binkofski blinked and smiled. They walked down the hall toward the chemistry labs, Binkofski delivering a monologue on the facilities, the teachers and the problems they were having with the Hispanic students. Half of them dropped out after sophomore year. How could they help these kids? Should they start up a special language class or go for a full bilingual program?

They discussed it at length over their beef sludge, Gin's rolling laugh alternating with Binkofski's bony cackle.

THIRTY-FIVE

A week later, the money ran out.

After arguing with Gin about it for forty-five minutes, Marcia finally called her mother.

Mary Beth Grimley picked up the phone in her kitchen. Marcia could hear her little portable TV in the background.

They exchanged pleasantries, and then Marcia took the dive.

"Gin and I are having a lot of financial problems," she said. "We're flat broke, we've got the house on the market, and it looks like I could lose my job."

"Oh my," Mary Beth said. "That doesn't sound very good, dear."

Marcia could hear running water; Mary Beth was washing dishes.

"Mom," Marcia said. "We were wondering if we could postpone the December loan payment a while. Until we get ourselves back in shape."

The water stopped. "Well, dear, I don't know," Mary Beth said. "Could you make a double payment in January?"

Marcia couldn't believe her ears. She had just told her mother that she was bankrupt; she and Gin couldn't make their $550 loan payment in December. Her mother had responded by asking for a $1100 payment only one month later.

"Mom, we're broke," Marcia said. "We can't make any more payments until we sell the house. That could take until spring."

"But dear," Mary Beth said. "Your father and I wanted to take a trip to Florida this winter with that money. Now we might not be able to go at all." She managed to get just the right amount of hurt in her voice without whining.

"Mom, I'm sorry," Marcia said. Why was she sorry? Mary Beth had nine money market fund accounts in four states; each account contained at least twelve thousand dollars.

The phone was silent except for the sound of Mary Beth's TV. Marcia recognized the music of her mother's favorite gardening show.

"Why did you borrow money from us when you knew you couldn't pay it back?" Mary Beth said.

"I didn't know we couldn't pay it back," Marcia said. "I didn't realize that owning a house cost so much. And I certainly didn't plan on having to find another job."

Mary Beth snorted in exasperation. "You kids don't have any sense about money. Your brother can't balance his checkbook; Camille spends every dime she makes on clothes.

"Your father and I loaned you that money in good faith. We trusted you. Now it could take us years to get it back. That was money we were going to use for your father's retirement."

"Mother, I'm sorry. I told you I made a mistake."

"You're trying to take that money away from us." Mary Beth's voice was developing an hysterical edge. It was the Depression again; people were stealing her money.

"Mother, don't be ridiculous," Marcia said. "Look, as soon as we sell the house, we'll pay you back everything you lent us—the entire fifteen thousand plus interest. If we get lucky, you could get your money in three months."

There was a pause.

"Well, dear," Mary Beth said. "I suppose that would be all right."

"Thanks, Mom."

They said nothing for a few moments. Somebody on TV was repotting begonias.

"Is it snowing out there?" Mary Beth asked. "It's snowing here."

"It's snowing here, too, Mom."

"It looks like we're going to have a white Christmas."

"It sure does."

"Let's hope the snow doesn't get too deep."

"Let's hope not."

"Dinner's at three on Christmas," Mary Beth said. " Why don't you and Gin come around one?"

"Oh Mother, I'm sorry," Marcia said. "I know I told you we were coming. But I forgot we had promised Gin's mom we'd have Christmas at her house this year."

Mary Beth was silent a few moments. The TV voice moved on to pointsettias.

"Well, dear," Mary Beth said politely. "I hope you have a nice time. Say hello to Gin's folks for me."

"Yes, Mother. I will."

"Merry Christmas, dear."

"Merry Christmas, Mother."

Marcia hung up. She dialed Alice Bernthal. Alice was delighted to add two more plates to her Christmas table.

*   *   *

Christmas was a grey, snowy day.

Except for her mother-in-law's cooking, Marcia hated Christmas. Every year, she and Gin spent time and money they didn't have buying presents for their families.

Every year, the recipients opened their package, feigning excitement.

"Oh, what a lovely sweater (or tie, or shirt, or book)," they would say. They would set it aside and open the next present with exactly the same response.

They could have been opening cans of tomato paste.

No worries about that this year, Marcia thought, staring out the car window on their way to the Bernthals. Everyone was getting chocolate-chip cookies.

She and Gin had made them yesterday from some prepackaged cookie mix. They packed them in baskets from the dime store, and wrapped them in cheap Christmas paper.

At least the cookies going to Gin's family were wrapped that way. Mary Beth was getting hers in a shoebox, wrapped in plain brown paper and mailed on December twenty-sixth.

Merry Christmas, Mother. There were some advantages to being broke.

The porch on the Bernthal's house was strung with Italian lights. A Christmas tree twinkled in the picture window. Inside, the house was steamy mayhem.

Gin's brother, Jack, was there with Claudia and their two little girls, Caroline and Fay. Gin's twin sisters, Lorraine and Berenice, both seniors in college, were home from school. The living room was filled with their friends. Lorraine was trailed by a shy boyfriend. Berenice was trailed by a shy husband and a big dog with a lot of German Shepherd in him.

She couldn't leave Zone-Out at school, Berenice told Gin as she hung up his coat. No one stayed in married student housing over the holidays; who would watch her dog?

Zone-Out jumped up on Gin, snagging his claws on Gin's sweater and drooling.

A matched pair of spinster great-aunts from Virginia, clad in print polyester pants suits, lumbered around the dining room. They laid out plates on the table and kept disappearing into the kitchen where they retrieved relish trays and crystal glasses.

In the TV room, Hodge held court from his leather recliner. Two beefy neighbors had stopped by for Christmas punch and to wish Hodge the best of the season. All three sat half-snockered in front of the big console TV, watching a football game.

Gin walked in to say Hi. Hodge gave him a firm, if distracted handshake: the Bears could score this play. Everyone watched in silence. The Bears blew it, the men groaned in unison, and the ball went back to Tampa Bay. When the commercials came on, Hodge introduced Gin to the two neighbors, Ernie and Jim.

They nodded politely.

Everyone watched a beer commercial in silence as if it were a message from God.

"Go help yourself to some Christmas punch, son," said Hodge, grabbing a handful of beer nuts.

No dinner battles today, Gin thought. He's got more important things on his mind than pounding lumps on me. Gin had told his family nothing of his recent financial problems. Why bother?

Hodge and Ernie began a detailed discussion of the passing style of the Tampa Bay quarterback.

Gin wandered back to the living room. Marcia and his brother Jack were hunched over the fireplace, poking a smouldering fire.

"This wood's too wet," Jack said, standing up. "I'll get some more."

"No, no. Don't bother," said Gin. "We'll get it."

"We will?" Marcia said. "I've got my dress shoes on."

"A little snow won't hurt them. Anyway, wear your boots."

He took her hand. She got the boots from the front hall. They filed through the kitchen, which resembled NASA headquarters during the moon launch. The room was twenty degrees hotter than the rest of the house. A huge cooked turkey sat on the kitchen table. Claudia was elbow deep in its steaming innards, scraping out hunks of stuffing.

A great-aunt stirred giblet gravy on top of the stove. The steam wafted up, filling the kitchen with the most wonderful smells. Alice mashed potatoes. She barked orders to the second great-aunt, who rummaged through cabinets retrieving serving platters.

Lorraine and Berenice ran in and out with water pitchers and silverware; Fay sat in her highchair and howled.

Marcia slipped her boots on.

Gin flung open the back door and pushed her through. The silence and cold air hit them like a wave. Chilled and giggling, they ran to the woodpile at the far end of the yard. Gin began pulling logs out from its center. Marcia wrapped her arms around herself and stamped her feet to keep warm.

The big blue house loomed over them in the dreary afternoon light. A gust of wind swept through the yard; the old oaks in the yard creaked, their black branches swaying. A squirrel hung over the roof of the birdfeeder, eyeing the seed behind its glass windows.

Gin assembled a pile of wood, and put his arms around Marcia.

"It's pretty, isn't it?" he said.

"Very pretty."

They watched the squirrel swing down into the feeder and nearly fall off. It retreated back to the feeder roof.

"Do you think we'll ever live like this?" she said.

He laughed and kissed her on the cheek. "Not in this life."

"I mean maybe when you get that Brookfield job?"

"That's a big 'if.' I've got two more interviews. Then, they don't make up their minds until February. If I do get the job, it doesn't start until next September. With the loss we're going to take on selling the house, I'd forget about buying another for quite a while. We've got to save our money."

Her shouldered sagged.

"Aw, Marsh," he said, pulling her into his arms. "There are some nice apartments around here we could afford. We'll drive through Cicero and Berwyn on the way home. You'll like them."

"Who wants to live with a bunch of cheap Czechs or whatever they are?"

"Two broke guys like us, that's who."

She nuzzled into his sweater.

"I really messed up our finances, didn't I?"

"Yep. You screwed us up royally."

She looked up at him."You're not much on the comfort and support front, are you?"

"Oh stop it."

She pushed his arms away, turned on her heel, and headed back to the house.

The first snowball hit her on the bottom of her skirt. She felt the snow melt against her leg.

She turned around. "These are my good clothes," she yelled. The second snowball hit her on the left breast.

"You're water-staining my silk blouse, you moron!"

She picked up a handful of snow and ran toward him, all rage and ungainly attack.

She looks like a rampaging Canada goose, Gin thought. He ducked behind the garage. She ran after him and threw her snowball, hitting him in the back of the neck. Cold water trickled down his back.

"Bull's-eye!" she screeched, bouncing up and down.

Gin ran around to the side of the garage. She scooped up a handful of snow and barrelled after him.

She ran right into his arms.

Not hesitating a moment, she threw the snow in his face, laughing wildly.

"Marsh, that wasn't a very good idea," he said. The snow dripped off his cheeks and hair; his nose was red. "You're in big trouble now, lady."

He pinned her up against the garage wall with one arm, and picked up a handful of snow.

She shrieked.

He plopped the snow on top of her head.

"Damn you, Bernthal!" she yelled. "Look what you've done." Her hair was a damp mess.

She broke free and stormed back to the house. He laughed, picked up his firewood, and followed. Dropping the wood on the hearth, he went upstairs. She was in the bathroom, combing her hair. It hung in thin, wet boards by her ears.

"How's Snow White?" he said.

"You lunatic. I look like a drowned rat."

"I think you look kind of cute."

"Buzz off."

He kissed her on the neck. "Make love to me on Hodge's bed, right now," he whispered. "We'll give the springs more action than they've had in years."

"Are you crazy?"

"Of course. I married you."

In spite of herself, she smiled. They heard Alice call everyone for dinner.

"Are you ready for this?" Marcia said.

He shrugged. "Are you?"

"I'm never ready for your family."

He bristled.

"Oh, come on, lighten up." She nudged him in the side. "Do me a favor this year."

"What?"

"Don't fight with your father until after dinner."

"What makes you think we're going to fight?" he snapped.

"Does water run downhill?"

He glared at her.

"Look," Marcia said. "One of your great-aunts made a pecan pie. I don't want to leave without having a slice."

"For God's sake, Marsh."

"Just planning ahead," she said. "You look so cute when you're mad."

"Touché," he said.

He took her hand and they went down to dinner.